"A remarkable piece of literature... a brilliant piece of prose writing...a must read for every Guyanese, particularly as a means of delving into the more sophisticated and complex issues of race relations, cultural tolerance, sociology, philosophy and politics.... For those who have read V.S Naipaul's Miguel Street, they would find a similarity in style, whereby serious issues of sociology and culture are related in lavish humour and hilarity, but the message remains firmly embedded in the story."
— *The Guyana Chronicle*

"The Brown Curtain's importance is owed to the comfortable manner in which it deals with intra-Caribbean migration along with all these other issues of race, politics and the East Indian ethos....It stands somewhat alone in the way it has brought all those themes together in one drama, including the issue of Guyanese running off to work in the West Indian Islands....The Brown Curtains is a novel that is prepared to give forthright treatment to race, ethnic divisions and prejudice. The ending is moving. An ageing Indian father sees traditional beliefs being wrenched from him and is pictured in the final paragraph in an emotionally wracking resignation and acceptance of change."
— *Stabroek News*

"Mr. Sankardayal handles language skillfully ... The contrast between life in Guyana and Saint Lucia is skillfully handled, often in flashbacks to the rigid cultural village and family life in Guyana and the freer more cosmopolitan approach to life in Saint Lucia....The Brown Curtains is an entertaining novel well worth reading .... There is some comic relief, reminiscent of Shakespeare .... Mr. Sankardayal joins that growing body of West Indian writers who have been making a most valuable contribution to world culture and to an understanding of the region and its peoples."
— Jacques Compton, *Fellc*
*Chavalier De I.*

D0921351

# The Brown Curtains

# The Brown Curtains

## Clive Sankardayal

**Jako Books**

New York  London  Toronto  Vieux Fort

Published in the United States by Jako Books, a division of Jako Productions.

First Jako Books Edition, January 2006
Revised Jako Books Edition, March 2007

Cataloging-in-Publication Data
    Sankardayal, Clive.
        The brown curtains / Clive Sankardayal.
        p. cm.
        LCCN 2005935099
        ISBN-13: 978-0-9704432-5-0
        ISBN-10: 0-9704432-5-0

        1. Guyanese--Saint Lucia--Fiction. 2. Immigrants--Saint Lucia--Fiction. 3. Racism--Fiction. 4. Saint Lucia--Fiction.   I. Title.

    PR9320.9.S28B76 2005      813'.6
                        QBI05-600165

Cover design/painting by Michael Ward
Author's photograph by Peter Jackson

Printed in the United States of America

Dedicated to my:
mother, Lucille
wife, Ramkumarie
daughter, Shrynessa Ann
son, Ravin Ricardo

# The Brown Curtains

# 1

"Damn!" I didn't need it to rouse me again from my sleep. I jumped up and went for my assailant. When I lifted the bedspread, its segmented reddish-brown body wriggled frantically for shelter. This creature was larger! I pressed the sheet to it, squeezed and rotated the thumb downwards. I could feel it squirming and lashing out. Fluid oozed through the sheet. It was messy. I would have to wash the sheet again, and hoped it wouldn't rain. Then the mosquitoes would be on the rampage. Fuming with pain, I pulled the sheet off the sponge mattress and shook it. Uncovering nothing, I upturned the mattress and peered under. I wished I could have squashed some more. Two centipedes in two days! Yesterday's attack on the lower back was mild compared to this one although the swelling was still there. Today, I would buy a strong repellent, and today too, I must plug that gaping hole on the floor under the mattress.

Just then, a rooster from the coop just three feet below the floor came on full blast. Others joined in. It wasn't easy too to escape their stench. There were many crevices on the floor and in the wall. I glanced at the little clock hanging by a string on the wall just beneath the light bulb, which we kept on all night.

"The light might attract the flies, but it would scare away the insects and centipedes," Raj had said one night after he had shaken a slimy thing off his foot.

It was fifteen minutes to four a.m., my usual wake up time.

I looked at Raj. This morning he did not stir. The burning pain right in the middle of my spine quickly enveloped my entire back. I reached under his bed and into the box again for the ointment. I rubbed it on the swollen part. This time the pain surged. I slumped on the sponge and squeezed my eyes shut. Time walked on crutches. I slackened my muscles and the pain eased. Encouraged, I tried to control my breathing to a steady, easy pace. The antidote seemed to work. Maybe if I take my mind off the pain and bolster the antidote, more relief would come. I allowed my thoughts to roam. And as usual they drifted back to Zeelugt, my village in Guyana.

Four o'clock had been my usual wake up time back home too. My brother in law who had migrated to the United States — they said that God had blessed him — had sold me his old Vauxhall car for five hundred dollars. My wife, Geetangali, and the kids, Alesia, Jenny and Curly, had to get up also. They had to push the car. The mechanic had said that the battery was run down. But my parking space beneath my house was inclined. They didn't have to exert much energy. In any case everyone would awake — the car's exhaust was rotten.

And whether it rained or not, I was on the road before four thirty. In fact I was happy when it rained. Few private hire cars would venture out. And no traffic cop would be on the road at that ungodly time especially too if it rained — well, except one. He had chosen a market day, that is, a Friday to check things out at the usually busy Parika Stelling end where vendors from the numerous islands of the expansive Essequibo River gathered to sell their produce and scarce banned items.

But I had to hand it to him. This guy whom they nicknamed Scorpion was extremely clever. When I deposited a few twenty dollar notes in his outstretched hand, he smiled and moved his index finger slowly in my face. "Don't let it happen again *comrade*." The following Friday he greeted, "Hi, *comrade*." And as soon as I deposited the twenty dollar notes in his hand, he drove off.

Minutes later, "Another cop, Christ!" a passenger exclaimed as we turned a bend.

"Step out, *comrade*," the faceless cop ordered. His flashlight blinded me. "You know..." he began. I plucked the two twenty dollar notes from my pocket and deposited them into the book that he had in his left hand. "Don't let it happen again, *comrade*," he said and left.

The following morning as I approached the main road, a fellow driver shouted, "Three cops ahead!"

I returned home.

One day I drove home slowly with Geet in the car. I said, "Geet, lend me some money to pay for the gasoline."

"Sell the stupid car!"

But Scorpion and I had become pals after he stung me on the two consecutive Fridays. "The other cops won't stop you," he said. However, soon after, he told me, "Teacher, this job don't pay. I leaving."

The following week, I paid two cops twice.

A few weeks later, while I lay under the car tinkering with the exhaust, Geet said, "Honey, you know I have been thinking."

"Oh, yes." I gripped the spanner.

"You wouldn't be exactly popular if...if they report that you, a school teacher, who is a university graduate end up in court. You know...charged with breaking the law. You remember what the Minister said...And if they fire you, what is going to happen to us?"

Straightaway, I recalled telling Geet what the Minister of Education had said at a meeting convened for teachers to deplore truancy among teachers.

"We, the authorities," the Minister had declared, "deem it highly unprofessional for any teacher to be engaged in any other form of employment that would hinder his perform-ance in this noble profession and defaulters will be dealt with appropriately. But comrades, we need not come to that stage. You are nation builders. Don't be misled by a paltry few dol-lars more. You must make sacrifices..."

I sold the car.

And how could I forget the sacrifices I had made even before that?

Those hectic afternoons when I had to struggle to get across the river to the lecture theatre of the University of Guyana (U.G.) for the 5 o'clock class? Those times when I had to devour a roti —sometimes Geet put a boiled egg or a piece of fried fish inside—as I boarded the packed bus to the campus? And those midnights on my way home when I had to sprint towards the only bus plying the West Demerara route, having disembarked in a mad scramble from the Makouria ferry at Vreed en hoop Stelling?

Would I ever forget that Geet didn't speak to me for a week when I bought a motorcycle?

And certainly not what happened about one week later on my way home from classes.

"Let go! You mother..." Iron claws had gripped my wrists and were wrenching my hand from the handle of my motor-cycle. The motor cycle skidded to a halt.

"What the...!" my pillion rider shrieked as four or more faceless beasts pounced on him. He fought and escaped. His screams, "HELP! HELP!" died away in the distance. Not a man or vehicle appeared.

"Let go the flipping bike!" another masked animal grunt-ed. I held on. Cuffs and kicks, grunts and curses rained. I tightened my grip.

"Stab him!" another barked. I saw the unmistakable glint in the night. The blade descended. Instinctively I shielded my face. A heavy boot landed on my stomach and I sailed through the air and landed in a nearby ditch. Two hours later the police asked me, "Black or Indian?" I walked out of the police station.

Geet said, "You too damn hard-eared. Motor bike...save gas...go anywhere, huh."

Thereafter I expended energy to practise my sprints to get aboard the midnight bus. I was never stranded, except on one night when the bus refused to start. I slept on a bench in the small bus shed on the car park.

"R-i-i-i n-n-g…! R-i-i-i-n-n-g…!"

The noise of the alarm in the other bedroom brought me back here on this humid morning in our little wooden, partially dilapidated hut. It was exactly four o'clock. Dogs barked and howled somewhere nearby. I stood and leaned on Raj's bed.

Still, Raj did not stir. He was curled up like a child, and his body partially covered with a white sheet. Raj and I shared the same room, but he slept on the bed. He had migrated before me and the room was too small to accommodate two beds. I slept on the floor on a two inch thick, three feet wide piece of sponge. Only twice did I have to remind Raj not to step on me when he got off his bed. Usually I arose earlier than him and pushed my sponge under his bed.

The chanting of a Hindu religious song began in the other room. As usual, Bram initiated it. This morning I did not hear Nar's voice.

"Nar?" Bram called.

No answer.

"Nar!"

"Uh."

"Get up."

"Time?"

"After four."

Bed sheets rustled…a loud yawn followed…someone farted.

Silence. It lasted for no more than a couple of minutes.

7

The chanting resumed. Nar joined in. The song picked up momentum and then collapsed suddenly. The tinkling of the bell followed immediately after.

Silence. It lasted for some time.

Toilet flushed...utensils clinked...someone farted...toilet flushed.

Outside the din picked up as the wind whooshed through the vegetation.

"Tea ready?" That was Bram, barely audible.

"Not yet," Nar drawled.

"You taking egg for lunch?"

"Uhuh."

Two slapping sounds came in quick succession. "Blasted mosquitoes!"

I sat on the edge of Raj's bed and waited. And just when I thought Bram and Nar had nothing to irritate them this morning, Nar said, "Bram, I read a clipping from Guyana Mirror newspaper yesterday. Boy, the flipping Guyana government too flipping corrupt...All of them in the hierarchy from the President to all the ministers, possess big land and property. Unscrupulous bastards!"

"THUD!" Something fell on the floor in their room. Raj turned in his bed and sucked his teeth. He pulled the pillow over his head.

"And Nar, my wife says they ban everything...And now they can't control smuggling. Ha! In any case the police taking bribe. She says Parika market loaded with banned stuff."

"You right about the ban stuff. Did you read the article, 'The IMF and You?' Boy, the IMF is holding the people by the scruff of the neck. Man, things getting from bad to worse. The Government gone to the IMF! IMF...! Lord Krishna!"

Raj turned. "Why the hell they don't go home and do something about it. Is the same crap every damn morning!"

I wouldn't describe it as that. The routine was the same nonetheless.

"Nar, remember to pick up the breadfruit the man said he

would give us," Bram's voice floated over more pleasantly.

"And Bram, don't buy any chicken today like Raj says. He is too damn sweet mouth."

Raj sat up and when he saw me, he clenched his fists. "Ron, I have to put a stopping to this nonsense."

"Raj, a centipede…"

"I have to block this space." He pointed to the top of the partition between the two rooms.

He reclined in bed and clasped the pillow over his head.

The room was getting warmer by the second. I gingerly opened the door and parted the curtain in the doorway. I clung to it for a while.

The shapely female on the Sam's Sports Shop almanac hanging on the wall didn't seem appealing this morning. My eyes rested on the three unmarked days in March.

Beads of perspiration gathered on my hands and face, and I thought maybe a fever was coming on. If Geet was here, she would have made warm tea and rubbed my back. That thought didn't help. In fact it only triggered my nostalgic malady. I cautiously stepped outside of the house into the murky daylight.

It was cool and I sat on a pile of wood near the steps. I closed my eyes and my mind went blank.

Suddenly the door to the outside squeaked again, and then gently opened. Bramnarine Tiwari emerged. It had to be six-thirty or close to it. Bram was dressed for work. He looked smart and professional in his white shirt-jack. Today the sleeves were buttoned to the wrist and the front, which climbed smoothly over his slightly protruding paunch, fell perpendicularly and covered his hips. It wasn't an ordinary shirt jack like the ones he wore on the first four working days of the week. The front of this one was embroidered with mercerized white thread forming lovely patterns of arcs and curves. And together with his cream pants, it also gave him that saintly look.

"Ron?" He had already descended two steps when he

9

noticed me. Rays of sunlight were filtering through the openings in the foliage. He peered at me through his golden rimmed spectacles. "Eh! What happening, Ron? You early, man."

I nodded.

He carefully pulled up the left sleeves of his shirt. "Hey Nar! Time to go. We going to miss the bus."

"Alright, I am coming, man. What's happening? Is your sweet woman waiting for you? You old fornicator." Nar's outrageous laughter filtered from within.

A few minutes elapsed.

"Nar!" Bram shouted.

"Coming."

Bram limped closer to me, muttering, "Sweet woman... sweet woman."

"Yes, Mr. Bram, you know what? Is a long time since you here. I must find you a *djabal*."

Both Bram and I looked around quickly.

Regis appeared from behind the brush. "Yes, a mistress to cook for you?" he chuckled as he got closer. He was wearing a black overcoat and a red cap.

Bram dismissed Regis with a vigorous wave of the hand. "Mr. Regis, you *phaglee* or what?"

"What did you say?"

"You phaglee...you have to be crazy. I don't need a woman, Mr. Regis."

"*Phaglee...phaglee...*crazy...*fou*," Regis repeated and laughed heartily.

"Bram, do you have any change for the bus?" Nar called, still within.

"Boy, didn't I tell you that I have enough coins?"

"Do you have your roti and egg?" Nar called out again.

"Yes. Hurry up, man!"

Narendra Chatterpaul appeared in the doorway grinning sheepishly. Standing around the same five feet five like Bram and much darker, he too like Bram was in his mid-forties. He

donned a yellow shirt jack. The one he had worn the previous day was lighter and the day before that even lighter. He
was wearing a pair of tight fitting gray pants.

"Nar, my brother, like you shrinking?" Regis said.

"I need a woman to take care of me," Nar retorted.

"What you need is banja, yam and beef," Regis said and
laughed. "Come to my shop this afternoon, and I will get you
the right ingredients plus your woman."

Bram glanced at his watch. Nar saw me, drew back a little
and then broke into a smile. "Eh, eh, like you are imbibing the
fresh air?" He looked towards the house and then added
loudly, "Out late again last night, my boy? Clandestine nocturnal activities, eh? Like your sweet women making things
hot for you or what?" He laughed.

Bram grabbed Nar's shoulder. "Come on," he urged, and
pushed Nar ahead of him.

"Blasted anti men!" Raj was awake.

Quickly I looked around at the two departing figures.
They didn't look back. Both had round bald spots at the back
of their heads; Bram's appeared larger. Their light brown
attaché cases swung simultaneously on the outside.

As soon as they stepped into the bus, Raj barged out of the
room. I heard a ripping sound before his five foot ten frame
appeared in the main doorway of the house. "Every morning
is the same blasted thing!" He was in his underwear. He came
down the steps and looked at me. "One of these days, I am
going to bash in their faces."

I smiled.

"Take it easy, Raj," Regis said.

"What they concern if I stay out late or have women? I am
young, just half their age." He was breathing heavily.

"Man, they say you attracting the girls like flies," the
bemused Regis told Raj.

"Eh? Is that what they tell you?" Raj hissed.

"Just joking," Regis said, and left.

"Is okay, Raj...let's...let's see what...we...we have for

breakfast," I said.

"You alright?" he asked peering at me as he followed me into the kitchen.

"Look, Raj, a centipede..."

"You know why I am still in this house? Is because I have to support my relatives back home...I can't afford to live on my own." He stared at the floor for a while and then asked calmly, "What have they prepared for breakfast?"

"Egg and bread."

"Egg! *Awa!*" he erupted. "You mean is egg they cook again. Is everyday they frying egg and cooking dhal...and...and rice."

"That's not true, Raj," I said quietly.

"Well, almost," he snapped, and in one sweeping motion, he snatched the frying pan from the stove and hurled it through the window. He stood staring after it.

I blamed myself for allowing the situation to deteriorate. I should have asked him about the fete he had attended the previous Friday or the beach bash at Praslin Beach on the Saturday or the cricket match in which he had scored a half-century on the Sunday.

"Raj, I am very uncomfortable with the way you, Bram and Nar relate. I don't know what took place before I got here, but things getting worse every day."

"Ron, I am uncomfortable myself. These guys like watch-dogs...Mama!" He pointed to his watch. "Already seven o'clock! Look, Felicity picking me up. What about you? Are you not working today?" There was a little sparkle in his eyes. He took two quick steps towards the door of the bed-room.

"Raj, a centipede...I think I will stay home today."

He stopped. "Again? Christ! Why you didn't tell me? Where? Look, I have to go...Use the same ointment I gave you last night...Sorry about the centipede."

"I already rub it and..."

"Okay, I will bring a better one this afternoon."

He flitted in and out of the room as he dressed. He shoved his head through the window and stared in the direction of the highway. He cracked his knuckles. "Ron, I am sorry I threw away the eggs. Use any of the tin stuff I have under my bed. Okay."

I nodded.

A car horn tooted.

"Ah," he said. The horn sounded one more time, louder and longer. He grabbed his black attaché case and was out of the door in a flash.

I looked through the window and saw the sunlight streaming through the canopy of breadfruit and mango tree leaves.

I stepped outside again. I looked up into the horizon, and then to the east and saw dark clouds drifting slowly towards me. I sat on the pile of woods again. I found myself even more powerless to suppress my thoughts. I closed my eyes and chose to ride a cloud over the ocean to home once again... home to Zeelugt.

# 2

I ALIGHTED on the Boeraserie Creek, the northern entry into Zeelugt. The twenty-foot span of the bridge  on which the railway lines run, stood out as a distinctive landmark. It separated the counties of Essequibo and Demerara. Immediately I recalled the conversation a friend and I had years ago while we sat chewing sugar cane on the  foot wide and twelve-foot high rails of the bridge.

"Boy, are you a Guyanese or a Venezuelan?" he asked jovially.

"Well, it depends, which half of the bridge you are on," I replied.

He dragged his behind a few feet in the direction of Georgetown. "I Guyanese, you hear. But seriously, Venezuela really wrong and strong to say Essequibo belong to them. Like our President said…they ain't getting a blade of grass and not a single curass."

Zeelugtians would always remember the days too when the smoking, monstrous locomotives clanged over the creek. The clatter awoke the village, and throughout the day it alerted everyone every hour on the hour. Its absence in the evening, signaled the residents to retire to bed. A void was left when the huffing and puffing, and the hooting and toot-

14

ing stopped in the early seventies.

The next day, the front page of the 'Guyana Daily' carried an article under the caption:

### RAILWAY SCRAPPED!
### A classical example of the cobwebbed minds and brains of the hierarchy

An opposition member of Parliament wrote in another column, 'This indeed is the work of power-drunk minds that overleapt themselves.'

During the day the villagers gathered in groups and spoke about it.

One of them said, "Even London, New York and Toronto have trains."

"He say he woulda do it, but me never expect he woulda do it," an aged cutter told his friends.

But our President, in his 'Talk to the Nation' radio broadcasts, said, "This is modern times, my people. Trains are too slow...too costly to operate. And besides, comrades, this highway that your concerned government has spent millions of dollars to build alongside the railway tracks is to provide you with cheaper transportation. You must see the scrapping of both the West and East Coasts railways as a step to prosperity."

But Zeelugt still came alive at first cockcrow. Most of the men who lived on the sugar estate owned by The Guyana Sugar Estate Corporation, worked in the cane fields. Lights emanated from lanterns and flickered from bottle-lamps. The familiar sounds of wood chopping, clashing utensils and cutlasses being sharpened grew as chatter mounted. The cane cutters left around four a.m. for the cane fields. Some rode bicycles and others boarded the pontoons that were pulled along the canals by teams of harnessed bullocks. The canefields stretched far beyond Zeelugt.

Then, there was a lull in the flurry of activities until at

around six a.m. when a large whining truck would enter the village to transport the few rice reapers to the rice fields, which lie immediately to the west of the cane fields. And it was during the rice harvesting season too that some of the unemployed villagers would be up early to roam the rice section with their fishing tackle. Apart from providing cheap nutritious food for the table, fish catching was fun except on only one day—as far as I could remember and I had witnessed—when piranhas were trapped in the net of Raj's brother. Knowing that his net would be torn to shreds if he attempted to bring the piranhas to the surface, he had cautiously entered the water and tried to free them. He resurfaced with tenfold speed clutching his left hand and shrieked until he fainted. Part of the index finger was missing.

During the day, those men who stayed home and were overcome with boredom would venture to the creek with their cast nets or shrimp seines. And it was not unusual for them to encounter boa constrictors or alligators in their fish or shrimp tackle. However, one Friday morning when I looked outside I saw men with cutlasses sprinting down the street, which was parallel to the creek. I dashed through the gate and down the street. On arrival, I saw men hacking away at a boa constrictor, nearly twenty feet long. The reptile was thirty yards away from the creek. They found a goat in its intestines. A mother shuddered, "God, it could have been my child!"

But when cane and rice harvesting were over, and spring tide flooded the creek, time crawled in Zeelugt, and events took on greater significance.

One day the screams of women pierced the air.

"What...?" I shouted to Geet, but she was already out of the gate.

"*Rass*...They kidnap a schoolboy!" a neighbor shrieked.

When Geet returned, she said, "Nobody kidnap. They saw a group of strangers passing by the school."

Nonetheless, word spread like burning canefields that little boys were wanted for sacrificial purposes in some kind of bizarre ritual.

"Uhuh. It got to be obeahmen or Kali Mai Puja people," someone said.

On the Friday afternoon when the Moslems went to mosque, they denounced this development. In the mandir, on the Sunday morning, the Hindus raised concern; Bram was the most vociferous. Members of both sects were urged to be vigilant. And on the Sunday afternoon, the few Christians who held services in the bottom flat of a house owned by a former Hindu named Tanman condemned the sacrifice thing forthright.

Tanman's house was located in the extreme north of the village, next to a swamp in the squatting section popularly called Shanti Town. In this bushy area, men gambled in the day and brewed bush rum in the night. At first the villagers were suspicious of Tanman's church, which only came into existence about a year ago when a group of white men drove up to Tanman's shack and, in less than two months, put up a sign, 'Bible classes held here,' on the door of the bottom flat of Tanman's renovated house.

But when Tanman drove through the village with his Morris Oxford car after services on that Sunday afternoon, someone commented, "Tanman stop cutting cane, stop drinking rum and he turn preacher. But Tanman and obeah? Nah...nah."

Fathers and big brothers with gleaming cutlasses, knives and forks swarmed the school compound every day for a week. The strange men were never seen again.

But the villagers had their days of fun and enjoyment too. Cricket was the only team sport played on the village's vast cow-foot holed field. Everyone in Zeelugt, be they African or Indian, man or woman, was a cricket lover. There were weekends when almost the whole village would turn out to support their team. Families brought along picnic baskets, and men and boys drank rum.

17

I recalled playing in the match on the Sunday, when our local umpire had ruled that a batsman from the opposing team was dismissed.

The batsman stood his ground and queried, "How out, umpire?"

"L.B.W."

The irate batsman grabbed a stump and chased the umpire around the playing field, screaming, "You know what L.B.W. mean? Eh? I tell you...it mean *Lash Backside Wild!*" The villagers rescued the umpire and sent the batsman galloping out of the village.

Cricket may have promoted harmony in Guyanese society, but politics was a different story all together. Who could forget election time in the early sixties when politically instigated race riots, pitting Indian against Africans, forever changed Zeelugt. Some said that the riots were caused not by internal politics but by the destabilizing agenda of interfering foreign governments. But the results were the same nonetheless. During the day, men joked, shook hands and slept. At nights, hell literally broke loose—gunshots, crackling flames, and agonizing screams pierced the air. In the morning the people gathered to look at the dead and the ashes of burnt houses. Helpless, they shook their heads and swore.

The riot spread over the land rapidly and destroyed the social fabric of society. One local singer summed up the calamity in a pitiful rendition. "Out rings one bullet...one man dies...one nation falls..." The local politicians themselves pleaded for the return of calm and sensitivity. "The monster that these two major racist parties have helped to create is out of control!" one politician from a lesser recognized party had said over the radio station.

The horror attracted international attention. Diplomats threw down solutions. Eventually, 'Brown beetles'—according to a famous Guyanese poet—were summoned to restore calm. British soldiers swarmed the land.

In those turbulent times, East Indians and Africans were

forced to exchange dwellings and settle in a community of their own race for the safety of their families. After the riots all of the thousand inhabitants of Zeelugt were of East Indian descent.

Like the scrapping of the railway, the riots brought an end to part of the good old days in Zeelugt. To the entire country too, part of the good old days had died. The harmony and trust that existed between the two races melted like the dwellings that were razed to the ground.

People in Zeelugt were afraid to venture far and stay late. Most of the men who worked outside the village, returned before four o'clock, gambled and drank cheap rum until it became dark. By seven, almost everyone was indoors, unless the village enjoyed the rare luxury of electricity from the Guyana Electricity Corporation.

The destruction put many workers out of work. Others simply refused to work in places where they felt their safety was threatened. Soon, the jobless young men pranced around the village like rich movie stars and interfered with the young ladies. Others looked in at prospective looting grounds — poultry pens and kitchen gardens included.

Few parents risked sending their children to school. All schools were located outside of the village. The children roamed the streets, played in the trenches, and got into trouble. The villagers promptly organised five or more classes in the bottom flats of some houses. Even before the riots, Zeelugtians were deemed to have sugar estate mentality — they were not credited with much academic intelligence. Parents welcomed the 'bottom house' school. In this safe environment more children were attending school.

"At least the riot made us get our own school even if it a bottom house school," one parent commented.

Gradually the people began to put the painful effects of the riots behind them. They continued to show the initiative displayed in organizing the bottom house school.

In the mid sixties the village leaders lobbied successfully

for a secondary school. The literacy level rose with the education zeal displayed by the younger generation. Soon the village produced university graduates. Bram, Nar and I were among the first set. The villagers often boasted to outsiders, "Who have sugar estate mentality now? Tell me, nah?"

But political instability followed and the opportunities for initiative and improvement for individuals at home were few. There was a craving to reach beyond. Many evenings I withdrew to the patio and pondered about the future. Should I apply for another job and move out of Zeelugt? Should I apply to do post graduate study? Should I apply for a visa to the United States or Canada?

One evening while I was on the patio, Geet came up to me. "What's bothering you? Why are you so sulky these days?" she said.

"Sorry..."

"Why don't you find something to do?"

"Do what in this God forsaken place?" I snapped.

"Well, apply for a new job and let's move out then."

"What job...and go where?" I almost shouted.

"Just a suggestion," she replied.

"Sorry, Geet. You know this place sucks. A man can easily get bored here."

However, one bright September morning at the beginning of the new school year, Bram limped up to me and pulled me aside in the staffroom at Zeeburg Secondary School.

"Ron, look," he whispered and slipped a piece of paper in my hand. "A cable. They send for me in St Lucia."

"Are you going?"

"If? Boy, I am leaving next week," he beamed and placed an index finger across his lips.

Two weeks later, the principal asked, "Mr. Singh, have you seen Mr. Tiwari? He sent in a medical for one week and should have been back."

I looked away and shook my head slowly. A slender ray of hope floated in my mind.

The following week the principal asked, "Mr. Singh, have you seen Mr. Chatterpaul? He sent in a medical and..."

I shook my head and walked away quickly. The ray inside me took root.

One afternoon in the first week of the second school term, he approached me again, "What about Javed...Mr. Khan?"

"What about him?"

"Mr. Khan sent in a medical for one month, saying he suffering from acute depression. Eh? What depression he has when he has no kith or kin? Eh? You tell me that!" He took a deep breath and exhaled.

I shrugged my shoulder. I was excited. The ray of hope glowed.

"The SS head said Mr. Khan was far from completing his geography syllabus and CXC is just round the corner." He shook his head from side to side. He leaned closer to me, "Between you and me, Mr. Singh, I believe the bastard gone like Bram and Nar and..."

"But the last time I saw him he was looking sick."

"Oh. Okay." He scratched his head and shuffled off.

Three weeks later, I sought the principal very early in the morning to write up my non indebtedness clearance letter.

"Where are you going, *comrade*?" he inquired without looking up. He withdrew a pen from the pocket of his white shirt jack.

"Trinidad." It was the only foreign country that I had visited. I hoped he wasn't going to ask about Bram, Nar and Javed.

"When are you leaving?"

"Next week."

"Do you know that you have to give the Ministry one month notice that you are leaving the country?"

"Yes."

"Why?"

"Why what, Sir?"

"Why are you going?"

21

"Business."

"Oh."

While he wrote, I looked around his office. The walls were dingy. In the center, a new picture of our President and a slightly fading one of our Prime Minister stood out. Two of the meshed, wooden framed windows hung on single hinges on the Northern wall. On the floor, books were scattered in one corner, and broken desks were piled in another. There was a standing fan close to his desk. This was how I remembered seeing it...at least for the past term. Today the fan was creating some noise.

He sat upright and looked me in the eye with his pen hovering over the letter. A faint smile appeared on his face. He slowly folded the letter, handed it to me and drawled, "We don't have envelope. Take this to the D.E.O. office at Vreed en hoop."

At the District Education Office, his superior looked at the letter suspiciously and remarked, "Do you know you were supposed to apply a month in advance, *comrade*?" He looked at me over the rims of his oval shaped spectacles. He wore a bright multi-colored shirt-jack.

I nodded and looked at the large framed picture of our President stuck firmly on the wall and that of our Prime Minister hanging loosely below. I hoped the superior wouldn't take much longer. It was a hot day. His room had little natural ventilation and his air conditioning system was not on.

He began to write on the documents. This took about five minutes. When he stopped, he turned them over, studied them closely, looked around, peered through the window, scanned the documents over again and stamped them. This lasted over five minutes. "Okay, take these to the Ministry of Education in Georgetown and tell the supervisor...What's his name? I can't remember his name. He knows me well. Anyway, tell him I send you." He smiled.

I left the office hurriedly for the Ministry.

"Where are you going, *comrade*?" asked the supervisor, exuding an air of professionalism and authority.

"Trinidad." I felt the coolness from his air conditioning system, which hummed somewhat irritatingly. He wore a dark, long sleeved shirt-jack.

"So you are going to the U.S. of the Caribbean?" he commented and shook his head affirmatively. "For what, *comrade*?"

"To buy a truck," came out smoothly.

"Oh." He thumbed through the pages of the document, tilted them and his head simultaneously sideways and peered at a particular section. He screwed up his face and nodded slowly for a few seconds.

Both pictures of the President and the Prime Minister on the wall behind him looked new. They were larger than those in the D.E.O. office and the frames were more expensive looking. The President and the Prime Minister appeared to be glaring at me. I looked away.

He sat upright and said, "Okay. Looks like we Guyanese have become workaholic. Anyway take these back to your D.E.O. office."

I arrived at the D.E.O. office minutes to four and approached a young male employee who was slouching at his desk, on which there were two folders and a penholder. He sat upright and looked at his watch. He slowly took the envelope I held out to him, and looked at me straight in the face with a no-nonsense air. Then smiling wryly, he asked and advised at the same time, "*Comrade*, in this guava season, when things rough, do you know what a box of fried chicken can do? A little show of appreciation can work wonders and make people work beyond the call of duty. Don't you think?"

I smiled.

I obtained the little pink paper they called tax exit at a cost of only three lunches, one dinner, a couple cases of Banks beer and a box of fried chicken.

Geet was angry. "The govment don't pay them? Why you

have to give them too."

"What would you have done if you were getting the pay they get?"

"Well...am...I..."

"That's it," I said. "They want to survive."

But when I told her about the truck part, she was very amused. "Yes." she said. "In the year twenty fifty, and a second hand one too!"

When the children returned from school that afternoon, she invited, "Come sit." They gathered around her expectantly. "If ever I hear anyone of you open your mouth and say your daddy going, see what I will do to you," she said, as she wagged a finger in their faces. They sulked for the rest of the afternoon.

I decided to give my close friends a farewell drink two days prior to my departure. Before I left for the beer garden, Geet said, "When you drink your beers, open your big mouth and tell every Tom, Dick and Harry...and invite bandits!"

I LEFT MY HOME on a dark, cold and wet Thursday morning. I couldn't recall when last it had rained so much—full moon rain, they called it. Geet and the children accompanied me to the bus stop on the highway, about one hundred yards away from our home. It was not yet six a.m. and the place was desolate.

I looked up and saw the enormous silk cotton tree that loomed about ten yards west of the bus stop. The face of the lifeless youth surfaced in my vision. It was under this tree that I and some residents had trapped escaping bandits. A shot rang out! The youth fell at my feet. That was exactly two weeks ago. The bandits were never apprehended. The thought of leaving my family behind was most daunting. But Geetangali was very supportive and brave. "Is for the children...go."

On the highway that morning she noticed my gaze. She squeezed my shoulder. "I know. But you must move on," she said.

A dark-blue fourteen seat bus pulled up. Instantly I recognized it. '**Journey to Hope**' was written boldly in white, forming a parabola that rode a yellow sun. Vincent Bagot alias Hustler, smiled from ear to ear when he saw the five of us, a shoulder bag and a suitcase. Hustler and I knew each other well from high school days.

"Glad to see you, Ron," he greeted me. "Where you going?"

"Georgetown."

"All five?"

"Nah. Me alone."

His mouth became a parabola.

"Alright. Okay." He took the small suitcase and dispatched it somewhere in the back of the bus and tried to take the green overused shoulder bag that hung loosely on my shoulder. I shrugged him off and handed him the small radio cassette player that I was carrying.

"Like you become trader now, Ron?" Hustler asked.

I smiled.

"Yes. You not teaching no more," he concluded and patted the shoulder bag at the same time. I glanced at the passengers on the bus. Most were looking at me, the suitcase and the shoulder bag.

"Sit in front," Hustler invited.

I turned and looked at Geetangali and the kids as the bus drove off. They waved until the bus turned the corner.

Someone touched me on the shoulder. "Ron, like you get that elusive visa, boy? American or Canadian?"

I turned around and smiled. He shook his head approvingly.

Hustler stopped for every outstretched hand. When a squashed passenger complained he said, "Me want to help everybody get to work."

"Drive the flipping bus fast nah!" someone shouted and Hustler accelerated.

As we turned the Vreed-en-hoop corner, a taxi driver hailed, "Hustler, the bridge break down!"

Hustler erupted, "Is the same freaking thing everyday!" He sucked his teeth, and then turned to me. "Ron, use the small boat."

When I got to the boarding point, scores of angry commuters were already jostling to get aboard the little fishing boats. Those who were strong and able bodied, bullied their way to get onto the narrow planks precariously placed from the beach to the boats. The captain into whose boat I clambered, collected his money as soon as the passengers entered. "Alyuh hurry up nah before the stupid Babylon come and charge me." He was alert to ensure that the vessel was not overloaded.

One angry female passenger left behind called out, "You too damn biased. You taking you own people. You is a crab-dog!"

"You mother big, fat, arse!" the captain retorted without looking up; he was busy counting and pocketing the cash.

The crowd went wild. He was a *dogla*, mixed of Indian and African heritage, so how could he be bias to either of the races? In Guyana, Indians were often referred to as crabs, and Blacks as dogs, so being a *dogla* the captain was either none or both.

The speedboat covered in less than five minutes the one-mile trip across the rough waters at the mouth of the Demerara River.

Thoroughly drenched and numbed, I scrambled up a ladder to the Georgetown Ferry Stelling where my suitcase was snatched from my hands by an over zealous tout who roughly ushered me into a taxi. I slouched and closed my eyes all the way to Timehri. Before I entered the departure lounge at the airport, I donned my oversized sunshades. In the lounge, I espied five of my colleagues from Zeeburg Secondary School huddled in a corner. We stared at one another in awe. "They never told me they were leaving," I muttered. But then it occurred to me I hadn't told them of my plans either. Later I found out that one went to the Bahamas, another to Miami, two others to New York and one to Toronto.

# 3

"FASTEN YOUR SEAT BELTS and prepare for landing..." jolted me upright in my seat.

I took off my sunshades and glanced at my watch. It was 7:10 p.m. I peered through the window and I saw lights like stars—in clusters of different symmetrical patterns—rushing up to greet me.

As the terminal buildings at St. Lucia's Vigie Airport glided past us, I felt lighter and more relaxed. When the plane came to a stop and the seat belt lights went off, I grabbed my shoulder bag and walked boldly to the front exit. Taking a deep breath, I stepped on St. Lucian soil. A light breeze caressed my face and made ripples on my shirt. I surveyed the immediate surroundings as I proceeded to the entrance of 'Arrivals' section.

"Hey, Ron!"

"Bram!"

He was standing under the bright street lamp on the road! He was astonishingly close to the aircraft and was waving frantically. I returned the wave with greater zest.

At the immigration counter, a broad shouldered officer with a thick moustache and an expressionless face glanced up and down my short figure without moving his head.

Suddenly he jerked his shoulder and head back, and asked, "Guyanese, eh?"

I nodded and he looked at me again. "Where are you going, sir?" he queried seriously as he brought his hand to his chin.

"I don't know exactly, *comrade*...ah mean, sir. But I am expecting someone from the Ministry of Education to meet me, sir." I was glad I said the ministry part; I felt important.

"Ministry!"

I couldn't really tell if he was impressed or aghast but then a frown appeared on his brow.

"To work, *comrade*...sir," I added quickly.

"Work?" He made it seem outrageous.

"Well, yes, sir."

"Where is your working permit?" His lips curled.

My stomach growled. "Don't have," I said hoarsely, "but..." I dipped my hand in the side pocket of my hand luggage and fished out a crumpled piece of paper. "I have a cable, sir." I held it out to him.

He looked at the cable for some time and sighed, "Go outside and see if anyone is there to meet you."

I didn't know for sure if anyone meant friend or official. I walked quickly to the exit, and with an effort, pushed the door open. I looked for Bram.

Staring at me was **RONALD SINGH**, handwritten in black on a green strip of cardboard. A stout gentleman, who was scanning the passengers and grinning from ear to ear, held it across his chest. I glided up to him.

"Hi, *comrade*, ah mean sir. I am Ronald," I said as I held out my hand.

"I am Joe. The principal of Soufriere Secondary sent me, sir." He shook my hand.

"Glad..."

Two hands dropped, one on each of my shoulders.

Turning, I looked into the beaming faces of Bramnarine Tiwari and Narendra Chatterpaul. Rajendra Rohan

Girdharry, who stood a little distance away, was smiling broadly too.

The rest happened quickly.

When I returned to the counter, the Immigration Officer said, "One day. I am giving you one day. The Ministry will do the rest."

"Thank you, sir."

The Customs Officer fingered some of the contents of my suitcase. He held up the flat disc like item. "What's this?"

"*Tawa*," I said.

He squinted.

"To make roti," I explained.

"Oh, roti."

He extracted pot, frying pan, rolling pin, knife, mosquito net, and plastic cups from among the other paraphernalia. He delved into the pot and plastic cups, and squeezed the net. "Come to work?" he asked.

"Yes." I nodded and he smiled.

As soon as I emerged through the exit for a second time, Bram guided me to the car park, which was actually the road adjoining the airport — the same road where I had seen him when I alighted from the aircraft. Only a fence stood between the tarmac and the road. Joe tagged along and stood some distance away. We stood under the lights of the street lamp. On the right, actually no more than twenty feet away from the edge of the road was a big almond tree. Other trees, just as large ran along the side of the road as far as the eye could see in the dark night. But, still on the right, I was more curious about the familiar lapping sound of water rising and falling. The water glistened in the light from the street lamp.

I pointed. "Is that the seashore?"

"Yes, a bay. Right there," Raj said.

The aircraft and the ocean couldn't be much more than a hundred feet apart!

"Yes, Ron. How was the trip?" Bram asked.

"Okay, but..."

"How much is the currency exchange now?" Nar inquired.

"One twenty."

"Yes!" Nar exclaimed, rubbing his hands together.

"Did you have problems with immigration at home?" Raj asked.

"No. Except that they disappeared with my passport and had me waiting at the immigration counter for a long time."

"How kick down door robbery? We have been hearing about it a lot." Nar asked.

"Yes, Ron. How?" asked Bram.

"Terrible," I said, "terrible." They listened with rapt attention as I told them about Tiger. "I was there...there within touching distance of him, when the pistol was discharged at point blank range in his stomach."

A wave of grief swept over me. They shared my grief for a while. I couldn't bring myself to tell them of the nightmares that followed and how I had been on the verge of canceling my trip.

"How is that kind of thing over here?" I asked.

"Nil," Nar said. "Nothing like that. You could leave the door open and sleep."

"Ron, tell us about the vigilante group. We hear you were the head. Does it still function?" Bram inquired.

"Yes, in a kind of a way." I told them about the vigilante group.

They were relieved.

"People over here are different. They nice," Raj said.

"Yes. But they like to fete and get pregnant...And spend money wild," Nar said looking at Raj. He began a simultaneous rotation of his left shoulder and his head until they glided across each other. Queer, I thought, if he wanted to scratch his cheek or brush away a mosquito, why didn't he use his hand? Somehow I couldn't remember him doing that back home.

"But wait, do you have money?" Bram asked suddenly.

"Oh, yes." I pointed to the two gold chains that I was car-

31

rying around my neck, the thick bangle on my wrist, and pulled out my hairbrush from my pocket. I withdrew a hundred dollar US note that I had tucked in a tiny compartment of the hairbrush. Bram and Raj were amused.

Nar said, "You right. What fifty US traveling allowance can do?"

"What else you brought?" Bram asked laughing.

"I couldn't bring tooth paste. They don't have," I laughed. "And...oh Bram, I have this letter for you."

He pushed the letter in his pocket.

"Anything for me?" Nar asked.

I shook my head. He hung his. I peered into the dark ocean.

The light breeze that had sprung up was soothing and refreshing. Music, albeit strange to my ears, floated in the air as a minibus cruised by. Just then, Joe came up and pointed to his watch. "Soufriere far and the road bad," he said politely.

"Ron, why don't you come with us?" Bram suggested. "I would show you how to get to your school."

"Okay," I said.

"Tomorrow is a school holiday in any case," Bram continued.

Bram explained to Joe, and soon we were on the white bus that the trio had hired. And when Bram said, "Let's go home," I already felt at home.

Their chauffeur invited me, "You could sit in front with me. You will see the place better."

I saw a dark but star filled night. Lights, thinly scattered, gave me a faint idea where people could be living, or where there could be some sort of human activity. As we turned slowly out of the airport premises, I saw lights somewhere ahead, high up. I pointed a finger.

"Hill. Anyway we are entering the city of Castries," the driver said.

"What's over there?" I asked, pointing to a brightly lit

place.

"The wharf," the driver replied.

I heard the heavy droning of an aircraft close by. Glancing to my left, I saw it was flying low over the water.

"The runway to Vigie begins right over there," the driver said pointing.

A few seconds later, he said, "We already out of Castries."

The bus squeaked and strained. It negotiated two goose neck turns—live goose necks, I thought, since we went up and down the necks. Those back home were dead ones; they lay flat. The bus rattled and screeched to get to the very top of the second neck. When it encountered level ground, its purring filled the night.

There was no sign of human activity. I saw no houses, nothing, only bushes, and trees especially mango and coconut, and banana plants, tall and thick, on the right side of the narrow and uneven road. I looked across to the left side— nothing—just a vast empty space and a few stars.

"Ocean," the driver said casually, "about one thousand feet below."

A cow or a donkey just has to dart across and we could be plunging down, just as we see in the movies, I thought with a slight shudder. (Two days later, when I told Raj of my fears then, he said, "*Awa*. There are no cows or donkeys in this part.") I glanced at the boys. They were engaged in light conversation. I asked over my shoulder, "How far away is home?"

"Not too far," Bram said.

The bus, which had no name, went up and down, and around numerous curves. It groaned and hummed. I thought of Hustler and was sure he wouldn't enjoy this. In fact, I could picture him swearing a lot. I didn't think his bus would have made it to the top anyway. From the light on the dashboard, I could see the driver's face. He was cool. As the bus ascended and the gradient decreased, twinkling lights grew thicker.

"Blasted road!" the driver said, as old fashioned designed buildings trotted and then hopped past us, and we crawled through a densely pot holed street. But the smile soon reappeared on his face. "Ah stopping to buy bread," he said, and we all alighted.

"Weapon," Nar muttered.

"What?" I asked.

"Look, tomorrow morning that bread could impregnate you and kill you, so hard it becomes!"

"You mean juk," Bram agreed laughing.

"Let's have a soft drink at the restaurant," Raj said.

"Indian!" hailed a pleasant voice from within.

I looked up in the direction of the voice, and saw two men at the counter of the bar grinning, and waving their hands.

"*Gason!*" Raj called back, jovially. "I didn't see you." He went up to *Gason*; they shook hands and spoke. Raj pointed to me. *Gason* smiled and raised his hands. I did the same. I collected my coke and joined Bram and Nar at the door.

The driver appeared in the doorway of a small building across the street, holding a bag in his hand. He offered us a loaf of bread each. The boys declined. I took one. It was warm, soft and tasty. He offered me another. I accepted.

"But what is the cost of bread back home?" Nar asked.

"Bread expensive and it hard to get," I replied. I hardly ate bread—Geetanjali cooked good cassava roti.

When Raj rejoined us after some time, he held out a bag to me. "Bread and cheese," he said.

I took it and ate again. The driver and the boys lingered around some more. I began to feel somewhat jaded. "I feeling tired. Do we have to go much further?" I said.

"Okay…to bed. Just down the hill," Nar replied.

We stopped about four hundred yards downhill.

"Mon Repos," the driver whispered.

"Home," Bram said, pointing to a light some distance in a track. Light filtered through crevices on the walls, door and windows. In the semi-darkness, the house appeared very small and dilapidated. When I entered the living room, I asked, "Is here you guys living all the time?"

"Uhuh," Nar answered.

"Since there is no sofa and no extra bed," Bram explained, "you have to make do with the piece of sponge Raj has under his bed."

After a while, he walked up to the calendar that was pasted on the wall and put an 'X' on Thursday, January 31st.

I AWOKE JUST AFTER SIX A.M. and tucked away the sponge mattress under Raj's bed. Sometime during the night I thought I heard chanting and the ringing of bells. I wanted to ask Raj about it but he was still asleep. On my way to the living room, I ran into the curtains that draped the doorway to our bedroom. There was a slit down the middle. A few tiny holes were noticeable at the bottom. I disentangled myself and entered.

I stepped outside at the front of the house and stood in the shadow of an enormous breadfruit and a tall mango tree. Looking around, I only saw more of the same trees, two dogs, and some fowls and chickens. Banana plants seemed to be all around. Something scurried by suddenly. I stood upright.

"It's only a mongoose. There are many around," Bram shouted from the doorway. When he got closer, he said, "So different from back home, eh?" He looked around and then asked, "Do you like the place, Ron?"

"Peaceful, but..."

"Take a walk, then. I am preparing some breakfast. Go over to Mr. Regis' shop and buy two pounds of potatoes." He handed me some money. "We told him about you."

"Where?"

He pointed. I could see part of a building jutting out behind a clump of bushes. It was thirty or forty yards away in a clearing, just next to the highway.

"There!" he continued pointing. "That little blue thing is the shop."

I walked to the shop cautiously. I could see a huge weather beaten, cork shaped Coca Cola sign nailed to the outside of the only window on the side that was facing our house — the eastern side, I presumed. The rays of light, which had managed to filter through the overhead branches, reflected off the red sign. The window was slightly ajar. As soon as I veered away from the thick clump of carrion crow bushes and a tangle of huge ferns and twisting lianas, I stopped in my tracks.

The bright little blue thing was clinging to a big, blanched appendage, nearly four times its size. It seemed to be sucking the life out of the appendage, much like the bird vine does to a mango tree. The appendage had two windows, both of which were clamped shut with straps of boards nailed in a crisscrossed way. A gutter on the window side of the appendage was nearly touching the ground. I looked from the shop to the appendage and back. A queer alliance, I thought. The shop stood about three feet high on concrete blocks, most of which leaned away slightly from one another. The appendage sat flat on the ground.

I walked around, placed my foot on the bottom of the step and looked up. Overhead, branches of a huge breadfruit tree were swinging loosely and threateningly in the strong wind. The top half of the door — definitely the 'smaller' half — was open. On the inside were two signs painted in white ill shaped letters:

**OPEN 6A.M.**
**MR CREDIT DEAD! DEAD!**

I climbed the four steps carefully and entered the shop. Two small boys were leaning on the counter. Immediately they looked up and stared at me, mouth agape. No one was standing behind the counter.

"Where is the shopkeeper?" I asked.

Both boys tilted their heads sideways, still looking at me.

Daylight came in from the open half of the window opposite the one with the Coca-Cola sign. A big freezer was humming away under the Coca-Cola window.

I scanned the shop but couldn't see much. There were so many things. Everything was blocking something else. Some items even hung from the rafters. There was no wall on the fourth side of the shop. It opened into the appendage. Only a narrow board, spanning right across, indicated where the shop area ended.

"Mr. Cal, my father has to go to work," said one of the boys.

"Well, let your father go to work. You don't see I can't find the thing yet!" The voice came from somewhere at the back of the shop at floor level. Irritable man, I thought.

"Here!" A small, fair skinned man with a partially bald head emerged. He was holding a pack of disposable shaving cartridges. He glared at the boy.

He saw me, and his face lit up. "Ah, you must be the new teacher? Good morning." The tone was tinged with an American accent.

Perhaps he had lived in the United States for sometime, I thought. "Yes," I said quietly.

Smiling, he gave the package to the boy, shot out the other hand and grabbed mine, which was on the counter. He shook it gustily. "Welcome! Would you like a malta?" His eyes held mine.

"Well...am...am...I..."

"Mr. Cal," the boy cried again, looking at the twenty-dollar bill he had placed on the counter, "my father..."

"Boy, *konpòté*. Don't you see I am talking with this gentleman?" He turned to me and smiled. "Children these days don't have manners. I am Regis Cauldron." The American accent was stronger.

The boy sucked his teeth.

Regis picked up the money, disposed of it under the counter and came up with some coins. He handed to the boy without looking at him. As the boy descended the last step, I heard him mutter, "*Salòp.*"

"You are Ron, aren't you? The boys told me you were coming."

"Yes."

"Well, how do you like it here? I mean our country, of course."

"I have not..."

"Of course, you have been here for one night only. But St. Lucia is beautiful, of course."

"Yes..."

"You know what your country needs? Good management." He pushed his hands under the counter and brought out a rag. "Yes, a new government," he said as he wiped the counter with one big swipe. The American accent was growing progressively stronger. His small bright eyes danced and darted in their sockets like balls struck around a pool's table.

"You know the Americans invaded Saddam." His bottom lip folded over the top one, stretching his sparse moustache. "But they can never remove him," he continued as his hand held on firmly to the counter, like the shop to the appendage, and the other thrashed about like a music director's. Maybe he was dissatisfied with America's foreign policy and that was why he had returned to St. Lucia. A mild gust of wind made me look up quickly as the items hanging overhead thrashed about recklessly.

"It is okay," he said, glancing at the swaying items. "The downfall of a lot of people in this world today is their greed." His face contorted. For a few seconds, his lips formed a circle as he stretched the 'down'.

So much like Kalli Balgobin, my cane cutter friend back home, I thought, and smiled.

"You see, you are thinking like me," he said, nodding.

He looked at my malta bottle. I turned away, and peered through the window, trying to see what was beyond the highway. I saw green undulating land, slopes, hills and mountains. I tilted my head to find an end to the green. He followed my gaze.

"Morne Gimie. Are you bringing your family?"

"Not yet," I said, still tilting my head to find out what was beyond the green.

"I don't live here, you know. I live far north."

I was now convinced that he lived in the United States.

"Where would you be working? May I ask?" he asked.

"A place called Soufri…air."

"Oh, Soufriere… S-O-U-F-R-I-E-R-E." He laughed.

I knew the spelling but he pronounced it so differently.

"So far away? That's in the west. When you see two mountain peaks sticking out like a woman's two breasts, ha …they call them the Pitons. They are in Soufriere. Yes, you can see them all the way from Vieux Fort in the south."

It seemed as if the entire west—again, I assumed that it was the west because the sun had risen in the opposite direction—was only mountains and hills densely populated predominantly with swinging and listing coconut trees.

"I live in a nice, very nice place they call Gros Islet. It is…let me see, about five miles north of Castries. I must take you there on a Friday night, my friend. They have roadside barbecues. Have you ever eaten barbecued chicken? Yes. They have barbecued chicken, fish, meat …And boy, the music is something you will never forget… jump up reggae…Mama! The fun goes on and on until in the morning. All the tourists go there…and the women…Mama! Look, I must take you there!" The end came abruptly as he exhaled noisily. He fingered a few bottles on a shelf and resumed. "And drinks, don't talk about that…*Gason*."

I looked behind me expecting to see *Gason*, the guy to whom Raj had introduced me the previous night.

"What?" he asked puzzled.

"Where is *Gason*?"

"Who?"

"*Gason*."

"Oh ho, I see." He laughed until his eyes closed. "Nobody name *Gason*. *Gason* mean boy. Ha…Yes, I must teach you some patois. Yes."

"Oh, I see. Many people living in the mountain, Mount Gimie?" I asked.

"No, not Mount. It is Morne. Oh yes, our agriculture area. Many villages are scattered all over. St. Lucia has many, many mountains, and hills and valleys. Yes, people live all over. Have you ever heard about Pigeon Island?"

"No. I…"

"Of course not. I must take you there, my friend. And you ever hear about the drive in volcano? No? I must take you there." He stopped, passed a hand over his forehead and removed beads of sweat. Mechanically, he shifted around a few bottles on the counter and wiped the top again.

I waited.

"You are a very quiet person…But I have heard so much about your country…Kaieteur Falls and…Oh yes, Guyana has lots of gold. People over here love gold, just simply love gold," he said, fingering the gold chain on his neck. "Ah, you have." He pointed to my neck and hand. "Will you like to sell? The boys sold when they came…"

"Mr. Cauldron," a thin voice interrupted from outside.

"*Awa*. Eh! Oh, Brother Paul, how are things?" There was a slight irritation in his voice. The American accent was almost gone.

"Irie, brother, irie. Can you spare 'I' man a minute?"

"*Wi*. Come in, man."

Brother Paul, tall and wiry, had a pronounced, aquiline nose and thin lips. His plaited, matted dread locks rode his shoulders and a few reached down randomly to his waist; even his beard was plaited.

41

"This is Mr. Ron. He is from Guyana," Regis said.

"Pleased to meet you, Mister Paul."

"Rasta."

"Okay, Mr. Rasta Paul."

We both smiled. I extended my right hand. He folded his right fist and held it out in front of him. I folded my fist and jammed his.

"Do they have Rastas in Guyana?" Rasta Paul inquired.

"Yes, a few," I said, remembering Lionel Long, a teacher at Zeeburg secondary.

Sensing Rasta Paul's desire to speak with Regis, I used the opportunity to make my exit after I had declined Regis' offer to have another malta.

"Okay, I show movies in here," Regis said, pointing to the open space in the appendage. "Tomorrow, I am showing 'Jaws.' You must come."

Bram and Nar were waiting for me.

"How many maltas you had? Two?" Bram asked.

"Why?"

"How many gold chains does he want?" Nar said.

"He didn't say."

"Where are the potatoes?" Bram asked smiling.

"Oh Christ!"

After they had spoken about Regis and laughed, they engaged me in a replay of the previous night. I repeated what I had said with minor alterations. Bram and Nar went in for a nap after lunch. I sat under the tree in the yard perusing some recent issues of the local papers. Suddenly I looked up and saw Nar standing in front of me.

"Ron, did you see my wife and boys? Meena didn't give your wife a letter for me?"

I shook my head slowly. He sighed and shuffled back inside.

The time passed quickly and soon the sun was disappearing over the hills. Raj arrived home about four-thirty.

"Mister Regis is a nice, nice man," I told him after he had

changed and settled down to a glass of limejuice.

"How many maltas did he give you and how many gold chains does he want?"

I smiled and shook my head.

Feeling tired, I decided to get into bed early. As I was about to pull the covering over my head, I heard the chanting and the ringing again.

"Raj...?"

"Bram and Nar. They are meditating."

WE AWOKE EARLY THE SATURDAY MORNING. Raj loaned me some cash, and advised that I buy whatever I needed in the city. "Things much cheaper there than in the countryside," he said.

"And besides," Bram said, "It may be useful that you know your way around in case you have to go on school business."

They all decided to accompany me to Castries.

Before we left for the city, Bram and Nar called me over to their room.

"Tell me what you see in the dark room," Raj whispered as I was about to go.

"What?"

"Just go and tell me when you return."

I had to push aside the entire curtain to enter since it was all in one piece. Unlike ours, no holes were noticeable.

The room, which smelled of camphor, was dark. There was only one window — it was on the southern side. The eastern wall separated the room from the washroom. A flickering light from a tiny lamp permitted some visibility. The lamp was on an altar. Miniature carvings of Hindu deities, a small bell, some books, fresh looking flowers, and a photograph of Bram's family surrounded the altar. Bram was lying on a piece of sponge next to the altar. Nar sat with legs folded under him on a wooden bed that was about four feet wide. Above the bed was a shelf with mostly books. Clothing hung on nails on the walls. I sat on the bed.

"Okay, Ron. What have you decided? Living with us or in

Soufriere?" Bram asked.

"Here," I said immediately.

He got up and stood in front of me. "Glad you have decided to stay with us. Well, then, there are some things you ought to know."

"Yes, Ron," Nar said. "For instance, we know you are a Christian, but no beef in this house."

I nodded.

"And you should help Raj cook in the afternoons. Nar and I usually come home late in the afternoon and so we cook in the mornings. But don't make him leave it on you."

They fed me with what I should do, know and expect.

As I was about to leave, Bram said, "And Ron, we are glad too that you brought a radio/cassette player. Sometimes things get boring here."

I told Raj what I saw, and about my decision to stay. I mentioned only about the helping part. He shrugged.

When we boarded the bus, it was cool and cloudy. Immediately the bus began to climb a hill; I remembered the night I came. The undulating terrain along the highway was indeed endless and abounding with vegetation. The lush green vegetation gave an overwhelming freshness to the morning. Everywhere was peaceful and quiet.

Today I saw more houses, but still very few. Most of those dotted and clung to the sides of the hills and hugged certain parts of the highway. I tried to visualise what it would be like to live amidst tall trees on high sloping land.

"Has anyone ever been to one of those houses up there?" I asked.

"Yes," said Raj. "You feel like you are on top of the world."

"And what if you fall?" Nar asked.

"You don't have to worry about that. In the first place you can't make it to the top," Raj replied.

"Ah. Go and jump off the cliff," Nar said.

I laughed.

Soon, we passed a long stretch with no houses. Mostly

banana fields were on both sides. Shacks peeped out from the fields and there were a few farmers around. The banana leaves waved in the high wind.

Nar pointed to the banana plants. "Ron," he said, "why do you think they have put plastic bags over these bananas?"

I shrugged

"Well, it is to guard against birds. Yes, in the banana industry..."

"Nar born and raised in the banana fields," Raj slipped in.

Nar paused, sucked his teeth and continued. "Yes, banana is the main foreign exchange earner. Many of the people are banana farmers."

When the bus began to ascend and seemed to be traveling in a southerly direction. Raj said, "We are approaching Praslin. There is a lovely beach in the bay. I have there many times."

From on top, on the right, and a few hundred feet below, I saw the bay arching into the mainland, and on its edge the lovely beach was sprinkled with coconut trees and shrubs. The Atlantic Ocean on the right ran as far as the eye could see. The water shimmered in the now bright sunshine. I felt light and relaxed. Maybe this was the top of the world feeling. It was a wonderful feeling...a grandiose feeling

After Praslin, there were very few houses along the highway. On the left side hills rose steeply from the edge in some places and stretched for some distances.

After about fifteen to twenty minutes drive we came upon a densely populated area.

"This is Dennery," Nar said. "It is a town. It extends all the way up to the sea." He pointed to his right. "There is a thriving fishing industry here."

Leaving Dennery, we encountered more of the same kind of vegetation and landscape on both sides if the road. Yet Nar's running commentary continued. The names of the villages came easily to him and he seemed to know each plant.

When we came upon another area thick with banana

plants, he said, "La Caye."

And further on there was yet another large expanse with banana plants. "Yes. This is Ma Bouya Valley."

Soon the bus meandered through a stretch where we lost the sunshine. It suddenly became cooler. The foliage of immensely tall trees actually covered the road way.

"Rain forest. This is Barre-de-l'Isle." Nar said. "You see those tall, tall trees. They call them blue mahoo or something like that…"

"Looks like the mahogany and greenheart we have back home," I said.

"Oh yes. I haven't been in the forest but I was told that these mammoth trees are loaded with epiphytic bromeliads…"

"What?" I asked.

Bram smiled. "He means plants that grow on other plants. And here he is talking about members of the pine family. But orchids and mushrooms grow on them too."

"And, they say, here you can see the Jako, the St. Lucian parrot…the national bird…" Nar continued.

"And so also are the yellow and red breasted finch, the St. Lucia peewee and St. Lucia oriole," Bram added

"Oh. And this?" I said pointing to an opening in the rain forest.

"Trail," Nar said, looking over his shoulder as the bus drove on. "There are others. Tourists visit here often…That trail can actually take you to the other part of the island…to Soufriere."

Raj turned to him, "Are you a Literature teacher or a tour guide?"

"What do you mean?"

"If you are a tour guide, get your facts straight."

"What facts?"

Raj did not respond.

"In any case, a man of literature makes an excellent tour guide. Not like you…dumb."

They glared at each other. I smiled.

Leaving the coolness of the Barre de l'Isle, we travelled in bright sunshine and soon glided through a long and relatively flat stretch of road. Houses were strewn alongside the road among the banana fields and other vegetation. I got the impression that this was one continuous village. But Raj pointed out that the settlement changed names as we moved along. First it was Ravine Poisson, then L'Abbaye, next Bexon, and then Odsan.

After Odsan, the land opened up into the largest expanse of banana fields I had seen so far, bringing to mind the rice and sugarcane fields back home.

"Cul de Sac banana plantation," Nar said.

When the bus began to ascend once again, Nar said, "We are going up The Morne. The tertiary institution I told you about...the Sir Arthur Lewis Community College is up there. Sometimes we attend seminars there. You may have to come here soon." After a while, he pointed. "This is the route you have to take."

Minutes later, "Castries," someone said.

Looking down from on top of The Morne, I saw a city which looked like the arena of an amphitheatre whose eastern edges rose unevenly into hills, and western bordered a bay that extended far inland. Buildings sprinkled the hills in a seemingly disorganized way. Sunlight glanced off the roofs of the buildings cramped in the flat middle of the town.

As we meandered down a steep hill, we seemed to be heading straight into two gigantic ocean liners docked in Castries Harbour in the bay. The ships dwarfed Castries.

"This is it?" I asked.

"Uhuh."

"I think I could throw a cricket ball to the other end," I said.

They laughed.

The bus stopped at the park, not too far from the edge of the bay. Close by was the market square. It was humming.

47

Many people moved around.

We walked through the streets gingerly.

"You see that building there," said Nar, pointing to a sign. "This is the Ministry of Education. You have to come here to receive your first pay."

And further up, Raj said, "And this is the Ministry of Health, where you have to know in case you have to bring Nar to check on his sanity."

We laughed.

"And there is Cable and Wireless." Raj turned his head to indicate.

"Over here is the Bank of St. Lucia," Bram said.

"M and C is up this way." Nar pointed.

We slipped in M and C Drug Store. "Would like to buy some aspirins," I said.

We took some time to locate it among the array of other drugs.

We proceeded to Brazil Street. "Perhaps the busiest," Nar said.

Cars lined the street and parking lots were crammed. There were many little food and haberdashery stalls on the sidewalks. We shouldered and squeeze our way through gatherings and lines of people.

Some hailed, "Trini..."

We waved.

Vendors beckoned, "GT..."

We looked at them.

Others called, "Indian..."

We smiled.

We entered a shopping plaza. Clothing, footwear, cosmetics and electronic equipment made in US, Canada, UK, China, Japan, Taiwan and Honk Kong were everywhere. We held and fingered them, turned them over, and checked the labels and prices. Raj and I bought a few items of cheap clothing.

As I was about to enter into another a shop, Raj said, "You

will see more of the same. Let's go to the supermarket."

The supermarket had flour, dhal, toothpaste, cheese and toilet paper in abundance. We inspected and checked prices. I grabbed several items, but Nar said, "Take it easy, Ron. Take it easy. All the stores have these." We bought a few food items.

It was around midday when we left the supermarket. On Raj's insistence, we went for lunch in a small creole restaurant.

"I would like a barbecued chicken and a cheese sandwich," I said.

"You are sure you don't want channa and dhal too?" Nar said, and laughed.

I got my desire, plus a small portion of what Raj had ordered — red beans, dumplings and salted pigtails; the latter didn't taste too badly. The ice cold passion fruit drink was very refreshing.

Nar glanced at our plates and screwed up his face. "Huh. The way some people are metamorphosing, one of these days I won't be surprised if they start to devour beef!"

I looked at Nar. He raised his hand. "Not you, Ron...You are Christian."

Bram and Nar ordered light snacks and soft drinks. Raj stood in front of Nar and opened the belt on his pants. "Oops...my pants falling."

"What's wrong with dieting?" Nar said.

When we hit the streets again, the sun bore down on us. We flitted in and out of stores that we did not visit in the morning, and again, the boys did not buy much. I bought some stationery. Soon we were overcome by the heat and exhaustion and decided to rest on the wharf at the water front before we boarded the bus to home.

When we arrived at around four, Regis was standing not too far away talking to Rasta Paul. Immediately he came over to us, and after shaking our hands in turn, reminded us about the movie. We assured him that we would be there.

Raj dressed and left before six. He told me he had an important meeting with some of his colleagues. Bram, Nar and I decided to take it easy until it was time for Regis' show. Bram and Nar asked me if I brought cassettes.

"Let me see...English oldies and a couple of Mukesh and Rafi."

"Ah, Mukesh. Yes. Play that," Nar said.

"Yes. I must get some Bhajan." Bram added.

While the music was playing, I took the opportunity to speak to Bram when he stepped into the kitchen. "Bram," I whispered, "What's going on between Raj and Nar?"

"Look, Ron, don't bother. They have been at each other like this for some time."

We went over at about 6:45 to Regis'. About ten patrons were already standing by the door. A light bulb hung over on a black oblong piece of plywood secured to the wall next to the door. On the plywood was written:

**Tonite: 'Jaws' and 'Ninja Action'. Price $1.00.
Chicken and Fish. $1.00**

We heard Regis' voice in the shop. "*Gason*, hurry up. Hurry up with the beer!"

It was already fifteen minutes past seven. The number of patrons increased to over a score.

"Cauldron, when the ass you going to start?" a heavy voice rose above the loud chatter.

"He too greedy. Why he don't close the shop and start the blasted movie? Is the same *maji* every time!" another shouted.

"*Awa*, if he cut the picture tonight I mashing up the T.V!" someone said.

The door rattled and the crowd now about fifty surged towards it. The door squeaked and the crowd tried to form a line. When the door was pushed open, they stepped forward.

"Alright, take it easy or else I cancel," Regis growled. In the dim light Regis stood with hands folded across his chest, red hat perched on top of his head, the sleeves of his black shirt buttoned to his wrists. The double queue shuffled in a single line. His eyes moved over the patrons slowly and he smiled.

When he saw us, the smile broadened. "Ah. Alyuh here. Come, come, pass."

Those by the door quickly made way for us and we entered the dimly lit hall. In front was a television—nineteen or twenty inches—resting on a table, about five feet high, and a video recorder perched on it. There were six rows of seats— approximately one by twelve, twenty foot boards—resting on concrete blocks. As soon as a patron got in, he or she would dash to occupy a seat up front. The seats squeaked and buckled whenever a backside landed on it. Some patrons stood and leaned against the wall. Those who couldn't find seats sat flat on the floor or balanced in a squatting position.

"Regis, what you waiting for? If I get vex, I break up this damn place!" brought an instant hush.

"Alright, alright, ah starting now."

When the movie began, I could hear the patrons breathing.

"Look, Robert ..."

"Shut up!"

"Mama, look at the shark teeth...*salòp!*"

"God, look, it coming again ...e...e...e...e..." the audience screamed in unison.

"*Salòp!*" The scream died.

Silence.

"E...e...e...e...e...!" The crescendo was building up. The shark was gliding towards Robert Shaw.

"*Salòp!*" The shark had Robert Shaw by the legs.

One of the seats crashed to the floor. "*Salòp!*"

When 'Jaws' ended, Regis locked the door of the hall from the inside and went into the shop.

"Buy! Buy! Buy before the chicken and fish get cold." Regis called out. The surge didn't come.

"But Mr. Cal, I want to pee," a boyish voice said.

"Alyuh want to see I don't show any Ninja picture."

There was a surge.

"But Mr. Cal, I want to pee," the same boyish voice pleaded.

"Boy, don't disturb me. Pee anywhere...Pee in the corner. *Pisé, pisé,* nah."

I was now sure others had peed in the corner.

We left after seeing about ten minutes of Ninja's Revenge. The youngsters were over enthusiastic, especially during the Ninja fights. The *salòp* thing was deafening. We encountered Regis at the door chatting with Rasta Paul.

"Enjoy the movie, brothers?" Rasta asked quietly.

"Yes, brother. It irie. *Salòp,*" I said.

"What did you say?" Regis asked laughing.

"What everybody is saying."

"But Ron, you too wicked," Regis said still laughing.. He scratched his head. "Well, it's a bad word, like when someone swears when he is excited or hurt. The boys didn't tell you?"

I shook my head. "You mean everyone was cursing throughout the movie?" I asked.

"Happens all the time," Regis replied.

"Okay. Back home," I said, "if a stone was dropped on someone's toe, he might yell 'Oh *rass*!' Maybe something like that?"

He laughed. "Ron, you too wicked. But what is *rass*?"

"Your backside," Nar told him. "You know, once in the Guyana Parliament, the leader of the opposition in an angry outburst shouted, 'Is sheer *rass* going on in here!' and the Speaker of the House promptly said, 'Either you apologize immediately or you are suspended for two sittings.' The opposition leader stormed out of the House."

"That is sheer *rass*," Regis said and burst out in a renewed fit of laughter and was still laughing when we left him.

At home, I asked Bram and Nar, "Is that the way the audience always behaves?"

"Always," Bram said.

"But tomorrow the same people would behave differently," Nar said.

"How?"

"Everybody would be going to church," Nar replied.

# 5

"YOUR FIRST SUNDAY," Bram greeted me the next morning. He was dressed in white and clutching a big book to his side. I hadn't seen this one next to his altar. When he noticed my stare, he said, "The Gita...Ron, bathe early and let us go to the Hawan by Laljeet, not too far from here."

"Next week. I want to prepare for my first day at school tomorrow. Okay?"

Nar joined us in the living room. He was wearing a yellow shirt and a pair of brown pants.

"Raj!" Bram called out. "Nine already. Are you not going to the Hawan?"

"Nah. Next week."

"Huh," Nar said and began to rotate his head and shoulders.

About ten minutes after they had left, Raj came out into the living room yawning. "How was the movie?"

"It was alright, but man, the people. They are something else."

"Yes, I know." He stretched and yawned again. "Man, I come in after midnight. I went to the Theater Guild in Castries with my girlfriend to see a play. It was..."

"Guyanese girl?"

"Nah. But anyway Ron, the play was fabulous. You know, it is the first time I have seen a staged play. It was a Derek Walcott play too. He is the St. Lucian who won the Nobel Laureate prize last year."

I looked out for Bram and Nar. As soon as they entered the house after one, I said, "Bram, Nar, tell me what to expect at school."

Bram's said, "Different from Zeeburg...Don't rock the boat."

Nar said "The children could talk and eat."

I stared at both of them.

On the Monday morning I left home at six thirty. It was quiet and breezy. The bus went up and down, and around curves. It passed a stretch of banana fields before it came to the populated area, Micoud, about which Regis had told me. "Just like Dennery," he had said.

After about twenty minutes, Hewanorra International Airport appeared on the right. It was much bigger than Vigie's. Soon, I heard the distinct sound of water lapping against land. The narrow road was squashed between the fence enclosing the airport and the shore. I looked to the left and there was the Atlantic Ocean bearing down on us angrily. There were two islets-one large, and the other lying close by, very tiny- not too far off shore. They had to be the Maria Islands, the boys had spoken about. They spiraled out of the sea.

The wind whistled through the bus. It was chilly for a while. I took in the pure smell of the ocean. Immediately after, we entered a short stretch of road about four lanes wide. An almond grove nestled on the left, hugged the Ocean. There was coziness about it.

At the junction where the wide road ended, and everyone disembarked from the bus, I looked up and saw the lighthouse. It stood protectively. This had to be Vieux Fort. I scanned my immediate surroundings. It was as flat as Zeelugt.

There were many people at the bus terminal at the cross road. I boarded a bus that was bounded for Piaye. Regis had said, "It would take a long time for a bus going to Soufriere to fill up. And the drivers don't leave until the bus fill up. So take one to Piaye and then join one going to Choisel or Soufriere."

But this one too was filling up slowly. Those on board became impatient. I glanced at my watch. Nearly half an hour had elapsed since I entered the bus. Inside the bus was getting humid. But as soon as the bus drove off a light breeze sprung up. I sat upright and looked outside. For a short while I had a fleeting glance of the Caribbean Sea on the left. The fence of the airport still ran on the right. When the bus climbed to a road on top of a hill at Laborie, situated three to four miles from Vieux Fort, I looked down to the left and saw the Caribbean Sea as far as the clouded horizon. It evoked that same conquering feeling as I had at Praslin. It was a peaceful view. The water appeared calm. A few boats dotted the surface. Then looking up and ahead, I saw two mountain peaks far away to the west. I pointed and asked the young lady sitting next to me, "Is that the Pitons?"

"Yes. It is," she replied, and looked at me closely.

I focused on the peaks for a while until the bus took a turn and a hill blocked the view.

The bus rattled and screeched around turns as it drove along the hilly coastal road to Soufriere on the West Coast. This was going to be a long rough drive, I thought. Regis had said that Soufriere was about twenty five miles away from Vieux Fort. And to think I had committed myself to travel daily wasn't comforting. Some passengers complained about the deteriorating road. Others closed their eyes. I craned my neck to see what was on both sides of the road. Mainly mango, breadfruit and coconut trees, banana plants and shrubs appeared all over, sometimes in thick clumps, and in other sections thinly scattered. After the bus negotiated a hair pin bend, the sea disappeared from view but the Pitons reappeared. They loomed larger. Lovely! Like two breasts indeed! Suddenly the bus pulled up at a junction and everyone got off. "Is this Piaye?" I asked the woman next to me. She nodded. I alighted and inquired for the bus traveling to Choiseul or Soufriere.

"That bus," said a boy as he raised his head in the direction of a yellow bus parked on the other side of the road, "is going to Soufriere, Mister." He was clad in a yellow shirt and a pair of maroon long pants. I joined the bus. The boy came into the bus and sat next to me. He extracted a book from his school bag and began to read. After a while I nudged him and asked, "Which school do you attend?"

He leaned back, stared at my face and said, "Soufriere Comprehensive," and pointed to the crest on his shirt.

"I am going there," I said quietly.

He tilted his head and looked into my face again.

I smiled. "At Soufriere Comprehensive what…"

Suddenly I heard screams and laughter. I looked around quickly and saw a set of children racing towards the bus. A few had on the same maroon and yellow uniform. The others donned grey and white. They jostled to get aboard the bus. Inside the bus, they tugged at one another and made a lot of noise. As soon as the driver entered the bus, he looked at them and raised his index finger, "Listen, if alyuh don't behave, I throwing the whole pack of you out!"

There was an instant hush.

The boy next to me said, "Is everyday they make the driver get vex." He resumed reading.

The bus left after seven. It shook even more than the previous one. The children twisted and braced themselves as the driver applied the brakes, as it seemed every second, and the bus screeched more loudly around the bends. The children became noisy.

"Driver, you driving this old bus too slow," one of them said.

All of them laughed. I smiled. The driver turned his head

to look at them. Immediately the noise died.

A sickening feeling was welling up inside me. I rubbed my stomach and clasped my hand over my mouth. I felt like vomiting.

The boy peered at me, and then touched my hand. "Mister, you okay?" he asked.

I nodded and closed my eyes.

"Mister," the boy said, "You ever travel here before?"

"First time."

"Mister, people who travel on this road for the first time does get sick. You will feel better soon."

I touched him on his shoulder and smiled.

After a while, the boy tapped me, "Mister, Balenbouche."

"What?"

"You will feel better," he said and concentrated on his book again.

The bus was running smoothly. When I looked ahead, I saw an unusual long stretch of straight road. It was smooth. Just like back home, I thought. I felt better. Most of Balenbouche was flat. Very few houses appeared on either side of the road. Both sides were lined with shrubs and vines and a variety of trees predominantly tall listing coconut trees. There were a few breadfruit, flamboyant, mango, tamarind and glory cedar trees.

Minutes later, the bus began to descend. The sinking feeling began to resurface. The bus seemed to be heading straight into a cemetery. But at the bottom of the hill it took an obtuse angle turn, and a small yellow building marked, 'Choiseul Police Station', came in view.

"This is a village? Isn't it?" I asked the boy,

"Yes."

"How far are we from Soufriere?"

"About ten miles."

He smiled.

Immediately after, the bus began to strain and groan more than anytime before. The double hair pin bend that it was negotiating was steep...really steep. I looked down. We were literally above the roof tops of the buildings on the left. I gripped the back rest of my seat. The boy glanced at me and smiled.

When the bus reached level ground, I looked ahead. More of the Pitons appeared in view. It was spectacular.

"That is really beautiful," I said aloud.

"What?" the boy asked.

"The Pitons," I replied, still looking at them.

"Oh, that," he said. He returned to his book.

I sat back and enjoyed the scenery.

Then some where along the route, I had a whiff of a strange smell. I sniffed the air. I looked outside. I saw fields of cocoa trees and banana plants. Maybe rotting vegetables or insecticides were left on the roadside, I thought. But the smell became more pronounced. I took a deep breath.

The boy tapped me and grinned. "Sulphur, Mister."

Immediately I recalled what Regis had told me.

"Sulphur Springs around here?" I asked.

"Uhuh."

Suddenly, on the left, one of the mountain peaks reared up before me.

"Majestic indeed!" I said.

"Petite Piton," the boy said.

It was tall and pointing to the sky. It rose from the sea.

"The one back there is the Gros Piton." His left hand moved further to the left.

Gros Piton appeared bigger and flatter. Both were studded with vegetation.

Less than fifteen seconds later, he said, "The town of Soufriere."

The bus was rolling slowly down a hilly coastal road. When it rounded the first bend, a small wooden sheltered structure with the sign, 'Viewing Gallery,' greeted us. I peered through the trees and shrubs on the side of the road. Down below, I saw the waves of the ocean slapping and washing the brown sand beach and the shoreline of a sprawl-ing town. I turned my head in all direction to see as much of the town as I could as the bus glided through a narrow street. All I saw were many cramped, small wooden structures of quaint architectural designs on both sides of the street, and many people on the side walks.

The bus was in the compound of Soufriere Comprehensive Secondary School within minutes.

"Mister, this is the Compre school," the boy said.

"I will be teaching here."

"Eh?"

I patted him on his shoulder and smiled.

He smiled. "Okay, sir."

I stepped on the sandy driveway cautiously, hugging my shoulder bag and surveying the surroundings. The com-pound buzzed and swarmed with students dressed in their maroon and yellow uniform. A few stopped and looked at me.

When I entered the administration office, the secretary who was sitting at her desk, looked up. I introduced myself and handed her the cable—the same one I had shown to the Immigration Officer.

"Welcome," she said, and immediately got up and knocked on the door of the Principal's office and entered. She emerged almost immediately. "You can go in," she said.

The Principal, a tall and bespectacled man, stood, wel-comed me, shook my hand and beckoned me to sit.

"How was your trip?" he said as he turned to his filing cabinet.

"Okay, Sir."

He plucked out an envelope and turned to face me again. He smiled, sat and nodded as he read the sheet of paper he had extracted from the envelope.

"Mr. Singh," he said without looking up, "your résumé indicate that you are a professional." He paused. "And I sure you will conduct yourself as one." He sat upright and looked at me steadily in the face.

When he looked at the paper again, I glanced around his office. It was small. Around him books were neatly arranged on the shelves. There was a small picture of the Prime Minister on the wall and next to it was another one of the same size with a group of people. There was a leather strap on top of the filing cabinet. He noticed my focus.

"Sometimes we have to resort to that," he said and smiled.

"Here," he said, and handed me a booklet. "In here are our mission statement, motto and so on....Teachers' roles and responsibilities. Collect a timetable from the secretary. Let her put you on to your H.O.D."

I took it and flipped the pages.

"You can do that later...Where are you staying?"

"Mon Repos."

"Mon Repos!"

"I have some friends there."

"Can be tiresome..." He got up. "But it's time you meet the staff."

He shook my hand for the second time. "Ronald, welcome on board. Feel free to see me anytime...problem or no problem."

The secretary introduced me to the staff members individually. They seemed a friendly and exuberant bunch. Only one male donned a shirt jack. Others appeared casually dressed. None wore a tie. The females were exquisitely attired. Most of the teachers asked, "Guyanese or Trinidadian? What subject area?"

When I entered the classroom at 8:30, a curious hush descended on the class. I introduced myself, printed my name on the blackboard, and began the lesson. At first, the students were quiet but gradually the chatter rose. Immediately after the period was over about five students surrounded me and asked many questions.

"Sir, are you married? How many children you have?"

I told them.

"Sir, you like St. Lucia?"

"I haven't seen much. But yes."

"Sir let me tell you..." one student began.

Another interrupted, "He doesn't know. Let me tell you..." In less than two minutes, he told me about a dozen different things.

The number of students doubled only minutes after. Hands wagged in the air.

"Me sir, me sir...Let me tell you about the Pitons." He raced on.

"He lie, sir."

"Look." A few fingers pointed. The two mountain peaks were clearly visible from the classroom.

"Ever see anything like this, sir? They are the majestic Pitons."

"I was looking at them all the way from Vieux Fort. Magnificent!" I said.

Soon I was completely engulfed by nearly half a classroom of students.

"And yes, sir, Soufriere is the oldest town in St. Lucia and it was the island's first capital under French rule."

"Oh, yes."

"And, sir, did you smell anything like boiled egg as you were nearing Soufriere?" a petite female student asked shyly.

"Yes. I did. It came from the Sulphur Springs? Right?"

"Right, sir. The Sulphur Springs is widely acclaimed as the only drive in volcano in the world. It was and still is considered one of the main tourist attractions in this part of the world. And, sir, the tourists too, are drawn by other natural enticements, all of which are within close proximity of the town," she reeled out proudly.

"Wow! Are you a Social Studies student?" I asked.

"Yes, and sir, I am hoping to work in the tourism sector, sir, after I graduate, sir."

"You will do well," I said.

"Sir, tell us about Guyana," she said.

"Big, big," I said. "It is eighty three thousand..."

"We know that, sir. But do you have hills and mountains like here?"

"Yes. But the people live mostly on the flat coastland. It is below sea level. Sea walls had to be built to keep out the Atlantic Ocean."

"So sir, when you have hurricane, where the water go?"

I smiled. "We don't have hurricanes."

"Don't bother with her, sir. I know that, and I already tell her that Guyana is not an island..."

"But, sir, how is it Guyanese playing cricket for the West Indies and it is not an island?" one asked.

"It's the only English speaking country on the mainland of South America."

"And that's why you Guyanese speak so funny! This morning I couldn't understand you," chuckled another.

"At times, I didn't understand you either," I said, lightly slapping him on his arm. "But each country has its own dialect although it is the same English. We ought to appreciate that. Okay?

"With time, we will understand each other..."

Just then, the school bell rang. I glanced at my watch. "I have to meet another class."

"See you at lunch time, sir?"

"Okay."

During the lunch break, I couldn't get away. My colleagues in the staffroom kept me busy.

"Lots of people leaving Guyana, eh? Why? Discrimination?" one asked.

"Well..."

"I hear the government ban a lot of things."

"Yes, many."

"Generally how is the political and economic situation in Guyana," another inquired.

"Well, not too bad," I said. "But I am here because I would like to broaden my experience."

"Is that so?" one of them commented. He was smiling. He extended his hand. "I am Adrian Felix...the Agri teacher. I wasn't here this morning. Welcome."

"Ronald Singh." I shook the hand.

"I spent two weeks in Guyana last year. I enjoyed it," he said.

He sat next to me. We spoke about familiar things until the lunch break was almost over.

"Do you drink?" he asked smiling.

"A few beers...occasionally."

After school we drove to the beer garden in his pick-up van.

"I think," I said laughing, "the carburetor of your pick up van needs cleaning."

"Why do you think that is the problem?" he asked.

"Look, back home I had a car and I had to take it to the garage at least once a week."

He laughed. "Maths teacher, eh?"

He was a very affable and easygoing man. He told me his wife was Indian and they had two children.

That afternoon he drove me to Vieux Fort. The ride wasn't bad.

On the following day, the students accosted me in the same cordial ambiance as they did the previous morning.

"Sir, sir, do they have lots of Indians there?" queried Rohan, the skinny little *dogla*.

"Yes. There are more Indians than Blacks, but not too many more. We have six races altogether plus *dogla*."

They giggled. "And they *még* like Rohan, sir?"

Rohan looked at his feet.

"No, they can't be *még*, eh, Mr. Singh? I hear you all have lots of sugar and rice and fruits..."

"But we have top quality bananas," another interjected, as he held his hand above his head. "We export bananas to all parts of the world. I will bring some for you, sir."

I was beginning to sweat.

"Make way and let sir get some breeze. But sir, I hear you all have gold...like you have on you... like in all streams...all over the place."

I looked at the bangle on my hand and smiled. "Yes, we have gold and diamond. But we don't get them as easily as you think. Another day I will explain."

I wiped the perspiration from my brow and got up to leave. Two girls playfully tugged at my arm, "Sir, tell us about the streams then, and the floating bridge?"

"I have to leave to catch the bus to Piaye. Next week. Okay?" At home, I told Bram and Nar about the students' interest in Guyana.

"Oh yes," Bram agreed. "They are very curious."

"You see how they like to eat, eh? Didn't they ask you to bring roti for them?" Nar asked.

Bram laughed. "Ron, you remember when Nar flogged a student back home for eating in class?"

"Oh yes, I remember it," I said laughing too.

I recalled when the boy's mother had walked up to Nar the next morning, held him firmly by the shoulder and said, "How dare you lay a hand on my little boy? You little imp!"

He shook off the hand. "I lay hand on you too if you behave like an ignoramus," he replied, staring up into her face.

The altercation gained ground like two fisherwomen arguing over a man on a hot Saturday afternoon, and the principal was summoned. By the time he arrived on the scene, Nar and the woman were screaming at each other. Most of the students had already formed a ring around the two. The Principal pleaded with Nar to calm down until he got tired. He sent for Bram who grabbed Nar's shoulder and led him to the staffroom.

"Nar," I said, "have you ever had any such problem here in St. Lucia?"

"No. You have to be really stupid to touch a student here."

"How so?"

"The students themselves could beat you. They are big and strong. They don't have to bring their parents."

Back here at Soufriere Comprehensive, more students quickly gathered around me at break time on Monday morning of the following week.

I explained the little I knew about gold and diamond mining. They were attentive. I also told them that Guyana was called the land of many waters and that the rivers and the numerous canals and trenches were filled with reptiles and fishes.

"Like tuna fish, sir?"

"No. Fresh water fish we call them."

"Okay, sir, tell us if you have any waterfall in your Botanical Garden. Tell us."

"No, but we have the Kaieteur Falls, found in the interior of Guyana. It is famed for having..."

"The highest single drop in the entire world..."

"Seven hundred and twenty one feet..."

"Okay. That's right. So how long is the floating bridge?" I asked.

"Fifty feet..."

"One hundred yards..."

The figures increased.

"None of you close," I said. "It is nearly one mile long."

"Eh?"

"Yes, it is made up of a series of pontoons. Some say it is the longest floating bridge in the entire world."

"Sir, now you joking...Okay, sir, I bet you never heard of the Jako parrot. You ever see a parrot, sir? Wait sir, let me... show...show you," Shantal, the prefect of Form 2A, said excitedly as she extracted a book from her schoolbag. "Look. It have blue feathers *here*... yellow tail *here*...green wings *here*... and a red spot...*here*," she pointed out slowly like a seasoned teacher. She watched me closely as she emphasized the colors.

"Wow! Very beautiful, I must say. Thank you, Shantal. I hope I can see it one day. We have lots of parrots in Guyana. At one time we had a macaw named Millie at a world fair. It was the most beautiful bird there, but it cursed bad, bad."

"A parrot cursed, sir? No, no. You are joking sir?"

One Wednesday morning, as soon as I entered the compound, Perry, another of my lower form students came up to me with a big green nylon bag.

"It is for you, sir. We have a lot." Smilingly, he held out the bag. His friends giggled.

"They say grapefruits are good for fat people."

"But I am not fat, boy." I threw an arm around him and squeezed lightly.

"Never mind, sir. Take it. Do you get these things back home?"

"Oh yes. The people plant lots of greens and vegetables. Plus we have a variety of fruits and there are markets on Fridays and Saturdays all over the place."

He shook his head in disbelief. "But sir, why did you come here to St. Lucia?"

I did not reply.

THE NEXT SATURDAY MORNING was as bright as the first. The boys decided they must show me Mon Repos. "Just in case you have to go on some errands and you feel adventurous," Nar said.

I put on my pair of faded track boots and waited.

Nar led the way. As we passed a church and bar, he said, "Everybody goes solemnly to church during the day and patronize the bar boisterously during the night."

"Ah, come on Nar, that is not true," Raj said.

About twenty yards further was a playing field. I pointed to it. "Small," I said.

"Yes," Raj said, "If you edge the ball over the slips, is six runs. On Sunday they have a big match. We will come."

Further up the street, I saw a 'Post Office' sign. It was

located in the bottom flat of a house.

"You have to collect your mail," Bram said. "Some of the streets don't have names, and the houses and the lots are not numbered."

"A delivery mailman would urinate in his pants with all this uneven terrain and the winding and meandering streets," Nar said with a grin.

Soon, smell and smoke filled the air. "A bakery," Raj said, "There are four more around."

"Eh? Why so many?" I asked.

"Everybody eats bread everyday, some morning, noon and night like how everybody eats roti in Zeelugt," Nar sneered.

While they enlightened me and joked, I scanned the thick and lush vegetation all around. The air was pure and the place cool. It was a windy day. I felt very relaxed and energized.

And when Raj said, "From now onwards is downhill," I forged ahead of them.

We ventured down the sloping acres of farmland leading from the back of the village to the Atlantic Ocean. We scrutinized everything in sight. We turned over rocks and poked at unfamiliar things. Raj and I ventured shakily up fruit trees while Bram and Nar caught and dispatched our plunder in nylon bags. Nar's pockets bulged with guavas. It reminded me so much of home, when I, along with my friends in Zeelugt hastily pillaged mangoes and other fruits from properties, a few of which carried the sign, 'Trespassers will be persecuted.' Here we did not see any sign. Here we were unperturbed.

As we plodded on, the trail became steeper. Sometimes we had to scramble over huge boulders and mounds. Nar lagged behind.

We finally arrived at the bottom of slope where we encountered a stream. The water was cool.

"Like the place, Ron?" Raj asked.

I looked up at the tall shady trees. "Simply cosy. I could live here."

"I could bring a feminine companion here," Nar slipped in between sips of water.

"Okay, let's return to the top and get your woman," Raj suggested. "We will use a different track."

"Nar!" Raj called after we had progressed some distance.

"Coming," the thin voice echoed way below. When he caught up with us he was dripping with perspiration. We sat and rested again. A few animals were grazing nearby in a small pasture.

"Still want to bring a woman here?" Raj asked.

Nar brushed him aside with a wave of the hand.

"Nar," Raj continued, "you are a man of literature. Have you ever heard the story of the old bull and the young bull?" He pointed to the animals in the field.

Nar shook his head slowly from side to side. "What about them?"

"Well the two of them were walking down the road when they saw a herd of cows, and the young bull told the old bull, 'Let's run down and do a couple of them,' whereupon the old bull said, 'No, let's walk down and do all of them.' Lecherous old bull, eh?"

"So, what connection that has with me?"

"Oh, nothing, Nar. But you remind me of the old bull."

Nar removed one of the guavas from his pocket and feigned to throw it at Raj.

We returned home with both our stomach and hands filled.

A Bhajan being played on the tape recorder awoke me the Sunday morning. At around eight, all of us left for the Hawan. The highway was busy.

Male churchgoers were soberly dressed in dark suits, with colored or white shirts. The ladies wore black, white or mauve dresses and most, intricately shaped hats. Children too looked smart, some with black or white socks reaching up just below their knees. Almost everyone held a book of some sort.

"Good morning," a gentleman in dark suit hailed.

We returned the greeting.

"How are you brother?" another one asked.

We each told him.

"Have a pleasant day," a young lady said.

"You too," we said together.

When we turned a bend about one hundred yards from where we lived, Raj pointed. "Laljeet's house," he said.

The house—small and white—was perched on top of a hill. At the foot of the hill was a spacious gas station.

Before we entered the patio, the pungent smell of curry greeted us. A short, curly haired young man appeared in the doorway. When I got close to him, he extended a hand to me. "You must be Ron?"

"Yes." I shook the hand.

"Laljeet, *namaste*," he said quietly. "Make yourself at home."

In less than half an hour, the number of invitees had grown to nearly fifteen. Aside, Lal told me, "All here are Guyanese except for one Trinidadian gentleman, who is married to a Guyanese woman."

We introduced ourselves and tried to become familiar.

"Ever been to Rosignal...?"

"Yes..."

"You know Rampersaud...?"

"No..."

"But you have to hear about the goldsmith. Bandits clean him out and killed his son..."

"Lord Krishna!"

"Ever been to Linden...?"

"No..."

"You right...only black people live there..."

We looked around, squinted and studied the environment.

Eventually someone said, "Ronald, I hear bandits killed a boy in Zeelugt."

"Yes."

"What happened?"

I told them briefly.

"Lord Krishna! It coulda be you."

"But that is nothing. Listen..."

We heard more bandit stories.

An elderly man raved, "Boy, bandits caused me to run."

A young man said, "Never going back home!"

Then I espied a familiar-looking figure trudging up. Javed Khan! When he saw me he broke into a wide grin. "You know, this is not surprising," he said. He came up and threw an arm around my shoulder.

I told Javed about the principal's inquiry. He laughed. "I know the bastard suspected I would leave."

The Hawan got underway around nine. We sat with our legs folded yoga style on white cotton sheets spread all over the living room. Bram sat facing us, next to a wooden altar, over which smoke hovered. Picturesque photographs of different Hindu deities hung on the altar. Raj, who sat next to me, was closest to the door leading to the patio.

Bram opened the Gita and began to read and chant in Hindi as he flipped the pages. He squeezed his eyes shut, and rocked his head and body as he sang. It was as if he were transformed into another person, transposed into another world. Then he opened his eyes, looked us all over, and explained in his own broken English style as he did back home.

Back home, he was the recognized pandit of the village.

"Mr Tiwari is a Brahmin, You hear. We don't want any Chamar for pandit," they said.

"Yes, you is a bright young man, Mr. Suku. And we know you know everything in the Gita and you even speak more proper English than guru Bram. But you ain't born in the right caste. How Lord Krishna go listen to you?" an elder of the church had appeased the deflated Mr. Suku as they settled a dispute about who should officiate at an important function at the Hindu temple.

The affluent and high class in and out of Zeelugt sought Bram. "We want the best. We want guru Bram to do our work," they said. Their drivers waited on him and returned him safely to his home. It wasn't long after he himself drove his own Toyota car.

Here in Laljeet's home, the congregation was spellbound. A bead of perspiration trickled down my face. I wiped it and looked at Raj. He was turning and twisting. He glanced at his watch. I did the same. Only ten o'clock! Only one hour had dragged by and they said it would finish at midday. I looked at Bram. His eyes were closed. Cramp was taking over both of my legs. I clutched them. Bram squeezed his eyes tighter and a pleasant smile appeared on his face. I squirmed and winced as the cramp slowly engulfed both legs. Raj straightened out his feet and leaned against the wall. I did the same. The cramp got worse. I reached for the upright of the door and pulled myself up and out of the doorway. I stamped my feet lightly for a while. The numbness began to subside.

"Yes, you would be born again. Yes, reincarnated...yes, but in what form? Your deeds on this earth will determine whether you born a rajah, a queen, a cat or a dog or a jackass or Rawan..." I heard Bram exhorting as I moved off the patio. I plodded downhill and struggled across to the gas station where I gulped down a refreshing drink of Sprite.

Suddenly, a blue, double cab pick up with several people on board, pulled up in front one of the pumps. The driver waited for a few minutes and tooted his horn in quick succession. Just then, the sound of the bell was heard distinctly. The people in the pick-up looked up at Laljeet's house. They squinted. They looked away after a while. But when the blare of conch shell pierced the air, they stared again. The conch sounded a second time. The people gaped. It came a third time, louder than the previous two. They looked at one another.

"Oh, I believe someone is selling tuna up there," one of them sighed and the others giggled. They relaxed.

A small thin cloud of smoke floated through the window of the house. "They grilling the tuna," a little one said, shaking his head knowingly.

The pump attendant came, and when he saw the occupants of the vehicle looking up to the house, he said nonchalantly, "Some Indians...Guyanese. Yes. They always do that on Sundays."

"Ah, a feast," one of them said. "I wish they invite me."

"A cult...maybe like that Jonestown thing we heard about Guyana some time ago. Mama!" another concluded as they drove off.

*Jonestown! That was so long ago.*

Raj joined me. "The place is hot and I got cramps," he said.

I told him about the Jonestown thing.

"Yes," he said. "Some of the St. Lucians even believe what takes place at Laljeet's is obeah. And on the Jonestown thing, many have their own version of what really happened."

"Well. No one is really too sure. It happened so long ago and so far away in the hinterland of Essequibo."

"My father told me about it but I have a hazy recollection."

"I remember the morning clearly when my wife roused me out of bed.' Is war, Venezuela attacking!' she was screaming. When I peeped out I saw and heard hordes of aircraft flying in and out as they do in war zones in the movies."

"Yes, my father did mention Venezuela and I remember asking him, 'Who is Venez who?' and he said, 'Soon we will be Venez who, and you have to speak Spanish.' For a couple of days, I gazed at those things flying overhead, and until they disappear."

"Imagine a man claiming to be the reincarnation of Jesus Christ and luring close to a thousand people away from their home...and getting involve in a kind of communal living..."

I said.

"And then forcing them to commit suicide."

"Boy, talk about religious zeal and fanaticism. Man, the things that happen in the name of religion."

Raj looked at me steadily for a while and then said, "Ron, You are not too keen about religion...are you?"

"Why you say that?"

"You were not too interested in attending the Hawan and...and what you have just said."

"Well, you can say I am put off by some things that have happened."

"Anyway, imagine it was our government that encouraged this thing, giving Jim Jones land and all that," Raj said, shaking his head.

"A state within a state...in your own land and you didn't have a say on what transpired."

"That's what I called senseless."

"I wonder what was in it for the government..." I said.

The loud ringing of bell interrupted us. When we looked up at Laljeet's residence, we saw people moving about.

"Time for our seven curry and sweet meat," Raj said.

They served puri and seven curries—channa (beans), dhal (peas), pumpkin, bhagi (callaloo), katahar (breadnut), allou (potato), and boulange (egg plant)—with coconut choka and mango achar along with the sweet meats—sweet rice, fudge, manbhouge, gulgula, jillabie—and fruits—banana, watermelon, cantelope and grapes.

While Raj and I were eating, Nar came up. "Enjoying the foods boys? That's what...and how should cook," he said, and walked off.

"So that he could stuff his backside full," Raj said under his breath.

Javed approached me while I was standing on the step. He threw an arm over my shoulder. "Ron, where do you live and where do you work?"

I told him.

"Can I come and live with you guys? I live and work in Dennery...not too far."

I beckoned Raj and Nar.

"Ask them," I told him and left to find Bram.

As I was returning, Nar walked up to me before I got to Javed. "Halal chicken and beef. No way!"

That was the last day I saw Javed.

WHEN WE TURNED INTO THE PATHWAY on our way home, we found Regis sitting under a breadfruit tree. Getting up, he said, "Been to your religious service, boys? This morning when I passed, I heard the bell and saw the smoke again. And, Bram, you had promised to tell me about it a long time ago."

"Okay."

He listened attentively while Bram told him about the bell and the smoke in less than two minutes.

Afterwards, Regis turned to me, "Anyway, I must take you boys to *légliz-la*, the big one up there, the Catholic Church, of course."

"How come it is bigger than all of the buildings, Mr. Regis?" I asked.

"Ah, let me tell you," he licked his lips and delved into history as I expected he would. "Yes, big because the white masters could have gathered all of the slaves and teach them Christianity...about the great teachings of Jesus Christ. Bless them. And it remained so big that we could use it as hurricane shelter."

He paused and looked at me thoughtfully. "Mr. Ron, what kind of a Hindu are you? I mean, are you Catholic or Presbyterian or what?"

We laughed, and when I told him that I didn't belong to any church, he laughed more than us. "You Russian or what?" Suddenly he turned to Raj. "You see him there, he ending up marrying a girl right here in St. Lucia in my church."

"Like you know Raj's girlfriend, Mr Regis?" Bram asked.

Regis ignored Bram and belched. I smelled beer. Raj sucked his teeth and walked away.

"Too much *daro*...too much *daro*," Bram told Regis and threw an arm around his shoulder. Nar moved closer to Regis and rubbed the back of his head.

As I turned to leave I heard Bram whispering, "You know her, Mr. Regis?"

I was too far off to make anything of Regis' garbled reply.

When we got home we changed into more casual attire and headed down to the Mon Repos playing field. The cricket match was already in progress. We spent the rest of the afternoon there.

We left at around 5:30. As soon as we reached home two ladies and a white man accosted us outside in the yard. "My brothers, we are Jehovah Witnesses," the white man said.

"Am..." Bram said.

"Have you ever heard of Jehovah?" one of the ladies said.

"Well..." Bram began.

"Jehovah is a God, merciful and gracious. He is slow to anger and abundant in loving kindness and truth," the man continued.

"Jesus Christ! Not again," Nar grumbled.

"Don't have much time but could read the books," Bram said quietly, pointing to the books one of the ladies was holding.

"A dollar each," one of the ladies said, holding out four booklets. We bought two and they left.

"Is over a dozen times they come already... Real nuisance," Nar said.

That night, I sat at the table to write my first letter home. This was the last sentence I penned.

*"Geet, everything is working out perfectly in St. Lucia. Tell the kids."*

Minutes later, Nar emerged from the dark room grimacing and rubbing his stomach. "Raj," he said, "Do you have any medication for constipation?"

Raj laughed. "No. But you can try Epsom salts. Not too much though."

"And milk or water," Bram added.

"Nar," Raj said grinning. "Have you ever heard the story about the Indian chief?"

"No. What about him?"

"Well he was constipated like you, and he sent a tribesman to the medicine man with the message, 'Big chief no shit.' The medicine man gave him a potion. Big chief drank. No relief. Tribesman returned to medicine man, 'Big chief no shit.' Medicine man doubled the potion. Tribesman returned to medicine man, 'Big shit, no chief.'"

Bram burst out laughing, "You mean he shit until he died?"

"Exactly. That is what can happen when you eat a whole truck-load of guavas."

Nar glared at Raj but then said, "Okay, I will take a small portion of epsom salts."

"Lord. It means then that we will have to use under the breadfruit trees as our toilet for a few days," I said.

At nine, Bram walked up to the almanac and did his thing. Minutes later, I heard the tinkling of bell coming from their room.

That night I slept soundly. I dreamt that Geetangali and the kids were smiling and waving from a brand new white truck that was floating in the air.

# 6

WEEKDAY ACTIVITIES fell into routine. Raj was always there when I arrived in the afternoon at five. Bram and Nar came after six. We would fix dinner—well, Raj mostly.

"Look Ron, you don't cook. You just pack away the extras, wash the dishes and clean the mess. Okay. I will let you boil the eggs," he said as he was putting salt in the stew.

"Raj..."

"Sorry. Listen Ron, if the food doesn't taste well, Bram and Nar will have something to complain about...And I am now sure your wife did all of the cooking back home." He smiled and I nodded.

One afternoon, when I reached home, Raj wasn't there. I decided to fix the rice. Bram and Nar arrived home just after I had finished, and Bram as usual went up to the pot first. He opened the pot and poked his nose into it. "Pop!" he cried. "This is a waste."

"Bram, I tried."

"Oh, it was you."

"Like the roving casanova is still exploiting the field," Nar said.

Raj came minutes later and invited, "Hey Ron, let's take a beer."

When I told him about the pop, he laughed.

The following afternoon, Raj arrived home later than the previous day, again with a smile on his face. Hastily, he prepared the dinner and retreated to the bedroom.

Seconds after Bram arrived home. "Dumpling! Oh Lord!" he screamed from the kitchen.

Raj clenched his fists and said, "Yes."

One evening, several days later, Nar got to the pot first. "Fig and salt fish! Lord Krishna, we have been violated. What next?"

In the bedroom, Raj responded, "Got them," and punched the air.

I decided that if Raj went ahead and prepared ground provision soup the next day as he had hinted, I would dump the remainder in the garbage bin after he and I had eaten.

He cooked dhal and rice and fried tuna fish instead. Bram and Nar ate and hummed Indian tunes.

The next day he prepared channa curry and roti. Bram and Nar joined us in the living room to eat.

After that it was pumpkin and rice. After Raj had eaten he went over to Regis' and returned with barbecued chicken.

The day after, Bram and Nar arrived home before Raj. They grumbled and told me, "We will cook." They cooked egg plant and rice.

Raj came home after eight. On entering the house he hailed, "Ron, I brought you some beef burgers. Come."

I quickly rushed out of the bedroom. "Raj, you can't do that."

He put his index finger across his lips, "Just joking."

"Come," I said and stepped outside.

He followed me in the dark.

"Raj, I think you should ease up on the guys and…"

"Ha. You should see how they treat me before you came," he said.

"How?"

"Like a small boy. Do this and do that. Go there…come

here!"

"But..."

"No buts! And don't spend money wild...don't buy this...don't eat that. Don't run after the girls!"

"Okay. But ease up. You are only making things worse. Okay?"

He sighed. "Alright, I will try. I can see this is bothering you."

When Raj came home the following evening, he prepared dinner quietly and retired to bed early. Bram and Nar arrived later, ate and grumbled.

The next afternoon as soon as we took care of the pot, Raj invited me to play cricket. When Bram and Nar alighted from the bus we were still playing. Raj and I went over to Regis' immediately after the game. When we got home, Bram and Nar were already in bed.

"We playing cricket again this afternoon? Right?" I told him before I left for work one day.

"Right."

We played cricket for three consecutive days.

One evening, Raj batted for nearly an hour. "Joined the local cricket club," he told me after he had dispatched one of our three balls down into the nearby ravine.

"You have the class to represent St. Lucia," I suggested.

"Yes, I am in good touch. But, I have to be a citizen first. Maybe I should marry a girl here and that will take care of that problem," he laughed. "But I toured the whole island already," he continued as he described an arc with the bat.

"Yes, if you become a citizen, you could represent the island."

"So then, are you saying I should marry a St. Lucian?"

"No, I am not saying that at all."

"Don't mind."

"Don't mind what?"

"Marrying a St. Lucian."

"Oh."

He scratched the batting crease with his bat. Then he looked up suddenly. "Ron, do you miss home?"

"Sure, I miss home. Do you?"

He combed his hair with his fingers. "At first, you know…my relatives, the boys, the Indian films, and the little teacher girlfriend I had."

"Did you give her up? Do I know her?"

"To tell the truth, we wrote one letter each. I don't even remember her now. No, I don't think you know her…And you know before I left my father was actually looking for a wife for me." He began brushing some foreign object off his pants, stopped and looked at me steadily.

"Ron, I want to ask you something?"

"Shoot."

"Supposing, just supposing you were to marry a black girl, what would your parents say?"

"Raj, I marry already, nearly fifteen years ago, man."

"I know, I know, but just supposing…"

"Okay. If that happens back home it will cause too many problems, boy. And where we live," I shook my head, "you and the girl have to run. I don't think your parents or mine would accept that…And plus she would not be comfortable."

"I know, I know," he said somewhat irritably. "Over here, look how it is different. People don't care about race, religion, color or anything at all when it comes to those things."

"Yes. It is so good to know people's judgment are not warped by these things."

"Look, back home," he continued, "if you belong to the same race, same religion and you fair and the girl black skin, they ask you, 'You color blind or what? Why you gone and marry that tar baby?' Oh boy!"

"Ha, if you of the same race, same religion, same complexion and she rich and you poor, they ask her, 'You don't have ambition eh? Why you gone and marry that poor arse church rat?' Yes, you can't please people," I added.

We both laughed.

81

"Ah, for heaven's sake I don't care about people. I care about what my parents would think." The worried look returned to his face.

"Raj, like you...?"

"Ah, forget it Ron. It just makes me mad to know how people think...this tradition thing. Why can't people let go? Why?"

I didn't forget it. I understood why he was so withdrawn at times.

SCHOOL WAS NOT EXACTLY QUIET and I had to swallow a couple of aspirins occasionally, as soon as I arrived home.

Many afternoons Raj sat at the table in the living room and read his medical encyclopedia. I sat in a corner on the floor and corrected students' workbook.

"Raj," I said one night, "Can you tell me..."

"Later, Ron," he said, turning the page of the encyclopedia.

Most afternoons when Bram and Nar arrived, they walked into the kitchen and ate quietly. Bram sat opposite to Raj in the living room, opened his Gita and read. Nar flitted in and out of the bedroom.

"Bram," Nar called out one night, "You know the IMF..."

"Tell me tomorrow," Bram replied, as he copied something from the Gita.

Shadows engulfed our house long before sunset and night seemed to step in earlier. Only the sparse twinkling lights filtering from Regis' shop reminded us that we were not alone.

One night I turned on the radio to listen to the eight o'clock newscast.

"Ron, please," Bram said. "I am concentrating here."

I withdrew to the bedroom and played the radio softly.

A few nights later, Nar interrupted, "You remember the man who fell in the black water creek and when he emerged his hair was as hard as concrete. Not even a cutlass could sever it?"

"Yes," Bram said. "But I think it was some chemical that was responsible."

I looked up.

"Nah," Nar responded immediately, "he disturbed the abode of the massacuraman!"

"Come on Nar, you don't believe in that nonsense about a creature roaming the river?"

I joined in. "But Bram there was this woman who jumbie hold. She gulped down four beers in less than a minute and spoke French," I said.

"Ron, you too believe that nonsense?" Bram chided.

"But it is true. I was there. She never touched alcohol before and certainly hardly spoke English much less French," I pointed out.

"And another recollection..." Nar began.

Bram held up his hand. "Ah, go to bed Nar."

A few nights later, Nar did it again. "Boy, the IMF really has its feet stuck hook, line and sinker in Guyana." He was reading the Guyana Mirror newspaper, which he said a Guyanese friend in Castries procures for him.

"Yes," he continued, "They say workers on the sugar estate..."

Both Raj and Bram stopped reading.

A debate ensued, developed into an argument and ended when Raj told Nar, "You don't know one shit what you talking about."

In the evenings from then on, I listened to the radio quietly in the bedroom, and I believed Nar read the newspaper in his bedroom too.

Gradually, I retired to bed earlier and squeezed my eyes shut. I drew Geet and the kids, and Zeelugt into the picture — Alesia and Jenny would be sitting on the floor doing their homework, Curly would be asleep and Geet would be reading — and fell asleep quickly. One night I was dreaming I was at a picnic on Zeelugt beach. A thud awoke me. I swore.

On the Saturday morning, Bram on entering the living

room said calmly, "Let's go down to the market at Vieux Fort."

Immediately I said, "That's a great idea."

"What?" he said.

"Let's go," I said.

When we got there after eight, the market, which extended about fifty yards on both sides of the main street in Vieux Fort, was busy and noisy.

Most of the vendors were women wearing big sombreros, and large pouch like aprons that were tightly drawn about the waist and tautly pulled down by something, presumably coins.

They displayed garden produce, clothes and footwear, cosmetics, bottled products and a variety of flowers on plastic bags spread on the ground.

Two men were selling water coconuts and eggs from the back of their pick-ups.

"Indian, you don't want coconuts?" one of the men called out. We bought one coconut each, drank the water and ate the jelly.

Two rastas went up to a group of white tourists nearby. They showed them bangles and necklaces. "Volcanic rocks," they said. "Only 5US."

Everyone in the group bought.

The rastas came over to us.

"We are not tourists," Nar said.

They left promptly.

Soon after a scantily clad young man with glazed looking eyes marched up to me and actually demanded, "Boss, buy me a bread."

Bram sucked his teeth. "Don't bother with him, Ron. You have to ignore them."

Nar tapped me on the shoulder. "Boy, you have millionaire look."

"Okay. I buying passion fruit," I told him.

"Don't purchase yet," Nar whispered. "Once they think

you are a foreigner, they increase the price twofold."

As we walked along, Bram and Nar sauntered from one side to the other, pointing and quoting prices.

We stopped to examine a piece of fresh looking pumpkin.

"Four dollars," the vendor said.

"Things really expensive here," Bram muttered.

"Buy," Raj said.

"Don't," Nar advised.

We continued walking.

"How much is your pumpkin?" Bram asked another vendor.

"Oh, *jonmou-la*. Three dollars, and it sweet," she replied smiling.

"God, one hundred and fifty dollars for a little piece of pumpkin," he grumbled as he cradled the piece of pumpkin.

"I said three dollars," the vendor drawled and pursed her lips.

"It okay," Bram told her as he paid for it.

"How much is your..." Bram or Nar or both in chorus would ask the vendors.

"Huh...too expensive," either or both would mutter and screw up their faces.

Raj who was tagging along behind suddenly sang, "Well, we can always travel back home and bu-u-y or we can eat the mone-e-y."

"You can devour their faeces as far as I am concerned!"

"No. A better idea is that all of us stuff our backsides with guavas and..."

"Hi, Mr. Girdharry!"

We turned and saw two young ladies approaching. They were smiling. Their eyes were fixed on Raj.

"Two of my patients," Raj said, and immediately walked off with them.

"You behold the sweet-man in action," Nar grumbled. "Boy, he has a harem."

We lingered around for some time. Raj was still with the

girls. Bram looked at his watch and then in Raj's direction. Nar sucked his teeth and said he was going to the drug store to get some tonic. After a while Bram and I decided to join Nar. We found him engaged in conversation with the salesgirl.

"What are you buying, Nar? Toilet paper?" Bram teased.

"Nah. Where I live, Coolie people use their hands, water and black sage bush. They are so natural," he replied coarsely and grinned.

The salesgirl giggled.

"But I am buying condoms," he continued. "They don't sell such advanced methods of birth control back home. Coolie people are so oblivious of that and that's why they have proliferated cricket teams of children."

The salesgirl laughed.

After Nar had paid for his tonic, we left the store.

Raj was still with the girls.

"I wonder how many decades we would have to wait on His Majesty Romeo Girdharry?" Nar said shrilly.

Suddenly I heard, "Hey, Ron!"

"Adrian!"

He came up to me smiling. "Been shopping?"

I nodded. I introduced him to Bram and Nar.

Just then, "Boss man, give me a dollar, nah." We turned and saw a young man clad in dirty clothing. He held out his hand to Nar.

Nar brushed him aside, "Go find work, nah."

The young man walked off and approached an elderly woman.

"Yes, Ron, if you give them, they are going to buy marijuana," Adrian said.

We spoke for a while and before he left, he said, "Next Sunday I am going to the beach bash at Praslin. Come along...bring these guys with you."

Meantime, Nar kicked at some gravel at his feet and lashed out at one that was unmoving, missed and overbalanced. He cursed and embarked on the rotation routine. Eventually, Raj came up to us, smiling.

"You are definitely aware that Bram and I have a little religious function to perform? Where the hell have you been all the time?" greeted Nar.

"*Salezon, gason, bèf, gason.* I went to check out some meat. I feel like eating beef curry."

"The day a Hindu start gormandizing mother cow, he should bury his head in its entrails."

"Gorman...who? I could eat that," Raj said, and Nar cursed.

We left Vieux Fort market in relatively good spirits, and with a few items.

THINGS PROGRESSED SMOOTHLY for a while. No one grumbled or complained. No one said much. I retired to my bed early and turned on the radio. I secured a pack of cards and played 'patience' all by myself.

Then one night Raj pounded the door from the outside. It was nearing midnight.

"Can't find my keys," he said as I let him in. His face shone as he peered at me and smiled. "But tomorrow," he whispered, "*Gason,* ah taking you to fete...plenty girls." He put a finger to his lips, tittered and wobbled.

We left at midday for the fete that was sponsored by one of his friends from the hospital. About a score of exuberant and friendly people were there. Raj introduced me to most of them, then said, "Make yourself at home," and disappeared in the kitchen

The people played the music loudly, served a lot of food and drinks, and talked nonstop. I tapped my feet to the reggae music and had barbecued chicken, salt fish and figs and Heineken beers.

At times, their conversation veered to things at the hospital, and mostly they raved about the lack of something or some administrative inefficiency. It followed a similar pattern as when teachers meet in a bar. They asked me if I was Trinidadian or Guyanese and if I liked St. Lucia. They pondered deeply, came up with some names of people and places in Guyana, and asked if I knew them. I disappointed them each time about the people. But their faces brightened when I nodded to the names of some places. They interrogated me thoroughly and told me things I did not know about the places.

After we had run out of names of familiar places, they still tried to keep me interested. "Most Guyanese love cricket, eh?" one of them said, and when I nodded, they spoke a lot about cricket. They argued, forgot I was there and slipped into their patois. I looked at everyone and became tired.

Just then, Raj reappeared, and asked, "Everything okay, Ron?"

I nodded.

"You have to teach Ron, some patois," the guy they called Justin told Raj.

"We have to teach *him*," another said, pointing to Raj, and they both laughed.

"But, I know…" Raj began.

"Remember the other day…? *Ban mwen ti aspirin la?*" Justin chuckled. He turned to me. "What happened, Ron, was that I was there at the pharmacy when an old lady who doesn't speak much English was asking Raj for aspirin, and he kept on asking her, 'What you say? What you say?' and she kept on asking for aspirin in patois." He stopped and looked at Raj. They all laughed.

"And Ron, the lady was mad as hell," Justin continued. "Before I could explain to Raj, she was screaming, "*Zot Guyanese konnet anyen!*"

"What…?" I asked.

"She was saying, 'You Guyanese don't know anything'," Justin explained.

"Ron, and you know what Raj told the old lady? Ha! 'Get you *rass* out of here!' Boy, Raj was going crazy." He looked at

Raj and shook his head. "And it was only his friend over there..." He pointed to a young lady in the far corner. "She had to come over and calm him down."

I glanced at the young lady and was about to tease Raj about his patois, but quickly looked at her again. I couldn't recall seeing her when we arrived, but I recognized her. She was one of his two patients whom we met at the market.

Raj too was looking at her, and when they made eye contact, he beckoned her over. As soon as she came over, she held his hand and played with his face. He slipped his hand around her waist and whispered in her ear. He turned to me. "You remember her, Ron?"

I nodded. "Your patient."

She smiled.

On the way home, Raj beamed, "I know you had a good time, Ron," and I replied, "I know for sure you did, Raj."

The following Sunday, I awaited Adrian to take me to the beach bash at Praslin Bay. Bram and Nar said it was prayer day and they didn't indulge in such things on a Sunday. I invited Raj who extended the invitation to some of his friends. Adrian brought along three friends, soft balls, a locally made bat, snorkeling gears, and a case of Heineken beers.

Praslin beach was even more captivating than I had pictured it from above. Wide and long, it was protected by the narrow bay entrance and enclosed by high hills with gross vegetation that provided lots of shade.

Scores of excited beach bashers were milling about and a few were already kicking the sand as they moved buoyantly to the loud music. Bikini clad young ladies strolled about, and others, especially children, were already wading in the clear water. The surf was gentle. Immediately, I dived in. Adrian joined me minutes later.

"Hey Ron, try this," Adrian shouted as he threw the snorkeling equipment to me. The mouthpiece found itself in the right position after I had swallowed mouthfuls of water. I looked under. The stunning beauty and the serenity filled me with awe.

Fishes that I was seeing for the first time, fishes with intricate colors, and fishes of varying sizes and shapes, hovered, dipped and raced, displaying acute alertness, as fins and gills waved and pumped ceaselessly. Some came curiously close in shoals, tilted gracefully sideways to inspect the intruder, and darted away in an amazingly organized fashion, much in the same way as children going down on cue in mass games.

Numerous seashells littered the rippled floor of sand and rocks, and glistened like the eyes of the fishes when the sunlight penetrated the surface of the water. The few islands of projecting boulders harbored scores of queer looking, tiny scuttling creatures, crabs and barnacles. Within the parameters beyond which Adrian had warned me not to venture, there was sparse plant life. But the mushrooms, ferns and green slimy things showed more life and vibrancy than terrestrial plants, as they swayed rhythmically in the mild underwater current. Nibbling fishes plucked tirelessly at them. Shadows skimmed over the water, dimming the view, but the place brightened again as the sunlight infiltrated.

Every time I surfaced and peered at the bashers, they seemed to gyrate and thrash about with greater frenzy to the heavy bass music. After a while Adrian joined them. About five minutes later Raj was pulled in. When I finally got out of the water, Raj was nowhere in sight.

"Raj left with the girl from the hospital. She came a while ago," Adrian disclosed before I asked him anything. "He said to tell you he will be coming home later."

The Monday and Tuesday were proclaimed national holidays to celebrate the anniversary of the country's independence, attained on February 22, 1979. Carnival was in the air. When I told Bram I did not know where Raj had gone, he said, "I hope nothing happens to him."

Nar said, "He has gone with his sweet woman to indulge in the recklessness of carnival in Castries."

I thought about Mashramani celebrations in Guyana

around this same time to commemorate Guyana's Republic anniversary on February 23, and if Carnival was anything like it, Raj must be having a whale of a time.

When Raj returned on Wednesday afternoon, he said, "Have to tell you about carnival," and retired to bed at once, and must have slept for twelve hours. When he awoke, he joined us in the living room and in a far away, dreamy look, he said, "It was simply fantastic and uninhibited! The calypso competition, the queen show, the masquerade band...The showcase of St. Lucia."

"Like Mashramani?" I said.

"Better."

"Population explosion time," Nar added with a sneer.

Raj spun around and wagging his finger in front of Nar's face said, "If you don't have anything good to say, don't say anything at all."

Later, I called Nar aside and said, "Don't you enjoy being in St. Lucia?"

"What do you mean?" he stammered.

"You criticize the people and place at every single opportunity."

He didn't reply.

WEEKDAYS CRAWLED.

I checked the post-office four consecutive days in the last week in February for mail and got none. I began to worry. But on a Friday evening I collected five letters. Three were for Raj and one for Bram. I ripped mine open. The last part read:

*Everything is okay. The children miss you. Fatman and Jughead chop up each other over a chicken. The bandits attack in the next village and killed a shopkeeper and they say they get away with one million dollars, but don't worry. My brother does sleep with us. Everybody is asking for you. Money has gone up one thirty to one. The cambio is doing bright business. There was a shoot-out at one of them. The proprietor and two bandits died. They took 10 million, my God. Is almost every night we are having blackout. I hear something bad about Nar wife. Don't worry we are okay, Love, Geet.*

Later that evening when Raj came home, he was smiling. His eyes shone. "Let's play dominoes," he invited.

"Eh?" Bram and Nar said together. They looked at each other and then slowly nodded. I joined them although I was feeling tired and sleepy.

Raj, Bram and I started the game. Nar was the spectator. Our small, roughly built, wooden table received a severe pounding from the time the first domino landed on it. Dominoes danced, rattled, jumped and flew all over the place. Mine slipped out of my hand with annoying regularity. I was the first to be ousted. Nar joined Raj and Bram.

I stood up and watched the trio battle. I had always enjoyed a game of dominoes—the dare, the challenge, the waiting, the tension, the luck—it was so much like life...our life. In the covered tickets, there were so many possibilities—one's ticket to doom or success could be lurking there. They held their tickets in textbook fashion and pondered over them. They shuffled them around. I scrutinized their faces and tried to assess the situation.

But then my mind drifted back to what Geet had written and I remembered the letters for Bram and Raj. As I delivered, Nar asked, "Any for me?"

I shook my head.

Raj glanced at the envelopes and pushed them in his trousers' pocket. Bram deposited his in his shirt pocket. Silence enveloped the house. The trio concentrated as if they were writing the examination of their life. The game had reached at that do or die stage. Hands passed over brows and legs shook nervously doing the Saint Vitus dance. Eyes roved over the line of exposed tickets and lips mumbled numbers.

"My wife says money gone to one thirty," I said.

"Eh!" Nar said. A ticket slipped from his grasp and fell under the table. "How much?" he asked, still looking at me as he felt for the ticket.

"One-thirty…"

"Everything that goes up must come down," Bram said as he slammed another domino.

"And they had a shoot out at one of the cambios."

"Lord Krishna, how many dead? You know any?" Bram asked.

"She didn't say."

Bram plucked the letter from his pocket. He rested his tickets on the table, tore open the envelope and glanced at the letter.

Raj looked at him for a while, and then concentrated again on his tickets.

"Lord Krishna…two dead!"

"You know any?" Nar asked.

"She didn't say who."

Silence. They looked at their tickets, mumbled and screwed up their faces.

"Any other news from Guyana?" Nar asked.

"My wife says things beginning to heat up for the elections," I said.

"I dread election time. Race! Violence! Why can't the people come off this race thing and vote for another party if they want change?" Bram commented. His domino came down heavily.

"Race! Race! Race! So disgusting!" Raj said.

"Bram, your wife tells you anything about Meena and the boys?" Nar asked.

"That was the first thing I would have told you, Nar."

Nar bowed his head. Raj and Bram looked at the tickets in their hands and those on the table.

Raj broke the silence. "Yes, Bram, no matter if their manifesto promise gold and honey, free electricity and toilet paper, come election time, it is sheer race."

"I wonder why she is not writing," Nar said, looking up to the roof.

Bram said, "Race politics is a dirty game."

"Yes, only Jesus Christ can save them," Raj murmured.

Nar looked at him steadily and Bram's hand froze in mid air with the ticket he was about to thump on the table. I looked at the chalk marks on the table. Bram had five games, Nar two, and Raj was yet to score. Suddenly Bram's ticket came down; the table rattled.

"I rap," Raj said.

"Got you!" Bram said and slammed his last ticket on the table.

Bram 'loved' Raj.

We retired to bed immediately after that game, and as I was pulling the bedspread over me, Raj touched me on the shoulder and said, "Ron, I am in love."

"I thought so."

# 7

"ONE MONTH and ..." A gush of wind drowned the voice and the fowls stirred in the coop below. Immediately after, heavy raindrops pounded the roof and lasted for a while.

The rains had begun on the previous morning when it had come down in sudden torrential outbursts after a crackling and sustained clap of thunder that had the students screaming and scampering. Once when it subsided, a rainbow appeared within the valley touching the base of the mountain on either side. It seemed within touching distance. I felt like walking through it. And the rains too settled the irritating dust that, for the past month or so, had been a real nuisance especially when there were pockets of gusty winds. However, its persistence had soon made that day a lousy one. In the past, unexpected showers had caught me unprepared on the nearby desolate highway. That day was one of those. The sky had been clear one minute and then from behind the mountains, dark foams of cloud had sprung up and begun pelting heavy droplets.

When I began to sneeze in the living room that night, Bram said, "Bless you, Ron," and smiled.

I replied, "Do you have any Vitamin C tablets?"

The smile left his face.

"Sorry," I said.

A few subdued roosters and mildly chirruping birds were up to usher in the first day of March. It was chilly — the effects of the winter in the north, Bram has said. Bram hummed a Hindi religious song and rang the bell. A car horn sounded in the distance.

I clambered out of bed and entered the living room. I folded my arms across my chest and tucked my hands under my armpits. My glance fell on the picture of the strikingly beautiful and scantily dressed female on Sam's Sports Shop almanac. She was perched on a bicycle and had a seductive smile. For just a moment, a warm tingling sensation rushed through my body.

Raj joined me in the living room, looking ridiculously bulky in his over sized, red jersey and green track pants. "Boy, it chilly," he said. He huddled his shoulders and pushed his hands in his pockets. "Need a thing like that to warm me up," he tittered, as he tilted his head towards the female.

"Look who is complaining," I said.

He aimed a playful punch at me.

Both of us left after seven for work. I missed the school bus at Piaye and arrived late for my first class of the day. This was not the first time I was late, and when I told Adrian that it was fatiguing to travel to and from work everyday, he raised his hands to the heavens and said, "I am lost here. Why don't you rent a house in Soufriere?"

"Can't afford at this time."

During the lunch hour, as I did regularly, I ventured into the town — it was two minutes' walk away — and then down to the waterfront where a friend, a fisherman, gave me a tuna fish. On other days previously, other newly-made friends heaped fruits and vegetables on me.

I left the school compound at exactly 3 p.m., and got home after five. The boys smiled when they saw the tuna fish.

Raj wasn't there.

At around half past five, a young lady came and inquired, "Is Raj home?"

Nar said, "Who? Do I know that person?"

"*Yes*. Mr. Girdharry, the tall Indian pharmacist. He lives here," she frowned.

"Oh, him...the player. He has gone out with one of his girlfriends. Would you like me to give him a message?"

She shook her head and walked off.

Bram too was annoyed. "It not fair," he commented when he saw me. "It is Raj's duty to cook in the afternoons."

"He has gone courting and wooing his woman, and I am hungry like a starved beggar," Nar said and shuffled off to his bedroom.

Everyone retired to bed early that night. Before I dozed off, I was sure that I heard the jingling of coins—not like when they were dropped into a bag, but like when they were continually milled and caressed through fingers. It lasted about two minutes.

But I could not hear the clinking of the coins—if it had become part of the routine—or the countdown or the bell for several days. The inclement weather persisted and I awoke later.

However, on the following Saturday, I heard the tinkling of the coins. Raj and I spent most of that pleasant morning playing softball cricket under the breadfruit tree. Regis joined us after lunch. He enlightened us on politics, sports and women.

"I always like a small woman," he mused and glanced at Raj. "Like Raj's."

Raj looked at him in the eye. "You don't know my woman, Regis."

"Gros Islet...?"

Raj stared at Regis.

About one o'clock, a car tooted on the highway. It was the brown car. Raj excused himself and left.

"Know her, Mr. Regis?" I asked casually.

"Perhaps."

Bram and Nar joined Regis and me. Nar looked around and then asked, "Where is Romeo?"

"Who?" I asked, feigning ignorance.

"*Mr. Girdharry, the tall Indian pharmacist,*" he mimicked, and broke into a fit of coughing.

"Oh, a friend picked him up."

"He is going to pick up *A.I.D.S.* one of these days," Nar sputtered and coughed again.

"Mr. Nar, you look sick…and thin," Regis said, peering at Nar.

"Sick! Don't be ridiculous! I am deprived of sex. When I pee…ah mean when I urinate, it smells sweet, sweet."

"Wait," Bram said, looking closely at Nar. "Say that again."

"Say what?"

"About the pee."

I SPENT MOST OF SUNDAY QUIETLY. Raj left for Gros Islet. "Going with Felicity to church," he whispered before he left. Bram and Nar went over to Lalgeet's and Regis wasn't around. I wrote home:

*Dear Geet,*

*I got your letter. Everything is great here. The children at the school are really very noisy. Those at Zeeburg are docile compared to these here. I snorkeled. I mean I could see under the water. It is clear, clear. I would like to live under the sea. The people are friendly and generous. The neighbor Regis who is the shopkeeper is a nice and funny man. I have a close friend at school name Adrian. Nar's wife is not writing him. Do you know what is going on? Kiss the children.*

*Love*

*Ron.*

AT AROUND FIVE, Bram, Nar and I were in the living room listening to Indian music when we heard a light rap on the door. I opened it quietly and was greeted warmly by a female voice, "Hi, we are Jehovah's Witnesses. Can we come in?" The male accompanying her, smiled. They were not the same Jehovah Witnesses who had come previously.

"Again!" Nar muttered.

"Sure. Come in," Bram said after a while and turned off the tape recorder. He invited them to sit. Claudius, the slim, bespectacled, white man, attired in a pair of black pants and white shirt asked, "What church do you all attend?" and looked at each of us in turn.

"We are Hindus," Bram replied, nodding at the same time as if to reinforce the point and suggest we couldn't be anything else.

"Oh, well, we are Jehovah's Witnesses," Brother Claudius repeated.

They watched Bram and waited. They glanced at Nar and me. Brother Claudius shifted his attention to his little attaché case that was resting on his knees. Opening the attaché case, he extracted his Bible. The sister delved into her handbag and fished out a booklet. The brother placed the Bible on top of the case, opened it, looked us over once more and began, "Listen to this. This is what the true God Jehovah …the creator of the heaven…the one laying out the earth and its produce…the one giving breath to the people on it said in Isaiah…verses…" After he quoted, he closed the Bible, scanned our faces and said, "Listen, Jehovah is the name of the God who made the universe, and created men and women on the earth. And you must know what kind of God he is and why you should listen to him." He continued non stop for a couple of minutes. He worked up a sweat, closed the Bible, looked us over once again, and said glowingly, "Yes, brothers, Jehovah is the only one who can save us from our sins!" He stopped and looked at us again.

Bram seized the chance. "Tell me…tell us about God, the Father, the Son and the Holy Ghost."

"Listen, Jehovah's Witnesses believe God being the father must be greater than his son Jesus who is certainly not equal with the father. Yes, Jesus is subordinate to God and his task is to make God's name and purposes manifest to others." He stopped and looked at Bram.

And Bram responded, "Okay, Hindus also believe in one God and call their religion Sanatan Dharma, which means 'Eternal Law' and you know, anyone can call himself a Hindu, if he practices Dharma, the code of life." Bram stopped and looked at the brother.

I glanced at Nar. His head was resting in the palm of his hands and his eyes were closed.

I seized the opportunity. "Brother Claudius," I said, "I have often heard, 'Repent and you will be saved.' Do you believe in confession? What I mean is if you confess, will you be absolved from the things you call sins?"

"Brother, I don't know much about that, but I believe that the only way to be saved is to be like Jesus."

"And do you believe in resurrection, Brother?" Bram asked.

"Oh, yes...Jehovah's Witnesses have complete confidence in future life. We believe in the resurrection from the dead."

"But..." Bram interrupted.

"Oh, yes. The existence of man really ceases when he dies. But the future life for the dead is based on God's remembrance of him in the resurrection."

"Yes. But we believe in reincarnation...the rebirth of the soul, but in a new body..." Bram began.

"And many living would survive when God has cleansed the earth." Perspiration began to gather on the brother's face as he worked up to a climax.

"What do you mean? Will there be another flood? Or do you think hurricanes, earthquakes, and wars are God's way of cleansing the earth?" I asked.

"Well, if not, it will be something of that nature. And don't be mistaken, survival is dependent on meeting Jehovah's requirements." He removed his spectacles as he spoke, and wiped his face.

Nar got up, stretched, yawned and coughed. "How many will survive? Am I one, or only Jehovah people?" he queried almost mockingly.

Bram raised his hand and when he got everyone's attention, he said, "Yes, Hindus believe in reincarnation. But Hinduism is much more than that. It does not preach obedience to authority. Rather it lays emphasis on direct experience. You know, the aim is not to make someone conform intellectually to inherited doctrine and teachings but for one to seek knowledge. It is concerned with absolute truth, not with systems of belief. And Hinduism makes allowances for atheists." Bram too was working up a sweat.

Nar sat and said, "Yes, Hinduism is…"

"Yes, I understand," interrupted Brother Claudius, "but Jehovah…"

About half an hour dragged by. I tried to make eye contact with Bram. Eventually I called out, "Bram, excuse me, the place getting hot, and we don't have anything cold. I am going over to Regis and get something." I left immediately.

I returned about five minutes later with a Coke and a Sprite.

"It was nice being here, but we have to go. We will be back some other time, but remember the last book of the Bible describes the quality of life you can enjoy in the Paradise Jehovah promises you…what a benevolent Father he is! Are you willing to learn more about him and what is required of you to live in Paradise?" Brother Claudius reeled off as he stood and carefully placed his Bible and other booklets into his attaché case.

"Sorry you have to leave so soon," Bram said. He too was on his feet.

I offered them the drinks. They sipped and looked around uneasily.

They sold us the booklets; Bram and I bought.

101

As soon as the door closed behind our two guests, Nar mumbled, "Jehovah, my foot. I hope they don't come again."

"I am glad I spoke to them," Bram said.

"Yes," I said. "At least we know what they preach."

Both Bram and Nar retired to their room.

I was passing the rest of the evening browsing through my booklet. The house was quiet except for the occasional sound of coins until, "What the hell? *Salòp*!"

"Raj!"

I jumped out of bed and headed for the front door. It swung open before I touched it and Raj entered.

The tinkling of coins coming from the dark room ceased.

"*Bonswè*, Ron," Raj greeted loudly and grinned. He slumped into a chair, rolled up his trousers and inspected his foot. His shining face was partly covered with his disheveled hair. He was dressed in a pair of black pants and white shirt—there were a few dark spots in front—with sleeves rolled up his arm. He wore a black tie that hung loosely from the neck and extended beyond his crotch.

"Raj?" I said, pointing to his attire.

"Funeral. I went to the funeral of a friend's father." He rubbed the foot. There was a dark red spot on it. I pointed to it. "Nothing serious. Some moron left a box in the pathway."

"Oh."

"Ron, after the funeral, *gason*," he said shaking his head, "it was like a wedding reception. *Gason*, it was food, drinks and laughter...only thing missing was music." He belched and drawled, "I am tired. I am going to bed." When he got up the floor squeaked and the chair fell over. He pointed to the dark room, grabbed his pocket and shook it, causing a few coins to rattle. The curtains entangled him as he attempted to enter the room in a rush. He grabbed it, heaved it aside and swore; a few of the pins came loose.

The tinkling of coins coming from the other room resumed.

"Misers!" Raj hissed as I entered our room. Beer smell

joined coin sounds. "Ron, you want some coins?"

"Come on, Raj," I said. "Leave the guys alone."

Sensing my annoyance, he said softly, "Okay, okay."

But then a heavy thud echoed from the other room.

I looked at Raj sternly and placed an index finger over my lips. He screwed up his face, lipped a few curses and aimed some punches at the wall.

"Don't!" I said quietly but firmly.

He sat on the bed and dangled his feet over the edge. He looked at me and smiled, "She really nice, Ron."

"Who really nice?"

He fell backward. "We really had a nice time tonight. We are going out again tomorrow. *Wi*, tomorrow..." He continued grumbling and when he stopped, I assumed he had fallen asleep. I got up from my bed and as I was attempting to hoist his feet on the bed, he murmured, "Yes, she is mine...mine..."

"Who is?" I whispered.

"Felicity...Felicity...Felicity," his voice trailed off.

THE FOLLOWING NIGHT when all of us were in the living room reading as usual, Bram asked suddenly, "Ron, what do you think about the Jehovah witnesses?"

I looked up and found him flipping through pages of his booklet.

"Bram," I said, "I really don't care about what any one religion preaches. What puzzles me most is why so much intolerance exists when most claim that there is only one God, regardless of the names the different religious sects give him."

"Yes," Raj said, causing Bram to look up immediately. "Yes, why does one think that one's religion is better than the other? Isn't showing tolerance and appreciation for others among the morals taught in all religions?"

"True," Bram agreed. "I would like people to think like the great Indian philosopher. What's his name...? Oh, yes.

Swami Vivekanand. He likened religion to a wheel. He said that the cog in the middle is God and the spindles are the different religions...and that everyone has the right to choose the way he wants to reach God."

"Indeed! But religious fanaticism, I fear, is defeating the very purpose of religion," I said.

"But I think Hinduism surpasses the rest..." Nar slipped in suddenly.

"That's exactly what I am talking about..."

"And once we think that way," Raj interrupted, "it can be used as a tool for discrimination. We know of people who have been turned away or preferred to others because of their religious affiliation. Not so?" Raj said, pounding his hand on his book.

"Oh yes. And ironically, it is the agnostics...the non-believers who show tolerance and don't discriminate," I said.

"Yes. But non-believers have no identity...no morals..." Bram was on his feet.

"Ah, come on, Bram," I intercepted. "Is it right, as is the universal tendency, to associate religion with worship of God and to relegate man to a form of animal existence if religion is absent from his life? Raj and I were talking about the Jonestown tragedy. Talk about animal existence. Look how many lives were snuffed out in the name of religion!"

"Well..."

I raised a hand. "People all over the world," I continued, "have devised religion in some form or the other to give purpose and meaning to their lives and have lived decent lives. What's so wrong if this God entity is missing? It is true that all religions preach high ethical values, adherence to which would surely carve a morally upright character, but..."

"Ron, are you an atheist?" Nar asked looking at me steadily.

"Nar, that is beyond the point. If the threat of fire, brimstone and burning hell and the reward of milk and honey in heaven or paradise can influence believers to do the right things, then religion is indeed playing its role. But does that mean that agnostics and atheists cannot cultivate equally high moral values based on their perception of what is right from wrong?"

"Yes. But..."

I stood. "Everyone has vices, I would think, and people should be judged on the qualities that they possess rather than their religiosity or lack of it. 'The whisky bottle in the hands of some men is sometimes better than the Bible in the hands of others' is a sober comment worthwhile to ponder on, however outrageous it may seem. Like so many good things, why can't something as abstract as God be seen as an option?"

"Ron, you seem angry. You sound like an agnostic. Are you?" Bram sat upright and peered at me over the rims of his spectacle.

"Again, that is beyond the point. But what irks me most is when one uses religion in a way that is contradictory to its teachings."

Nar smiled. "Ron, you were unusually vociferous tonight. It seems that you are studying theology these days?"

"Nar, I don't have the least interest in theology. When people talk about religion, I prefer to become a pedestrian."

"What?"

"I prefer to walk."

They both stared at me.

I WATCHED OUT FOR BRAM AND NAR on Monday afternoon. They came after six. "What did the doctor say?" I asked.

"Diabetes Mellitus," Bram said.

"Eh!"

"He has sugar in the blood and urine. He has to avoid sweet and drink plenty water. He must exercise and lose weight too."

"My father had it," Nar explained wistfully. He collapsed into the chair. "Yes. He died in his early fifties of a heart attack one afternoon in the cane fields."

I recalled that, and also when his younger brother died a year later in a motor vehicle accident on the Parika Vreedenhoop highway. I remembered too that Nar suffered a mental breakdown immediately after and was advised to take three months medical leave.

"Okay, Nar, take it easy. I will do all the house chores. I will go and buy your tablets at the drugstore," Bram said, and left to get some water for Nar.

Nar began nodding his head. "Ron, Bram has always been there for me in times like these."

Bram returned with the water, two bananas and an orange.

"Take these," he said as he offered the fruits to Nar. "They are good for you."

After a while, Nar said, "If my health doesn't improve, I will return home."

"No. You don't have to go," Bram said as he placed a hand on Nar's shoulder. "Listen, take leave and I will send money for Meena and the boys and let her know about your condition."

"Yes, Nar stay," I said. "And Bram, you should go home. There was no need for you to come to St. Lucia."

"What?"

"Just joking."

"How you think Nar would have been here?" he replied and rubbed Nar's head before adding, "And Nar, you were there for me. You remember the explosion in the Science lab at Zeeburg?"

"Of course. You were very brave, Bram," Nar said, nodding.

"No. I don't mean that. I mean you stood by my side when I was in hospital. But okay. You must be brave like me, now."

"I remember. Yes, the explosion, and you darting past us and plunging into the trench." I said.

"Yes, and the government so concerned that they sent

heaps of CID men to check on you at the hospital," Nar added, shaking his head.

"Rawans! They wanted to know which political party, I belonged to," Bram declared.

When Raj came home around ten, I whispered to him about Nar.

Raj awoke earlier than usual the next morning, and shouldered Nar lightly as he stepped into the kitchen. "Take it easy, old boy," he said.

"I am alright," Nar replied quietly.

"You need a strong woman...a *djabal* to look after you now. Yes, if you know what's good for you, you would find a woman here," Raj said and patted Nar playfully on the back.

"You didn't have to do that, you know," I told Raj later.

"Yes," he said, "I am sorry. But my sister said Meena is not behaving herself."

"What you mean? Like seeing somebody else?"

"Something like that."

Regis and I waited for Bram and Nar the following afternoon. As Nar came up the pathway, Regis hurried to meet him. "Come. Let me help you with your attaché case, old boy."

"I am alright, Mr. Regis."

"You know, there is a man here who can cure those things. He has plenty herbs. I will tell Rasta Paul to check him for you. Okay? Or maybe you want a *gadè*?"

"It is okay, Mr. Regis, I bought things from the drug store already and I don't believe in obeah."

Regis touched him on the shoulder. "Come on, Nar, *gason*, Mr. Regis is there for you."

"Thanks, Mr. Regis," he said, and ambled off.

When Nar returned from work on the following day, he nodded to me and headed straight for his bedroom. He emerged three hours later drank a glass of water and retreated. In the morning, I heard Bram chiding him, "You didn't eat. Did you?"

The next afternoon, Bram said, "Hi," entered his room and did not resurface.

Early in the morning I joined Bram in the kitchen. He was emptying the pot in the garbage can. "He didn't eat again," he said.

THUD! It was at around seven, several nights later. Bram, Raj and I who were in the living room at the time dashed to the dark room. Thankfully, it was only the bed that had collapsed! When Nar saw us, he grimaced, "Blasted bed like it has arthritis!" and we couldn't help laughing. His elbows were bruised and he disclosed, "I wouldn't be able to sit on my posterior for a few days."

Before I left the room, I threw an arm over his shoulder. "Nar," I said quietly, "Becoming a recluse won't help."

Most of the following days were humid and I saw little of anyone.

Left alone, I sought the schoolboys in the neighborhood to play cricket or explore the ravine or pick fruits.

One morning before Raj left, I said, "Raj, you know Bram helps me to prepare dinner."

"Ron," he said quietly as he placed his hand on my shoulder, "I have some extra work to do. See what you can do."

"But..."

"See what you can do. Please."

One day I told Bram. "I will do it alone."

He looked at me for a while. "It's okay, Ron. I will help you."

A few days later, Raj beckoned me outside and placed an arm on my shoulder. "Ron, the truth is I spend some time with my girlfriend in the afternoons." He stared into the heavens.

"Is her name Felicity?"

"What? Who...?"

"You called her name in your sleep. But Raj, why are you so secretive about her?"

108

"Listen Ron, you know how my parents are. Bram and my father are good friends. My relatives would kick a racket. Already they are trying to fix me up with a rich man daughter."

"How you know?"

"My sister, Seeta, wrote me."

"Okay. But at least you can tell me."

"Listen, Ron. It is not that I don't trust you. But I know Bram and Nar and you are good friends too..."

"But you can trust me."

"Now that I am beginning to know you better...Okay."

"Raj, is she the same girl I met at the fete?"

"Yes."

"Patient or colleague?"

He laughed. "Didn't want the guys to become suspicious at the market. Yes, we work at the hospital. She is also a pharmacist. She lives in Gros Islet."

"She is okay," I said.

"She isn't just okay, she is fantastic."

"I don't doubt you."

He smiled. "She lived in Guyana for some time...got her degree from U.G."

"Oh yes? So you met her in Guyana?"

"Nah. Met her at the hospital."

"And Raj, try to make it home some afternoon."

"Okay...okay."

THE MORNING OF SATURDAY the sixteenth was exceptionally humid. I got off the bed and went outside. It seemed as if the rooster from under the house had disappeared. A few birds overhead screamed annoyingly, and a couple of dogs were yapping somewhere behind the bushes nearby. The breadfruit and banana leaves appeared to droop. Soon the others joined me.

"Hot, eh?" Nar said.

Suddenly Bram turned to Raj, "Look, Raj, I have something to tell you. I have been wanting to for a long time."

"What?" Raj snapped and stared at Bram.

"Look, you are a young man but I think you are overdoing it." Bram's tone was mild, almost pleading.

"Overdoing what?" He dismissed Bram with a wave of the hand and pivoted to walk away.

Bram wagged a finger at Raj's back, "I am sorry I fixed you up with this job."

Raj stopped in his tracks and turned around. "But what have I done wrong?" The tone was almost begging.

Bram wagged the finger more vigorously this time in Raj's face. "I regret I fix you up."

"A packed harem of concubines," Nar butted in.

Raj turned on Nar, "Pé la. Shut your sick arse! And don't bother. You will beg me for one of my concubines soon."

"Confess…confess and be saved," Nar threw over his shoulder when he was safely out of reach.

"What?"

"You become Christian now," Nar said.

Raj looked at me.

Bram raised his hand like a policeman at a major road. "Alright Raj, alright, listen man, you could get into trouble. You are a dispenser of drugs. You know about these things…these diseases."

Raj, with mouth set tight, stood as still as the leaves above. Dark clouds were forming overhead. Raj cracked his knuckles before he opened his mouth slightly. "Are you finished?" he asked calmly and trudged off to the house. A drizzle had sprung up.

"You will put your parents to shame. You will drive them to their grave," Bram muttered.

Nar rejoined us. "I don't care if the sweet-man contract A.I.D.S. or not!"

Bram turned to me and said hoarsely, "Ron, it is his father who told me to keep an eye on him."

"But it is clear that Ron is on his side. Or am I a Philistine?"

Nar said as he looked steadfastly at me.

I felt like slapping him.

The afternoon of Wednesday, the twentieth was hot and cloudy. I was standing shirtless by the window. Raj was sitting on the steps. Suddenly Bram and Nar appeared in the pathway. With some brisk strides, Bram forged ahead of Nar, entered the living room, dropped his attaché case on the table and immediately delved into it.

"Where is this stupid bill?" he bellowed. When he found it, he flung it on the table and cried, "I ain't paying this light bi...i...ll. Who burn, let them pa...a...y!"

"Yes, let the nocturnal prowlers reimburse," said Nar. He was standing in the doorway.

Raj withdrew to his bedroom.

He exploded the following day, "Who leave on the cooking gas, pay!"

Two days later, Nar flung, "Some people are only flirting unashamedly behind women and are neglectful of their prescribed household chores."

My old Nar, I thought. I smiled and patted him on the back.

He glared at me. "You find this amusing, eh?"

"Not when I have to do what everyone refuses to do?"

"What?"

"My turn to complain," I said.

One evening I found Raj pacing to and fro in the living room. "What?"

"Like Bram making sand castles in the toilet!"

"Why you don't go under the banana plants and then use the leaves," I joked.

Raj glared at me.

"Sorry."

"But he really full of shit, eh?" he said.

One Saturday morning Raj left with his towel around his neck, and returned about fifteen minutes later with the towel wrapped around his hand, sucking his teeth.

"What now?" I asked.

"Like he masturbating in the bathroom!"

"Who?"

"Nar!"

On Sunday. Raj left very early for Gros Islet—I supposed he was going to church—and Bram and Nar for Laljeet's. I played all of my music cassettes twice, turned on the volume full blast, and screamed along. I exhausted myself and slept for most of the afternoon. I wasn't even aware when the guys returned home.

Nobody complained about anything for a few days after. And I supposed on the last Sunday, the 'Love thy neighbor as thyself' or 'Remove the mote that is in your eye before you attempt to remove the mote in your brother's eye' thing was featured in the sermons.

But at eight o'clock the next night, Raj wasn't home, and I began to worry.

About half an hour later, he entered the front door noisily. He had a few drinks; all the signs were there. He smiled, flung the attaché case on the table and walked straight to the kitchen. He returned to the living room minutes later and was actually singing a Lord Kitchener's calypso, in the same tune but with a few words replaced: *"Guyanese I am a born Lucian, I don't like to fo-o-ight, but who take the meat out of the ro-o-ice...I didn't tell anyone to take the meat out of the ro-o-ice..."* He dropped the plate on the table, dipped his forefinger in the rice and looked at me feigning disbelief. His face shone.

A muffled sound came from Bram and Nar's bedroom.

"Raj, I don't know you could sing so well...and Kitchener too, besides," I said. He glared at me and for a moment I thought he was going to throw the plate through the window. He took a few uneven steps and entered the bedroom. The bed creaked.

A few days rolled by incident free and uninteresting.

However, one evening Raj invited me to have a cold beer

at Regis'. I accepted right away and walked ahead of him. He smiled a lot and enjoyed his beer. He spoke little. I was disappointed. But he did say, "I know that you know I love Felicity."

Just as we were about to leave, Regis said, "You know what, guys? Something is bothering me. It doesn't seem right. Bram and Nar hardly come over and when I check them they are always locked up in their room."

"You know Nar is sick," I explained.

"Yes, but they don't take strong or even a shandy. They don't go out. They don't play cricket like the two of you. They don't have anybody checking them out—man, woman or child. You think they bulling each other... homo...you know what I mean? We have persons like that here, you know."

"Nah, they are highly religious men and they meditate most of the time when they are not working." I said.

"But..."

"And besides too, they are writing a book!"

"Oh, I see,"

"Homo! Ha! Book! Ha!" Raj sniggered and gulped a mouthful of beer.

"And Raj, I hear about her. I live in Gros Islet too," Regis said, looking steadily at Raj.

Raj dismissed him with a wave of the hand.

At home, I told Raj, "I am positive Regis knows Felicity."

"That is what I am afraid of. He would tell Bram and..."

"Okay, I understand. And I feel he already told them you are going to church with her. So why don't you ask Felicity."

"I don't trust that Regis, but I will think about it."

The following Friday, I got a letter from Geet, part of which read:

*Everything is alright home. The children are growing big and they want to know when you coming home. The police kill a bandit who killed the Indian jeweler in Uitvlugt and raped his wife but don't worry, we okay. There is a rumor going around about Nar wife like she seeing somebody. The money devalue to one twenty. You know they can't get qualified teachers for the high school. Like all the teachers going away. You must bring cheese when you coming home and tooth paste and toilet paper. The government banning everything and what we have too expensive here. It is sheer black market. God!*

I began replying that very night but scrapped the letter.

# 8

I DIDN'T SLEEP MUCH that night. In the morning, I wrote the letter. There wasn't much to say...

*Find out the price of a good second-hand Toyota car...find out if they have vacancy at Zeeburg Secondary School...but think also of you and the children coming back with me to St.Lucia next term. Nar sick. He is a diabetic.*

It was a wet morning and when the rain subsided around nine we left for Regis' shop to make our weekly purchases.

"Hey guys!" Regis, wearing a red cap and a raincoat, and carrying a Heineken bottle, appeared from behind the big breadfruit tree. He gulped the beer and said, "Yes, let me see how I can help you boys out today." He slipped his hands around Bram's waist and said, "Let's seek wisdom and fortune in my little parlor."

"I can see you went partying last night, Mr. Regis," Nar said, tapping him on the back.

"*Gason,* for most of the night," Regis replied.

Bram handed Regis the list of groceries. Regis hummed and sang as he deposited the items on the counter.

"Why you boys so quiet today?" Regis asked suddenly.

No one replied.

"Like you all had a fight or what?"

"No, Mr Regis. We thinking deeply," I said.

"Oh."

Suddenly Raj said, "Why don't we buy more canned stuff?"

Nar remarked, "But you have under your bed."

Raj stared at him, "How you know that? And in any case, I bought those."

"Okay!" I almost screamed. "Let's get on with what we have to buy."

They all looked at me.

As we were about to leave, Regis whispered, "Have a malta on the house." He opened a beer for himself.

We glanced at one another, sat and waited. He stood by the window and looked outside.

"Look," he said, and we all peered through the Coca-Cola window and saw light raindrops. "I mean," he lowered his voice and beckoned all heads closer, "I mean, I could get an infinite amount of U.S. currency! U.S.!" His eyes roved over our faces slowly and his mouth was slightly agape. "Cheap...cheap, of course."

We glanced at one another.

"Oh, yes," Bram said. He drew up his shoulders and began to rotate them. I thought he was about to do a Nar.

"At what exchange, may I ask?" Nar asked.

"It's only two fifty, cheaper than the bank, of course. Any amount."

We sipped the maltas in the silence that followed. I reckoned each of us was pondering on this unexpected good fortune that had landed at our doorsteps, and this laudable exhibition of man's geniality.

"I will get back to you," Bram said eventually.

"See you boys this afternoon, then. I have to know today and don't worry the green thing safe, safe."

After lunch, I borrowed Nar's textbook, Selvon's 'Lonely

Londoners,' chuckled over the Moses character and drifted off to sleep.

When I awoke, I heard voices in the living room.

At one point, Nar said, "Bram, I have decided to ask Regis for two hundred. What about you?"

"If I could get five...that will do."

I got up and sat on Raj's bed. He was awake. "Raj, are you taking the US?" I asked.

"Yes...for my parents."

"You?"

"I am thinking of bringing over my family to live here."

"Good idea, Ron."

I had another quiet Sunday. The boys went to pray and Regis wasn't there.

But on the following day, which was a national holiday, I was awakened by loud singing. I peered at the clock. Minutes after five! I sat upright. Pagwah songs! Yes, it was around this time back home when Pagwah was celebrated. How Bram and Nar would have loved to have a tassa drum and a pair of cymbals. I thought. The voices, which sounded like a blend of soprano and bass, rose and fell.

"Christ!" Raj was awake.

Over in the other room, the jubilation continued.

"Boy, we must soak Ron and Raj," suggested Nar.

"Yes. Even the black people who pass through the village don't get vex when we soak them, even if the water dirty," said Bram.

"I will really miss it," Nar said, before he alone embarked on another song in his unique bass voice.

I decided to join them and opened the door into the living room.

Splash! Bram was laughing his guts out. The water trickled from my head to my toe. It was awfully cold. I dashed to the kitchen for a utensil to return the compliment. Bram scampered through the back door. Nar came out of the bedroom at the same time, and I poured the bucketful of water on him. He giggled, and sputtered the water that ran down into his mouth.

"Let us wet Raj," he whispered.

As soon as we opened the door, Raj shouted, "None of that damn stupidness!"

Nar halted with basin poised in mid air. He stared at Raj for a few seconds before he turned and left. When Bram rejoined Nar, they spoke in hushed tones.

"The metamorphosis of the butterfly has begun," Nar flung over his shoulder, before they retreated to their bedroom.

Bram and Nar hummed Pagwah songs. I was disappointed.

An hour later, Bram said, "No rank today, Ron. We are preparing some sweet meat. Okay?"

"Okay."

Raj emerged from the bedroom around eleven o'clock. Bram went up to him with a bowl of sweet meat. "Try some, Raj."

"Nah. I think I will go over at Regis and get some barbecued chicken."

Bram looked at the sweet meat, then turned and walked slowly to the kitchen.

"This new butterfly is emerging faster than I thought," Nar said, looking up to the ceiling.

Both Bram and Nar returned to their bedroom.

"Why, Raj? Why?" I asked him as soon as they disappeared in the bedroom.

He didn't look at me and he didn't say anything while I ate the fudge and metai.

"Even if you are going to a Christian church now, wasn't it part of your culture and your growing up? What about the tolerance we spoke about the other day?"

He bowed his head.

"Or is because you have so much against Bram and Nar?"

"You know they irritate me a lot. Judases, they are!"

"Come on, Raj. We have got to work things out."

Raj and I were still in the living room when Regis came over just before lunch all excited, "My brothers, my party has a meeting on the playing field. Let's go."

Bram and Nar came out of their bedroom but Nar immediately left for the kitchen. I heard the water tap flowing.

"Yes, Ron, it would be exciting," Regis said.

Nar returned with a bucket and stood behind Regis. Bram and I began to chuckle.

"Yes, Regis," Bram said, "You would enjoy it, my brother."

Nar raised the bucket and began pouring the water on Regis.

"What the ...?" Regis spun around and attempted to grab the bucket. He glared at Nar.

"Take it easy, my brother," Bram said, as he held Regis by the shoulder and giggled, "We are celebrating a Hindu religious festival."

"Celebrate who? What nonsense?"

"Okay Mr. Regis. Sit and let me explain," Bram beckoned.

Regis was still glaring at Nar as he wiped the water from his pate. After a while he sat.

"Today is the anniversary of the most vibrant Hindu festival. They call it Pagwah. They burn something called Holika, symbolic of the triumph of Good over Evil."

"Who? What?"

Bram told him about the festival.

Nar came with a bowl of sweet meat "Taste this, Mr. Regis."

Regis smiled.

Bram explained further while Regis ate.

Raj and I went to the meeting. When we arrived, the small playing ground was swarming with people. It was like an ocean of red. The ruckus was terrific. Everyone was speaking to someone else at the top of his voice. The hoarse voice over the public address system was singing and screaming, cooing and drawling.

"Our party will form the new government."

The crowd clapped.

"The ruling party is a dismal failure."

The crowd screamed.

"Our party is the best."

The crowd approved.

"We will kick them out."

The crowd roared.

Regis bellowed, "We going to bust their tail good and proper at the next elections. Long live the St. Lucia...!" The people around him took up the chant. Regis looked at Raj and me and gloated, "Yes, we go kick their *rass* out."

Suddenly the wave of loud cheering gathered momentum. Everyone turned and looked excitedly and expectantly in the direction of the highway. The sound of pan music floated in and rose above the cheers. Arms, legs and torsos began to move with the music.

Regis pranced.

Vehicles—trucks, pick ups, vans and cars-rolled in steadily with revelers chanting, clapping and dancing. Each wore a red jersey with the party symbol splashed across the front in white. Many held bottles, placards or pieces of cloth in their hands.

The crowd hastily parted as a black, expensive-looking jeep appeared. It drove into the playing field, straight up to the unfinished tent, which covered the entire cricket pitch. The podium appeared to be exactly on one of the batting creases.

"My leader," Regis said gleefully, as a tall, broad shouldered man glided up to the stage. There was a sweeping hush. Only the man with the microphone was screaming about something. Then he paused, looked at the leader and said more soberly and slowly, "Let us give a big, big cheer... no, three cheers for our great, brilliant and strong leader... our next prime minister, the Honorable Mister..." The leader's name was lost in the clamor that rose. The leader raised his right hand and the noise died quickly. He sat regally on the only cushioned chair.

Two speakers did their stints on stage but the humming and buzzing drowned their voices. I was distracted by a minor political issue, hotly debated by two young ladies nearby.

"And now my friends, our leader..." rose clearly and distinctly above the noise. Silence quickly closed in as the leader strode up to the rostrum. "Brothers, sisters, my people...thank you, thank you..." He was calm. He plunged into his policies and plans. "We will make St Lucia the Paradise it is supposed to be...the Helen of the West. We will build roads...we will increase salaries and we will provide employment for everyone...yes everyone! We want change...we must change...things must change, *Tout bagay!*" His voice rang out louder with every promise. The clamors reached new heights. And every time he paused to let the outburst subside, he withdrew a red handkerchief from his shirt pocket, and wiped his face.

He then attacked. "They can't even do a proper barbecue or run a fete. They are really and truly pups...yes, P U P S. They haven't grown yet. They should rename their party. And another thing, they are divided, not united, and divided they will fall...fall...fall! And another thing, they don't represent the workers. Get rid of this bourgeoisie government!" He reminded me of the way Regis' face contorted when he held on to a word. He paused again and looked over the gathering.

I glanced at Regis and the others around. Some were preoccupied with other things and their own animated conversation. Others with mouths agape waited expectantly.

"And the Prime Minister is a sparrow, how can he run a government when he running behind women...women, I say!" the leader screamed. The crowd went wild. "His deputy too is a real jackass!" The crowd hit the roof. "He needs a bridle to lead him. How can he lead people?"

The sun blazed down on the ebullient supporters. It seemed like most of them were intoxicated either from the contents of the bottles they were carrying, or by the words that poured forth out of the mouths of those who spoke. The funky smell of perspiration mingled with the piquant smell of alcohol pervaded the atmosphere.

When the leader retreated to his seat, a bald, grim faced gentleman grabbed the microphone and began singing lustily.

"Party song," Regis said, looking at Raj and me, before he joined the others who sang with gay abandon. The grim faced man was very efficient and seemed to be very popular with the crowd. He stamped the podium, much in the same manner that a batsman taps the batting crease when he is in form. Suddenly he stopped, raised his right hand and folded his cuff.

"They must go...go, I say go!"

"Yea-a!"

"And all the foreigners they bring here too!"

"Yea-a!"

Regis glanced at us anxiously. He jabbed Raj. "Don't bother with him. He is a damn kounoumounou," he said and sucked his teeth.

"Let us go now," Raj suggested to me.

"Wait on. Don't leave yet," Regis coaxed, holding on to Raj's arm.

"Let us go and have a drink," Raj said.

"Okay," Regis agreed, and walked on ahead of us.

When we caught up with him at the beer garden, he asked "What happens at your political meetings?"

"Totally different from here...not much fun. A lot of heckling from the opposition...violent at times," I said.

"Here is power play. See if we don't call a strike in the banana industry."

There was a strike the next day. That night the boys told me to bring the radio set from the bedroom and turn up the volume when the eight o'clock news was aired. The government called the strike 'wildcat' and 'political'. There were reports of some violent clashes between members of the rival parties. However the strike lasted only two days.

Wednesday 27th passed incident free. Around midnight, I felt a sudden pain. "What the...?'I jumped up and looked down. A centipede was scurrying away before I could lay my hand on anything.

"What?" Raj said.

"Centipede."

"Bit you?"

"Yes."

"Where?"

"Back."

"See in the box under the bed...insect bites ointment. It will help."

It helped and I settled down again.

Thursday afternoon, everybody was home early. We listened to the radio again. On the national front, there was still some tension around.

We had warm sunshine. Surprisingly, Bram and Nar joined us to play cricket. I didn't bat. My back was still swollen.

At around four, a blue bus pulled up and Regis, wearing dark sunshades, alighted. He took several brisk steps in our direction, before looking up. He stopped and scratched his behind. Then he turned and began heading away from us.

"Ah, Mr. Regis!" Bram shouted.

Regis stopped and turned around slowly, "Ah, Mr. Bram, I didn't see you, of course."

"Is everything okay, Mr. Regis?" Bram asked good naturedly and began walking towards Regis.

"Sure, sure. But I am not feeling too well," Regis replied, without looking at Bram. He stood his ground and resumed scratching his behind.

"What about the thing, Mr. Regis? You said today," Bram

asked while he was still some distance from Regis.

"What thing? Oh, the thing. It is safe, of course." Regis removed the hand from his behind, and brought it to his mouth to make a half funnel. "Is today I did tell you? Boy, I clean forgot with the strike and all that. Tomorrow it is, for sure."

While we walked home I asked, "Nar, did you ask Regis to get you U.S. too?"

"No. I am not sure that I want to take home money," he replied and sighed. "What about you?"

I explained to him. "And you know the situation with taking money out of Guyana."

He nodded. "You have made the right decision."

Regis came over about six thirty. "Bram...Raj, the thing safe," he said straightaway. Then he lowered his head and whispered, "I have a movie...A blues."

"Eh?" Nar said.

"Blues," Regis repeated. His eyes smiled.  He waited.

We smiled and looked at one another.

I remembered blues nights back home too. During the day people had responded with wide eyed and scornful expressions, "Who? Me? See that? Huh!" But the few nights I had attended, the cinema was jam packed!

At eight o'clock, Nar and I left for Regis' after both Raj and Bram had declined.

There were four of us. The other was one of Regis' female friends. She stood in the shadows in the hall. She was clad in black attire that concealed from her neck to her toe and appeared shy. "She is okay. She is my pussycat." Regis laughed as he drew her close.

Regis was at his expressive best. He cooed, shrieked and commented loudly and lewdly. In intonation, excitement and West Indian jargon, his running commentary surpassed any soccer commentator's when a goal is scored. In the dim light that reflected off the television screen, I saw him slap his thighs in quick succession then reached over and shook

Pussycat by her shoulders as he mirthfully carried on in his patois expletives.

"Regis, behave!" she responded. But then a broad grin appeared on her face and she leaned slightly away from him.

For the most part, Nar's eyes were riveted to the T.V. Once or twice he glanced at Regis and Pussycat, and murmured, "Uhuh."

On one occasion, Regis playfully punched Pussycat and she nearly fell over. "Man, behave!" she warned and giggled. His invectives in patois with a few English words thrown in filled the room.

For a while there was absolute silence. Only the gurgling sounds of the actors in the movie were heard.

"I warn you! Okay!" Pussycat's voice rang out suddenly. She deftly slapped Regis' hand away and proceeded to cover her breasts with her hands.

"What now?" he asked.

"You touch..."

"Accident."

"You lie."

Immediately after the movie, we asked Regis about the three words that featured most prominently in his commentary. He confirmed that they were the patois words for the human sexual anatomy. And without any prompting, he revealed others and expounded on equipment and stimulants he would recommend for sexual pleasure. "I am an expert in this field," he concluded.

He would score a ten out of ten on my score sheet any time for his expertise in the field.

Nar and I walked home quietly and as we entered the living room, Nar succinctly remarked, "Oh God, how I want a woman!"

I rubbed some more of Raj's ointment on my back and poked around my bed with a cutlass before I settled down.

Friday 29th turned out to be a long day...

# 9

BOOM! I was jolted back to the present in Mon Repos shortly after midday on that Friday. Somewhere in the vicinity, a tree must have fallen. This was not unusual especially when gusts of strong wind swept over the banana fields, but on this occasion it had to be a huge tree. Perhaps a coconut tree had been deliberately felled. The sound echoed throughout the surroundings.

I sat upright. I remembered the frying pan that Raj had dispatched through the window and I got up to retrieve it. From what I could see of the sky, only light cloud floated above, but that was no bother. The upper canopy of breadfruit and mango branches and leaves, and the second tier of banana leaves made the place cool. I rubbed my back. It didn't hurt that much.

I began to trudge down the slope at the back of our house. It was always soothing down there. Mostly banana plants, tall coconut, papaya and mango trees lined the way. The descent wasn't difficult. The gradient could not be more than forty five degrees and the terrain was sheltered. A light, refreshing wind picked up and the place brightened.

Suddenly a dry coconut landed about two yards in front of me, startling me and halting my progress. It bounced and raced ahead of me down the incline. I looked back and up anxiously. I gathered a few pebbles and aimed at ripe mangoes. Birds, especially the agitated black ones, heralded my intrusion with their loud twittering and sudden flights. A few were carrying out a concerted attack on a ripe papaya. I poised to throw an imaginary missile. They retreated with a flurry. Their harangue continued and my back ached a little.

My descent ended in a narrow stream that flowed at a slow, steady pace. I threw a few pebbles that disturbed the calmness, and sent angry ripples racing. A lizard scurried by, stopped, snapped at something and then disappeared. A light breeze rustled through the leaves bringing a whiff of the sweet smell of ripe sapodilla.

My stomach began to growl. There were lots of guavas around but I remembered Nar and ate only two. Now and again the pain in the back returned but slightly. Then a thought hit me. Maybe I should cook when I returned to the house. The boys wouldn't be annoyed with Raj and it would even ease up the tension. Yes, that is what they call killing two birds with one stone. I would make cook up rice like Geet did, with lots of rice, dhal, spinach, okra, pepper and even a few pieces of chicken if there was any, although Raj had said that he couldn't stand that heavy stuff anymore. I jogged part of the way up. I panted. My legs gave up and I settled on a boulder. Maybe I should jog daily. Yes, that was it. A healthy body makes a healthy mind and my thoughts wouldn't race off so easily. Yes I would start jogging tomorrow.

At three thirty, I was still outside when the same, small dark-brown car pulled up. Raj alighted and greeted me warmly. He leaned over and spoke to Felicity. She waved, and I heard a faint "Hi."

Yes, I remembered her small round face, and the captivating smile. She was indeed very beautiful. Raj and Felicity spoke briefly. They chuckled. She waved and drove off.

Raj was all smiles as he approached me. "How are you

feeling? Let's play some cricket."

"Take it easy," I said.

We played cricket. In all, the game involved one batsman at a time, three bowlers, because we had three soft balls, four fielders who were spread out in the outfield among the banana plants. Our only spectator, Regis, emerged from his shop when Raj was batting.

"She is very beautiful," Regis said.

Raj dropped the bat.

"Ask him," I urged quietly.

"Regis, do you know her?" he asked

"Who? Felicity? Of course. Remember, I live in Gros Islet."

"But you never told me."

"Of course. I was telling you all along. Did she never mention me?"

"No."

Regis shrugged.

"And, Regis...Have you told Bram and Nar about her?" Raj asked.

Raj should have been more subtle, I thought.

"No. Why?" Regis asked.

"Why what?"

"Why you want to know if I told Bram and Nar?"

"You would not understand, Mr. Regis."

"If you say so."

For a few minutes everyone seemed lost in his own thoughts.

"Mr. Regis," I said, "Do you have anything to scare away insects and things like centipede?"

"Oh yes. Baygon will do." He left immediately and I followed him. When I looked around Raj was already on his way home.

In the shop I asked Regis about Felicity.

"Mr. Regis, how long have you known Felicity?"

"Very long...since she was a child." He looked through the window. "A very beautiful woman now," he said softly.

When I returned home I found Raj in bed.

"Raj," I said. "Regis says he knew her from childhood."

He shrugged.

"Anyway, I hope I don't disturb you. I want to patch this hole on the floor where I think the centipedes come through."

"Oh I forgot. Still hurts?"

"A little."

The next evening when Raj came home, he greeted me coldly, dropped his stuff on the table and crawled into bed.

I sat on the edge of his bed and said, "Raj, what's bothering you? Is it the boys again?"

He sighed. "Well, if you should know. I asked Felicity about Regis as soon as she picked me up yesterday morning." He paused.

"Well...?"

"She said she knew him and that they both live in Gros Islet. I told her I knew that, but asked her why she didn't ever mention that she knew him." He paused and took a deep breath. "She said that she didn't think it was important."

"But what I can't understand is why Regis and Felicity didn't let you know that they knew each other."

He sat up. "That's exactly what I asked her. And you know what she said...She said she knew him before I came and they were acquaintances."

He was breathing heavier. "Ron, then I lost my cool. I asked her what kind of acquaintances and he was more than twenty years older than her." He paused again. "She didn't say anything and I told her to stop the car and let me out."

"I think..."

"No. Let me finish. She didn't stop and I said, 'Did he screw you?' It was then she stopped."

"I don't think you should have..."

"Yes, I know. She asked me if that was what I thought of her and began sobbing."

He exhaled again. "I told her I was sorry. She said nothing happened between them."

"So you made up?"

"Yes. And Ron, I am glad you asked and I told you."

"And Raj, don't say anything to Regis."

"Okay."

Regis was standing under the breadfruit tree when Raj and I got there to play cricket at around five o'clock the next day. Raj looked at him briefly, and Regis waved his hand. It was a dull period of play. No one said anything much.

About half an hour later, Bram and Nar descended slowly from a black bus. As soon as Bram saw Regis his face lit up. He lumbered up to Regis. They exchanged courtesies.

"Nice shot!" Regis suddenly shouted, as Raj clouted the ball over the highway and into the gully. Bram's eyes followed the ball. The boys dashed after it. Raj turned his back to Regis and scratched the batting crease.

"Oh, Mister Regis, did you get the thing?" Bram inquired suddenly.

"What thing? Oh, the thing…yes, the thing…Nah, I didn't get it. But it safe, safe…next week," Regis replied.

Raj looked up and stopped the bowler who was charging in. He took a mighty swipe at the next delivery and hit it far into an irretrievable part of the gully. Raj retired. I chose not to bat. My back was still swollen.

As we were leaving for home, Regis told Nar, "Come across to the shop at about eight tonight."

"Why?" Nar asked.

"Just come," Regis replied.

At eight, Nar invited me to accompany him. When we got there we found Regis chatting away with Pussycat.

"Ah, Mr. Nar," he greeted. "This is Pussycat…I mean Candida. I call her Pussycat. You remember her, of course…the blues night."

"Hi," Pussycat said to Nar and smiled down to him as he sat on a stool. Her trim petite figure stood out in her white top and tight brown shorts. When she opened her mouth, her beautiful white teeth gleamed in the light and contrasted heavily with her dark complexion. Her braids were neatly arranged in corn rows. She was a very good looking woman. Nar squinted and Regis explained, "I told her about you. She would like to become your friend."

"But Mr. Regis..."

"No buts."

Pussycat appeared embarrassed and turned away. Nar was tongue-tied but finally managed, "Later," and walked out of the shop.

Regis scowled. I hurried to catch up with Nar. When I caught up with him, I patted him on his back. He sucked his teeth.

When we arrived home, we found both Raj and Bram reading in the living room.

Nar sat next to the window. After a while he looked at me and smiled.

"Nar," I said, "Regis was..."

"Yes, Ron...me too. I don't like this weather. The inclemency is most aggravating."

"What? Oh yes," I said. "This weather can really freak you out." I smiled

"What Regis said?" Bram asked without looking up from his book.

"Usual thing...bad weather. Ron," Nar said, "I was teaching the students how important the punctuation mark is and I told them the anecdote of the Amerindian who was accused of killing his wife." He paused and looked around. Raj and Bram were still totally absorbed in their books.

"Look, Ron, I told them the police recorded that the Buckman—I mean Amerindian—said in his statement, 'She is me wife, I mind she, I kill she,' and the prosecutor said that was a confession." He stopped and Bram looked up.

He continued, "The Amerindian's lawyer said, 'Oh no, my worship, the police doesn't know English. He forgot to put in the exclamation and question marks at the end. My client was saying, 'Me mind she! Me kill she?' And you know the

131

Amerindian was exonerated."

Raj looked up smiling, "You were that Amerindian or Buckman or whatever you call them. Sorry, I forgot to say question mark."

"But Nar, I think that was cleverly explained. I mean, the punctuation mark thing," I said.

"Nar, if you kill your wife that's how you hope to get off?" Raj slipped in.

Nar looked at Raj. He sat and sighed.

"You will. I think you are a man full of technicality or whatever you call it," Raj concluded himself.

"You are..." Nar began as he jumped up and pointed a finger at Raj.

I was about to intervene when Bram said, "Oh, I just remember, I got a letter from my wife. She says that Balgobin says I must find work for him here since I am finding work for everybody."

"What! My wife didn't write," Nar said, turning his attention to Bram. "But you tell Savitri to instill in Balgobin that here they only employ people with doctorate. And furthermore police beat up people brutally with cricket bats, especially coolie people, when they find them intoxicated on the street, and sometimes pound their balls."

"He is not coming here and..." Bram said.

"Boys!" Regis was standing in the doorway. He looked at Nar. "Nar, why?"

Nar raised his hand quickly, "I will see you tomorrow, Mr. Regis," and headed for his bedroom.

"St. Lucian girls are so beautiful...too sweet. Ah must find one for you, Mr. Bram, and Ron too. I have cock fighting on this coming Sunday. Many will be around," Regis said, breaking into a near convulsive laughter.

"Mr. Regis, you ..." Bram began to say.

"Yes, I know. I *phaglee...* wi, *fou.*"

The rain eased into a drizzle.

"Mr. Regis. What about the thing?" Raj suddenly asked.

The smile left Regis' face. "Oh, that. This afternoon, I was telling Mr. Bram about the thing...it safe, safe. Next week." He took a deep breath and added quickly, "See you boys." With that he hurried out into the drizzle.

Another shower of heavy, pelting rain drowned the silence that ensued. When it subsided, Bram walked wearily to the almanac and painted 'X' on the '29' with his black ink pen. I felt like doing the same. Then he turned to me and said, "Ron, I would like to hear the weather forecast."

I went into the bedroom to get the radio/cassette player. As I turned it on, Nar emerged from his bedroom smiling, "Ron, how about some Mukesh tunes?"

"How about some Reggae, Ron?" Raj said.

I returned to the bedroom with my set.

# 10

SUNDAY the 31st of March was cockfighting day. On the Saturday afternoon, we watched Regis and his work force dumping board, zinc, tables and other materials in front of our house.

"Ron, are you coming tomorrow? You must come," Regis hailed when he saw me. "There will be lots of fun and games, *gason*." He waved and did a little dance before he resumed barking orders to his workers.

It rained that night and persisted lightly on Sunday morning.

"Ah glad if it rains so the whole day," Bram said as he peeped through the window.

"Still," Nar said, "I would like to see some curvaceous backsides."

"You had the chance last Friday night," I reminded him.

He looked at me quickly and zipped his mouth with his finger.

The drizzle did not deter Regis and company, which included his wife and five boys. I joined them and helped in shifting things around. The workers struggled, working under these sodden conditions as Regis ranted and bellowed orders. But he got the work done. He led by example.

134

His wife moved about slowly. Pieces of materials slipped from her hands regularly, and each time Regis looked at her she took some time to recover them.

"Why the ass you don't go home?" he told her.

She glared at him, sat and massaged her legs.

He stood upright. "All you fit for is to stuff you fat back-side with food!"

Her mouth was clamped shut and her cheeks bulged. I was sure that if she had only opened her mouth, she would have shrieked, and I thought she didn't cry out because I was there.

I followed Regis into the cock fighting amphitheatre — he called it Madison Square Garden. The Garden, which was anything but square, had an arena which I was sure was meant to be circular, but which was enclosed by four different arcs — one large and three small — of cardboard, about two feet high, held in upright positions by wooden stakes. The diameter must have varied from eight to ten feet.

There were three tiers of seats made from long boards — some slender and uneven — resting on concrete blocks. The ringside seat was one concrete block high.

The wall that was nailed to the breadfruit tree — the same one that we used as our cricket stump and wicketkeeper — was made from old galvanized sheets nailed upright. The wall opposite was about two feet shorter. The other two walls were built in identical fashion: the wattles and coconut branches were secured closely to bamboos, arranged in a checkered pattern.

"I usually charge five dollars for them to go in. Ron, this thing was a big, big business." he continued. His left hand came up gradually, until it extended above his head. It rested there for a while. "But these days people mean, mean." The hand dropped with double speed by his side as he shook his head forlornly.

"But I also rear a lot of cocks where I live and I sell them."

"I see."

135

"You see me setting up these dominoes tables?" He said and pointed to three sets of wooden fine legged tables with three benches next to each set some distance off, near to the bar that was shaded with coconut branches. "Well, the men do play until they get drunk..." He paused and beckoned a little boy nearby. "Boy, remove this board, nah. What you think I am paying you for? Is why you so blasted lazy?"

The boy stiffened and grabbed the board.

"What the hell!"

Regis grabbed his left foot and hopped about in rage and pain. He spat out about half a dozen foul words in quick succession.

As it turned out the board had slipped out of the boy's hand and landed heavily on Regis' foot. His face contorted, his eyes closed and his cheeks rose to meet them. He glared at the frightened and motionless boy. He took an unsteady step forward. He lost his balance and barked, "Boy, you best haul you lil tail from here before I mash it up." He made a swoop with his right hand for something, but the boy had already disappeared among the banana plants.

"That's it. It is coming." Regis' tone changed as he pivoted his head in the direction of the highway even though he was still rubbing the foot.

"What is?" I asked.

"The truck that is bringing the music set."

It was only then that I heard the groaning of the truck. It grew louder as it turned onto the pathway. It rattled and creaked when it climbed over uneven ground.

"Brother Paul, what took you so long?" Regis shouted angrily.

"Brother Cauldron, the old truck is no good." Rasta jumped out of the truck and walked briskly towards Regis. "I man tell you, rent another truck next time," he continued angrily. His face shone and his eyes glazed.

"Brother Ras, you talking *maji*. But next time I am renting a helicopter," Regis retorted.

Rasta Paul left to unload the music, Regis for the bar, and I for our house.

As soon as I entered, Raj came out of the bedroom and said, "Come on Ron, go and get ready and let's have some drinks. Don't bother with those anti men."

I looked at him sharply and pointed to the dark room.

"Don't worry. They are gone." In less than fifteen minutes, the music came on. It filled the air and drummed in my ears.

"Lovely," Raj said as he rocked his body. His eyes smiled.

I stood by the window for a while. One …two…three…four vehicles pulled up. Over a score of men, women and children jumped out. The children were instantly attracted to the six enormous speakers, like pins to magnets. They began twisting and turning slowly and gradually increased the tempo as they gyrated and contorted their bodies. Other 'pins' were sucked in. Alesia, Jenny and Curly would have been fascinated by this, I thought. The men and women stood in little clusters, watching the children, and talking and gesticulating. Some men gravitated towards the refreshment bar.

The crowd was swelling.

"The fun is already starting," Raj called out from behind me. Turning around to move to the bedroom, I pulled back a little, instinctively brought my hands to my waist. "*Gason!*"

Raj was dressed in a pair of dark pants that bulged around the hips and thighs, and tapered off at the heels — almost like an upside down isosceles triangle. The shirt, which was definitely about two or more sizes larger than those he normally wore, was multi colored. He stepped back, pulled himself up to his full height and squared his shoulders. The smile never left his face.

"Is it alright? It is the style, you know."

"Yes. It looks nice," I said.

"By the way, Felicity will be coming."

"It figures," I said.

"What?"

"Nothing."

I got dressed in a pair of blue jeans and white jersey and donned my pair of dark sunshades.

"That look nice too," he said as he put a hand around my shoulder and steered me through the door.

We moved into the crowd. Many men and women stood around the bars and drank. In another section, a group of young people danced lustily to the jump up music. The children screamed and darted in and among the crowd.

I invited Raj to drink a beer.

He looked at his watch. "Not yet. Won't mind a piece of chicken, though."

As we approached the food section, the smell of barbecued chicken floated across. We found ourselves on top of the smell.

"Raj."

No answer. He was looking at his watch.

"Raj!"

"Uh."

I glanced at him. His head was shifting around like a weather cock. I nudged him, pointing to the chicken. "Wing or leg?"

"Am..."

He jabbed me lightly. I glanced at him quickly and he said, "Felicity." He raised his head and eyebrows in her direction. His face immediately lit up and the eyes laughed. There was a slight tremor in his voice when he clutched my arms and whispered, "Come, let's go and meet her."

I removed my sunshades.

When she saw him coming, her mouth opened and her white teeth glistened. She took two uneven steps forward but stopped. He was practically on top of her. Her face flushed.

"Hi," she sang. The thin soft voice was barely audible. He put an arm around her and she nestled up to him. Clad in her short white pants and red shirt, her petite figure was lost in his bulk.

"This is Ron," Raj said, leaning towards her.

She tilted her head. The large, conch shell shaped earrings dangled. "Of course, I remember him...the market...the fete," she said with a smile. She looked at me steadily and extended a hand. She looked at her feet and the earrings danced.

Raj bent over and whispered in her ear. She looked up at him and shook her head in the affirmative. The short nose twitched and the earrings danced faster. We all stood rooted for sometime. We looked around.

"Well, how do you like it here?" Felicity said eventually, taking me by surprise.

"Well...a...it is okay," I managed to say.

Raj and Felicity looked at each other and smiled. A sudden breeze rushed across and shifted her hair slightly out of place. The reddish brown and wavy hair came all the way down to her shoulders and flipped up. Her right hand went up and patted the hair back in place.

I bent to draw the laces of my boots tighter, and, straightening up, I felt in my pocket for my sunshades. "Raj," I said, "I think the cock fight is about to start. I am going."

"Wouldn't you like..."

I was already on my way. After I was some distance off, I looked over my shoulder. They weren't there.

Soon I found myself in the domino arena. A lot of people shuffled around the three tables excitedly. I strode up to the table with the least spectators, and positioned myself where I could have a clear view of the players. On the left was a bald headed player; on the right a bearded one, and sitting directly in front of me was the other who had dreadlocks. The tickets of the game in progress had already taken a right turn on the table. Beardman's gaze shifted from his tickets to those on the table and back to his. "You have deuce...deuce!" he called out to Baldhead, slamming the deuce at the same time. The other tickets on the table rattled. Baldhead looked at his tickets for some time and then drawled, "If I have deuce?" He removed a domino from his left palm, raised his right hand to the level of his right ear, held it there for some seconds, then added, "What deuce you talking about...orange juice...passion fruit juice...mango juice...eh...I have it...all. *Tout bagay!*" and brought down the hand with lightning speed. The dominoes on the table jumped into disarray. Dreadlocks straightened them, looking at his tickets at the same time, and hesitantly knocked three times on the table.

"Yes, too much for you!" Baldhead said.

Beardman looked at his tickets and brought them closer to his face. He squinted, shook his head and said, "Knock."

Just then, a guy, cuddling a rooster hurried past. He was heading in the direction of the Garden. Immediately I followed him. I wanted to get a ringside seat. And it wasn't that I hadn't seen roosters fighting before. In Zeelugt practically every household had roosters squaring off everyday. But I was told that here in Mon Repos these roosters were professionals.

Regis was not the doorman; Rasta Paul was. I had to pay to enter. Ringside was filled. I managed though to squeeze in on tier three. The large empty space between the seats and the walls of the Garden, which I called the pit, was filling up quickly with excited trainers, managers and cocks.

Cocks cuddled under arms appeared sleepy. Those left tethered to walls, while their handlers must have gone to negotiate their place on the fighting card, glared at one another, scratched their territory and poised to attack or defend. They were all athletic looking—slender with long limbs and necks, and shiny coats. They differed from the sickly looking cocks that slept under our house, and certainly were much smaller than those back home in Zeelugt where they ate too much, became obese, fought over the hens, and ended up in the frying pans or on the grill.

After a lot of arm flinging, finger pointing, clock watching, debating, and some confusion, the fights got underway. Two warriors held firmly by their trainers, found themselves in the ring. Money began to change hands.

The warriors—all of whom were given famous names— one white and the other brown were released. Immediately their heads fell forward, feathers stood up and tails lifted. There was a hush. Chavez, the white one, much smaller, and Tyson, the brown, took cautious steps sideways, their eyes riveted to each other. Spectators craned their necks and waited.

Then it happened. I thought I saw Chavez blink, and believed that was the mistake. Tyson sailed through the air and dealt Chavez a series of rapid pecks as Chavez was coming up. Blood spurted from Chavez. He staggered, fell, tried to get up but was counted out.

A roar went up. Money changed hands.

Fight number two did not live up to expectations. One of the fighters flew out of the ring and disappeared among the banana trees.

By the time fight number three began, the Garden was packed. The crowd had grown bolder, wilder and coarser with each fight. The smell of beer, liquor and sweat grew heavier. Regis entered the scene at the end of the fourth fight and immediately took control. "This is the last, the biggest...the title fight. It's North versus South," he shouted above the noise.

A hand suddenly dropped on my shoulder; Raj and Fecility had found me. He was excited. "How is it going, man?" he asked.

"Exciting, man...really exciting," I shouted in his ear.

"The last fight is usually the best," he said.

Felicity clung to his arm and looked sad. "I really don't enjoy this...You know, the blood and all that." Her face contorted.

Geetangali would have cursed me if I had brought her here.

"This is the last fight," Raj coaxed, squeezing her arm.

North's champ was dark red with abnormally big feet. The owner called him Ninja. His opponent, who was from Regis'

141

gym, was brown, smaller than Ninja and had an unusually big comb that Regis patted and called Big Brains.

"Are you afraid? Don't be a chicken," Regis shouted as he ducked and weaved among the spectators, flashing five…ten…twenty dollar bills in his left hand and holding Brains in the other.

Regis stepped into the ring caressing Brains' comb. The crowd roared. Ninja was brought from the other end. Part of the crowd bellowed and heckled. The two trainers glared at each other. I thought they were going to have a go at it first.

The two champions, freed at last, squared up like true pugilists trained in the art. They feigned. Silence descended on the Garden. Eyes, heads and gaping mouths of fans followed every maneuver. Perspiration trickled down faces. I glanced sideways. Felicity glued to Raj's side, clutched one of Raj's hands with both of hers.

Brains and Ninja sparred. Brains attacked. Ninja backed away, but suddenly counter attacked. Spectators jumped to their feet and shouted.

"Ninja! Ninja! Ninja!"

Ninja sprang like a basketball player about to dunk, and landed squarely on Brains' back. The crowd went wild.

"Ninja! Ninja! Ninja!"

Felicity shrieked.

Brains' comb was an easy target. Ninja landed a barrage of scratches, digs and pecks. Brains staggered and groaned. He tried to get out of the clench. He succumbed.

Pandemonium broke out.

"Foul! Foul!" the Southerners shouted.

"Yes, he is a fowl, not a cock," the Northerners retaliated.

The Southerners cursed Regis. They stampeded. Regis would have to buy more galvanized sheets than he had originally planned to, I thought.

Raj, Felicity and I escaped to the refreshment bar. While we sipped malta, we espied Regis and Rasta Paul still standing in the Garden. What was left of the walls did little to conceal them. Both men were drinking. About half an hour later, when I looked again in the Garden, they were pointing their fingers into each other's face and shaking their heads. Soon after, Regis left hurriedly in the direction of the food bar. He saw us, and staggered over.

"Is everything okay, Mr. Regis?" I asked. He pouted and shook his head from side to side.

"Ah, Feli! Feli! I didn't know you were here...I...I saw the car but thought Old Johnny was here...here. He does always come...come."

When he got close, he suddenly thrust out his right hand and curled it around her left shoulder. She stepped aside. He attempted to rest his head on her right shoulder.

"Mr. Cauldron!" she protested and moved further back, pushing him away at the same time.

Raj stared at him and his jaws stiffened.

"You are drunk, Mr. Regis," I said annoyed.

He ignored me. "I know her since she was a little one," said Regis amusedly, as his right hand hovered at waist height.

"How did the cockfight..." I began.

"Wait." Regis muttered as he extended his neck like a rooster's and stared in the direction of the Garden. "That Ras," he fizzled under his breath. Suddenly his right hand shot out and slapped Felicity on the buttocks. "See you guys," he flung over his shoulders, hurrying off immediately.

Felicity jerked upright and stood paralyzed. She bit her lips and stared at Regis' quickly departing figure.

"Regis!" Raj took a step in Regis' direction.

"Don't, Raj," I said, grabbing his arm. "The bastard drunk!" He stood still and gritted his teeth. He was breathing hard. Time stood still. Eventually he said quietly, "Felicity, let's go."

She drew circles with the tip of her shoe on the dusty ground.

"Felicity, let's go!"

"I would like to use the washroom," Felicity said quietly,

clinging to Raj's arm.

As we approached the house, I walked ahead. I saw Bram in the living room. "Someone is coming in," I said, and proceeded to the washroom.

"Go in," I heard Raj telling her as I came out of the washroom. "I am waiting outside."

"Hi," she said as she passed Bram.

"Oh, hello," he replied and quickly pulled together the front of his partially opened shirt.

I joined Raj outside.

"How is the washroom?" he asked faintly.

"It is alright. Only a few pieces of clothing scattered about."

"Oh." He combed his disheveled hair with his fingers.

"And the place doesn't smell too nice but I fix everything."

A wry smile broke on his face.

When Felicity came out of the washroom and joined us outside, her face was wet. She pushed her hand directly into Raj's pocket, withdrew a handkerchief and dabbed her face dry. He was staring at the ground.

After a while, he said, "Let's go," and walked ahead of her. She took two quick steps and held his limp hand as he escorted her to her car. He returned promptly, and went straight into the bedroom. I retired to bed, and above I heard his bed creak for some time.

The music stopped. Loud and incoherent voices, mingled with foul language, rose and fell. Eventually the place was quiet. Madison Square Garden was empty. I felt exhausted. Sleep was overpowering me. Still, I heard a faint voice saying, "Ah see she…"

# II

RAJ WAS STRANGLING REGIS! I jumped up and found Raj curled up and sound asleep. I wiped the perspiration from my face and settled down again. I awoke a second time—this time with a start. A utensil of some sort had dropped to the floor. The noise came from the kitchen.

"What the hell!" Raj growled.

Then all was quiet. The minutes dragged by.

"I think you should tell his father about her," I heard Nar say eventually.

"Yes, I am sure he is serious about her," Bram replied.

I slid off my sponge mattress and looked at Raj. He was clasping the pillow over his head. I strode into the kitchen.

"Ah, Ron. The penultimate week, boy," Nar said.

"And it could be my last two weeks here."

Bram stopped peeling the potato and looked at me steadily. "Why, Ron? You seem annoyed."

"I am."

"Well, how will we know why if you don't tell us," Nar said.

"Listen, I don't like the way both of you and Raj get along. This morning for instance, you deliberately drop something on the floor to wake him up, and then you want him to know that you know about his girlfriend and his father should know. Why?"

"Did he put you up to this?" Nar asked.

"Ah, shut up!" I said.

Nar dropped the spoon he had in his hand and folded his arms. "You on his side and..."

"Okay, take it easy, Nar. Look, Ron, I know what you are talking about too..." Bram said.

"This is not a matter of taking sides. Every morning you all create a racket and I know it is to annoy Raj..."

"And he doesn't annoy us too? Why don't you talk to him," Nar returned.

"I did and..."

"And..."

"Nar, let Ron finish."

"Listen. The point is we are all big men and we are far away from home and we should rally around one another and...and not behave like little boys."

"Well said...well said..." Nar began, and clapped.

I turned to him. "You are an idiot."

Bram raised his hand, "Okay, Okay. You right, Ron, we must behave like intelligent people. But you don't see anything wrong with his behavior?"

"Of course. There are certain things I do not like. But he is a young man and...and this is a different place and a different time. I could tell him but I can't stop him."

"But Ron," Bram said calmly, "Don't you care what this can do to his relatives. Don't you think I will get some blame? After all I was the one who helped him get this job over here." He stopped and sighed.

"Okay, Ron, do you approve of his drinking?" Nar asked calmly.

"Certainly not. But what I can tell you, he socializes a lot. Again his age..."

"Bram and I don't drink. No body drinks in our houses back home."

"Well, it is not what goes into..."

"Yea, yea, yea...defile the man."

"That saying fits you perfectly, Nar," I said.

"What do you mean?"

"Think about it. Going to Hawan and shouting God's name is not everything."

Bram tapped me on the shoulder. "Okay, okay. Let's not get too worked up here..."

"And another thing..." Nar interrupted.

"Oh, yes..."

"He is running wild behind women...And a black one in particular." He turned up his nose.

"How do you know that?"

"Don't bother. We know; and you know."

"And even if that is so, what's wrong with that?"

"You don't see anything wrong?"

"No...Black or White. And again, he is a young man."

"You don't know his father? Do you?"

"Not much."

"Find out."

I turned to Bram.

"Bram," I said, touching him on the shoulder, "I understand, but let's try to make things work out. Okay?"

And back to Nar, I said, "Nar, I am sorry I got vexed. Let's try to make things go smoothly. Okay?"

They both nodded. No one said anything for a while.

I broke the ice. "Nar," I said, "How is your sugar?"

"Eh? What? Oh, that. I am taking my medication."

"Good. Go on. Fry the egg."

The sizzling of frying eggs filled the kitchen, as Nar poured whipped eggs into the pan.

I turned to Bram, "Did Regis get the thing for you?"

"You know Regis..." Bram began. He was kneading the dough. "Ah, never mind."

"Don't worry. Didn't he say tomorrow?" Nar said.

I heard Raj stir in the bedroom. Minutes later he joined us in the kitchen.

"Raj," I said immediately, "Did Regis get the thing for you?"

"That Regis is playing the arse!"

"Don't worry, didn't he say tomorrow?" Nar said.

"What? Oh, yes," Raj replied.

I smiled inwardly. Making Regis the common enemy wasn't a bad idea, I thought.

And as soon as Raj and I were alone I said, "Why don't you ease up on the drinking? You know it is not good for your health."

"Did they complain about that too?"

"Nah. Your health, man… your health."

"Okay, my father," he said, and laughed.

"More like, 'Doctor, heal thyself.' What you say, Raj?"

"Ah, drop it."

Bram and Nar left on the stroke of six, but not before Nar had walked up to 'the girl', smiled wickedly and stroked her buttocks.

"Simply provocative. Black girls have nice behinds."

"Nar!" Bram chided.

"Is it not true? And Coolie girls have bottoms flat like a frying pan. Not so?"

"Boy, you are something else," Bram said, and laughed with Nar.

"Have to find someone for you, Nar," Raj joked.

"He already has one," I said laughing.

"Ah shut up, Ron," Nar said, and showed me a clenched fist.

As it turned out, that very afternoon when all of us were in the sitting room Pussycat came to see Nar. She went straight to him and implanted herself on his lap.

"Eh? Eh? What…what is this?" Nar responded.

Bram sucked his teeth and marched off to his room. Raj laughed. When Nar eventually succeeded to push her away, she said, "Sponsor me a barbecue chicken, nah, and I come when you don't have company. Sorry I come now."

Hastily, he gave her the money and literally hustled her through the door.

Two days later she came up to me and inquired for Nar.

When I told her, she said, "I will wait," and sat on the steps.

As soon as Bram and Nar came around the brushes, she got up and sang, "Oh. Hi Nar. I have been waiting for you."

"Watch yourself, Nar," Bram said angrily, and walked ahead of Nar into the house.

"Oh, I have to see someone up the road," Nar said. He pivoted and departed hurriedly.

When I entered the house, Bram was waiting. "You know something about this, Ron?"

"Well...well, in a kind of way."

"I thought so," he said and went into his bedroom.

For a few days I didn't see or hear anything about Pussycat until Regis told Nar, "Pussycat say you are a homosexual."

That was the end of Pussycat. I looked at Bram in the face again.

But then Nar told Regis, "Find me an Indian."

"*Gason*, that's like finding a needle in a haystack, but..."

The next afternoon when we went over to Regis', he welcomed, "Nar, your Indian."

She looked much older than Pussycat. She was wearing a blue, knee-length dress, and she couldn't have been more than four feet, ten inches tall, and more than eighty pounds. Her long, loose hair floated around her small head.

"Mr. Regis, I didn't ask you to get me an Old Higue!" Nar said, turned and left.

"Ron, who or what is an Old Higue?" Regis asked.

"An old woman who sheds her skin in the night and sucks the blood of humans."

I left Regis scratching his head.

When we entered the shop two evenings later, there were

two young ladies sitting on the stools. Regis said, "Mr. Nar..."

Nar held up a hand, "Forget it, Mr. Regis."

"I was going to ask you about your diabetes."

THE LAST WEEK of the school term had arrived. I left early for work on the Monday morning. I wanted to get my end of term records out of the way as quickly as possible. When I got there Adrian was already at his desk in the staffroom

"Ron, your last week," he said without looking up. "You must be anxious. You must be thinking of the family, sweet water fish, and El Dorado rum?"

"Yes. Very much."

"Is Raj going?" he asked—he had met Raj on a few occasions after the beach bash, and they seemed to be getting on well. "He told me he has a girlfriend at the hospital."

"Nah, he is not. But, you know, he doesn't have holidays like us." I settled down at my desk and tackled the pile of examination scripts before me.

When I got home that afternoon I swallowed two aspirins, lay on Raj's bed and closed my eyes.

A sudden noise awoke me. I opened my eyes in time to see Raj about to step out of the bedroom door.

"Raj," I said. "You early."

"It's okay, Ron. You look tired. You can stay on the bed."

I sat up. "Yes man...Don't want to remain next week."

"Anxious, eh?"

He sat on the bed.

I asked, "Are you going home soon? How many times have you gone home since you here? And..."

He held up a hand. "Take it easy, Ron. No. I have never returned home. You know the contract thing. And no, I don't plan to go in the near future."

"Raj, how is Felicity?"

"What?"

"How is Felicity?" I repeated. "You don't seem yourself these days."

"Don't know," he snapped and fell across the bed.

"Raj, you mean to say that you and Felicity had a quarrel over what Regis did?"

He nodded.

"*Gason*. Regis was drunk."

"I don't know what to think, Ron."

"You mean to say that you don't trust her."

"I said I don't know what to think."

"I think you are extremely jealous."

He looked at me, "But Ron...." He turned away and buried his head in his pillow.

On Tuesday, as soon as I arrived home, I invited Raj to play cricket.

"I don't feel like playing," he said.

"Come on," I begged.

He was dismissed twice in two overs and each time he pounded the bat into the ground. Bram and Nar arrived shortly after, ate and joined us. I allowed them to have my turn at the crease. Bram hopped uncomfortably on one leg and pulled at most of the deliveries. He connected a few times and bounced about on both legs. Nar made a few lusty swings and started to pant.

At five thirty, Regis Cauldron disembarked from a blue bus. His eyes never left the ground. Bram saw him, dropped the bat and hailed, "Mr. Regis!"

"Oh. Hi, Mr. Bram. I am tired now. I will speak to you later."

At seven o'clock, all of us went over to Regis. Inside the shop was unusually dark; two light bulbs were missing. Immediately Raj said, "Howdy, Mr. Regis. Give us four maltas and a beer for yourself."

"Don't want your beer," he replied, and slowly put four maltas on the counter without looking at Raj.

We sipped. We heard buses flitting by, outside on the highway. A rooster crowed far away in the distance. Mingling insect sounds rose in spurts in the still night.

"Mr. Regis, did you get the thing?" Raj asked suddenly.

Regis slapped his arm irritably. "Blasted mosquito! Oh, the thing. Oh, yes, the man at the hotel says sure, sure. How is Felicity?"

Raj didn't reply. He cracked his knuckles slowly. We finished the maltas and went home.

Inside the bedroom, I asked Raj, "How is Felicity?"

"Don't know."

"Sorry."

"Listen, Ron, I need to work out things. Okay. I am sorry."

On Wednesday, at exactly five p.m. Bram, Nar and I were loitering on the highway. Two buses passed, but didn't stop. Bram kicked at some gravel.

At five twenty, a white bus came over the hill. Our eyes rode it as they had done the previous two, but unlike them, this one stopped.

"Ah, he is here," Bram said.

Regis stepped off, followed closely by Rasta Paul. They stopped and talked. Hands went up to waists, and fingers began to tap the air furiously as their voices rose. Regis saw us, dismissed Rasta with a wave of the hand, and headed in our direction. He turned and hurled a few more words in patois at Rasta, who stood motionless, staring after Regis who in turn addressed us loudly, "What I am going to tell you. This world has a lot of thiefing people. *Vòlè!*"

"Mr. Regis..." Bram began.

Regis sucked his teeth loudly, spun around and hurried towards his shop. Bram took a couple of uncertain steps in the direction of the shop. He stopped, changed course and limped back to the house. Nar and I followed him.

At seven p.m. Bram and I went over to the shop. Bram stepped boldly to the counter, smiling. One light bulb was still missing from the corner of the shop. I couldn't see Regis' face in the shadow, but saw the smile disappear from Bram's face.

"Like you had a bad day, Mr. Regis?" Bram said.

"What I going to tell you, these people here are really thiefing. *Vòlè!*"

"What?" asked Bram.

"It is a long story," Regis grumbled and busied himself.

"Give us two maltas and a beer for yourself," Bram said quietly.

"Don't feel like drinking a beer."

A shirtless boy appeared through the doorway. "Quick, give me one dollar bread," he said, and dispatched a twenty dollar bill on the counter.

"One dollar bread...one dollar bread," Regis mimicked.

"*Wi.*"

"With twenty dollars!"

"*Wi,*" the boy said, drawing back and looking at the twenty-dollar bill at the same time.

"Boy, haul you little tail out of my shop before I mash it up!"

The boy grabbed the money and bolted out of the shop.

Somewhere outside two boys were arguing. Bram turned to Regis, "Get the thing, Mr. Regis?"

Regis bent over, came up with a crate and slammed it on the counter. He took out the canned drinks, one by one, and slowly deposited each under the counter. When he was finished, he took a deep breath and drawled, "Oh, the thing...yes...Didn't I tell you that I give the man at the hotel? Well, he said the hotel didn't have many tourists today. Tomorrow, it is...sure, sure."

Bram returned home quietly. The raised voices of the two boys trailed behind us.

At around nine, Raj came in and slammed the door.

"What happen now?" I inquired anxiously.

"That blasted man tell me that the man gone to Barbados and hasn't returned yet." His face shone in the light.

"Man gone to Barbados! He told me business at the hotel slow," said Bram.

Raj dropped his attaché case on the table and headed for

the door, "I am going to ask him for my money now."

I reached out and held him by the arm. "Wait. Take it easy, Raj. Let me go with you."

At the shop, Raj said calmly, "Mr. Regis, I run out of cash and I don't want the thing anymore." He squeezed his eyes shut and cracked the knuckles.

When he opened his eyes, he found Regis glaring at him. Both stared at each other. Both waited. It looked like an hour had passed before Regis tried to speak.

"But..."

"Mr. Regis, I really need cash, EC dollars."

"Alright...tomorrow."

"Okay, okay," Raj drawled. "Mr. Regis, give us two barbecued chicken, two guinness and four packets of nuts."

Regis delivered slowly. And as Raj crammed the bottles and nuts in my hands he said, "Mr. Regis, tomorrow when you give me my money, I will pay."

"Eh?" Regis' mouth fell open and still was opened when we left.

At five ten on Thursday afternoon, Bram, Nar and I sat on the buttress root of the breadfruit tree throwing pebbles at a beer can. Fifteen minutes later, Regis appeared on the highway, wearing dark, over sized shades. He spotted us, broke into a grin and walked up to us directly. He threw an arm around Bram's shoulder and said pleasantly, "What happening, man?"

"Am. I...I..." Bram stammered.

"That man from the hotel...I didn't tell you? He has gone to Barbados. Yes, I told Raj. He missed the flight back this afternoon. But it safe, man... tomorrow...sure, sure, sure."

He patted Bram on the back and hurried to his shop. Bram got up, flung the remaining pebbles far into the banana plants and limped back to the house.

Raj came home about seven thirty. The table shook when his attaché case landed on it. Nar and I looked up instantly, and Bram rushed out of the bedroom. "Come, let us go to

Regis' and take some drinks," he almost yelled as he clutched at the table to maintain his balance.

Bram declined.

When we got there, Raj strode up to the counter and said, "Mr. Regis, give me four bottles of guinness, four barbecued chicken, four parcels of nuts..." He paused, looked at Regis thoughtfully and continued, "And oh, the things I want to send home to my relatives. Let me see...two boxes of Tip Top cheese...eight bars of chocolates...eight packets of corn curls..."

Regis glared at him dumbfounded.

Raj grinned, "I serious, Mr. Regis. Lend me four nylon bags too."

Regis, with mouth pouting and eyes blinking rapidly, slowly put the items on the counter.

"Okay, Mr. Regis, add yesterday's to today's and give me the change."

Regis began to breathe harder as the muscles on his face twitched and perspiration appeared on his brows. He inhaled and snorted, "What you trying to do to me, eh?"

"But..."

"Alyuh foreigners feel alyuh can come here and do anything."

Raj pulled himself to his full height and glared at Regis. "You yourself told me that you would return my money today."

Raj breathed loudly. Regis shrank back a little. Uncomfortable moments of silence followed.

"Cal owe the Indian money. *Vòlè!*" The voice came from outside.

We looked through the window with the Coca-Cola sign and saw several shadowy figures.

"Cal rob the foreigners. *Vòlè!*" This time it was louder and clearer.

"Indian, you ain't know who you dealing with," another gruff voice mocked from outside once more.

Regis shifted his glare from Nar to the open window. "If I come over this counter!" he said, still looking through the window, as he attempted to jump over the counter, but couldn't or didn't want to. He stretched his neck forward like an agitated rooster and said, "Alyuh better get away from me shop before I get flipping mad and go for my cutlass. I don't like little boys!"

The audience outside roared, "*Vòlè! Vòlè!*"

Nar folded his hands across his chest like someone feeling cold. An anxious look swept over Raj's face. I shuddered.

"Mr. Regis, don't bother with them. Give me three more guinness and a beer for yourself," Raj said.

Regis gaped at Raj.

Raj returned the stare, and seethed, "Don't want… your… beer." He slapped the counter with the palm of his hand. "Don't know how Feli could like somebody like you…you…you Coolie! Is you who make she stop talking to me. Don't know how any black girl can like any Coolie. You all too damn mean!"

Raj took a step towards Regis. I stuck out my hand and held his arm firmly. "I am coming for my money tomorrow," Raj said, "and then you would see who is mean."

I literally pushed him down the steps.

When I awoke on Friday morning, it was already six. It was raining heavily and I didn't hear Bram and Nar leave for work.

The students' concert had to be postponed and the staff's get together too was called off. I returned home much earlier than usual under a drizzle and was surprised to see Bram and Nar already there.

At exactly four fifty p.m., Bram took his umbrella and stepped out into the light rain. I watched him as he stood there—a forlorn figure at the corner of the highway, huddled under the big, black umbrella. A strong wind had sprung up causing the branches and leaves of the huge trees to shake and deposit sprays and droplets of water like ducks shaking off their backs. Bram struggled to keep the umbrella steady.

At five fifteen, Bram was standing under the breadfruit tree.

At five twenty he was leaning against the shop.

Around five thirty, I saw a tall woman, wearing a black hat and yellow coat, walking towards the shop. She looked like Regis' wife. Bram approached her. They spoke briefly before she pointed in the direction from where she came. Bram started to walk back towards the house.

The rains came down heavier.

At six thirty Bram was sitting next to the window with his hands folded over the sill, staring into the gathering darkness. The rain began to subside.

At seven, Nar emerged from the bedroom, and went up to Bram. He threw an arm over his shoulder. "Did you get the thing?"

Bram didn't answer.

"Man, you are a born loser."

"What?" Bram said, pushing away Nar's arm.

"Sorry, man. I was just recalling when your cousin Snake Eye Balgobin borrowed your bicycle and didn't return it...But don't worry, Bram, Regis must appear."

And then in a sudden fit of anger, Bram leapt up and hissed, "Alright, I going over to see if the bastard come." When he returned, we knew.

At seven thirty, Bram grabbed his umbrella, left and returned five minutes later. He said nothing. Then suddenly, "I wish Rawan would DROWN the bastard!"

Howling winds and steady raindrops drowned the silence that followed.

Raj came in when I was already in bed. I whispered to him what had happened.

"I am not surprised," he said. "I could SMASH his skull!" He staggered and fell into bed.

For most of the night, heavy rainfall, sliced lightning and the rumble of thunder kept me awake. I remembered how much it had rained before I left Zeelugt. I began thinking of the following day.

# 12

My BRAND new, night dial watch indicated that I awoke at exactly five minutes past four. Two competing cock trumpeters under the house were heralding the Saturday. I lay for a while with the sheets pulled right up to my chin, and listened. The thunder, lightning and heavy winds had stopped.

"Exactly seven hours and fifty minutes before we touch down," sang Nar. He too must be wearing his brand new, night-dial watch.

"Yes," Bram said and I wondered if he also was wearing his new watch.

The bell rang louder and longer than anytime I could remember.

Other roosters added liveliness to the morning.

I joined Bram and Nar in the kitchen.

"What was the weather forecast for today?" Nar asked immediately.

"The eight o'clock report last night was not too promising. But they said it would not be too severe to cancel flights, if that is what you are thinking," I said.

"Packed already?" Bram asked.

"*Wi*. Since last night."

"Boy, you sound like a born St. Lucian," Nar said.

159

"*Awa, gason.*"

They hummed Indian tunes as they flitted in and out of bedroom, kitchen and living room with bags, suitcases and attire.

Minutes later, Raj joined us in the living room with two parcels, which he handed to Bram. "Give these to my father and tell him I am okay."

"Sorry you can't go, eh?" Nar told Raj, slapping him lightly on the back.

"Can..."

"They lock you up."

"Okay, Nar, you win."

"Don't bother, I will check out your chicks."

"Forget about the girls, Nar. Check for hassar, houri and cat fish."

"Yes, I am bartering cheese, toilet paper and colgate for them."

"And Bram, I can imagine how many people waiting for you to do their Hawan. You could buy another Toyota," Raj joked.

"True. My wife actually said that."

"Eh?"

"Not the Toyota...People waiting for me to officiate at their functions." He laughed.

"And Ron, drink a couple of Banks for me."

Bram got up to put Raj's parcels in his hand luggage. "No letters?" he asked Raj.

"No. I will write my sister later."

"What you want me to tell them?"

"Nothing. Just tell him I am okay."

"Raj, old Girdo would want to hear something. You know how much they look up to you and worry about you."

"You haven't already told them."

"What you mean?"

Raj slumped in the chair next to him. Nar looked at Raj and Bram. Bram's chest heaved and his nostrils flared. It was

160

drizzling outside.

"Is not you who tell them I staying out late and running behind women?" Raj said eventually.

"Boy, don't irritate me."

Raj got up and pointed a finger at Bram. "Is not you who tell them I going around with black girls?"

"Who...?"

"You want to see the letter Seeta wrote, eh?" Raj sprang up and headed towards the bedroom.

"Boy, don't make me get vex!"

Raj stopped. "You get vex? You don't make me get vexed!" He dropped into the chair.

For a few seconds, there was a respite.

Abruptly, Bram got up and planted himself before Raj like he was about to scold a truant at school. "Even if I tell them, is not true? You come here. You fornicate with the black girls. You spend your money wild, wild...you..." He reeled out the grievances and shook his head as if to suggest the list was endless. Raj blinked after every accusation.

"Raj," Nar joined in, "what Bram says is true. Like you forget where you born and grow...your culture."

"And you," Raj said, pointing a finger at Nar, "you best look into your own house before you say anything else." He swung around to face Bram again. "If I spend money is my money...I am not a mean old crow like you!"

"Mean old crow?"

"Mean old crow?" Nar echoed.

A few seconds passed.

"You calling me a mean old crow?"

"Raj," I said, "Please..." Heavy raindrops began to hit the galvanized roof.

"But who you calling mean old crow?" The racket on the rooftop drowned Bram's near scream. A brief lull followed. The cocks seemed to have gone asleep again. A gush of wind swept across and the rain subsided.

"I have to save. I am not here to swill my money on beers

and women...you...you worthless casanova!" Bram screamed his shrill voice edged with a note of hysteria. He hobbled to the window furthest away from Raj and looked through it.

"Which women are you talking about?" Raj drawled through clenched teeth.

"You think I don't know. You think Regis don't tell me about them."

Raj gaped. "Shit!" he exploded, "You mean to say all this time you all gossiping about me like women...like...!"

"Boy, is who you calling a woman? Eh? You see how you change. I nearly old like your father, and I trying to guide you, and you calling me a crow and...and woman!"

Raj pointed a steady finger at Bram, "You can't be my father. My father don't...don't... mind other people business like you."

"What? All right, I write. Yes, I write. What you can do about that?"

I intervened quickly. "Boys, cool it." I had hoped the rain would pelt down. It came but not as heavily as I wished.

Bram and Raj glared at each other.

"Boys," I begged.

They shifted their gaze to the floor. They began to breathe lighter. A cock crowed somewhere in the distance. The seconds ticked away slowly. They picked up momentum. The hatchet had gone through the floor and was in the process of being buried, I thought. I sighed and relaxed.

"But...my God! You all write them!" Raj suddenly belched. "Write them!"

The hatchet resurfaced. Bram looked up sullenly but said nothing.

"You are a dirty, scheming, cunning, old bastard!" Raj continued, pounding the table harder after each adjective and rattling it after the last noun.

We were stunned. Bram clasped his hands and squeezed them between his legs. Nar leaned on the wall.

"You call yourself a man! You are nothing but a damn anti man!" Raj screeched.

"Raj," I pleaded.

"Boy, is who you calling anti man?" Bram retorted and hopped up suddenly. He took two quick steps towards Raj. Nar instantly stretched out an arm and blocked him.

"You dump your culture...your tradition...Yes. Is me who tell you father? You can't do me anything." Bram threw over Nar's hand.

Raj sprang up and sent the chair toppling. "Every flipping day is the same flipping thing! Snide remarks! Gossiping! Back stabbing! Why don't you all lift your dirty old brown curtain?"

"What curtain?"

"The curtain that imprisons you in that cocoon...the hole...the jail...the dark room...you trapped in, you freaking ass!"

"Eh!" Bram was stunned.

"*Culture! Tradition!*" Raj mimicked, and then screamed, "Whatever! You fossilized piece of shit!"

Bram glared at Raj wide eyed, mouth agape. Suddenly, he snatched one of the two parcels that Raj had given to him, and hurled it at Raj.

Raj caught it in mid-air and mocked, "Ha."

Bram feigned to throw the other then hissed, "To hell with you. I chop you up!" and dashed to the kitchen.

Nar darted after him, and I tried to shoulder Raj into our bedroom. As I steered him past the door, Raj grabbed the brown curtain in our doorway and ripped it off.

A noisy downpour followed. I breathed a sigh of relief. Raj slumped on the bed and I threw an arm around him. He was shaking. The quietness, now heavier than the downpour, hung delicately. I listened. Nothing stirred. I closed my eyes.

Easily my mind drifted back to Shanti town.

"*Rass!* Me can't believe this. A house on me land!"

We dropped our playing cards on the rice bags, grabbed

our money and dashed towards Baldeo just a house lot space away.

As it turned out, in less than nine hours while Baldeo was in the cane fields, Jamal, his next door neighbor had implanted a house on a piece of squatted land that Baldeo had earmarked as his.

Baldeo was marching up to the house with his sledge.

"Hold it!" Jamal emerged from among the bushes. "You own land? Who the *rass* give you land?" His six-foot four overweight frame bore down on Baldeo. He fanned the cutlass in his hand.

Baldeo stopped. He rested the sledge at his feet and looked up into Jamal's face.

Suddenly, he screamed, "You wrong and strong!" He brought the sledge up and rested it on his shoulder.

Jamal retorted, "You thief estate land!"

Baldeo's hand slid half way up the handle of the sledge and he brought it down. The sledge hovered around waist height.

The crowd multiplied quickly like carrion crows drawn to a carcass. All around, curse words flowed like the rising tide.

Someone shouted, "He *rass* wrong. Chop him up!"

Jamal took two steps forward.

A woman screamed, "Hold him back!"

Two tall men grabbed him. One said, "Take it easy, me brother."

They beckoned Baldeo to come closer. They spoke for a while. Jamal walked away, saying, "Okay, I will pay him for leveling the land."

"My God!" Raj suddenly breathed out loudly here on his bed. I looked at him. His body quivered. He reclined on the bed and closed his eyes. I ventured into the living room, collected Raj's two parcels and returned into the bedroom. A strong wind swept across, causing the zinc sheets to rattle, and leaves to rustle. When the rain subsided, whispers floated from the kitchen. Once, Bram raised his voice, "I am going to tell his father everything."

I looked anxiously at Raj. He wiped away beads of water that had settled in the corner of his eyes. When I promised to take the two parcels to his father, he didn't say anything.

"Lord Krishna! How can he say all those things?" Bram's cracked voice rose again. I was sure he was crying or very close to it.

Gradually the house became quiet. Dead quiet. When Bram and Nar joined me in the sitting room before we left for the airport, Nar came up directly to me. "And you, Ron, you are conniving with him," he said, with a hint of animosity.

"But what can I...?"

"Your torpidity under the circumstances is pathetic to say the least, and you have given credence to his despicable deeds."

I dropped my bag.

Bram looked up briefly, "You two...cool it."

I felt like kicking Nar between his legs!

Nar sucked his teeth and stepped ahead of Bram and me into the drizzle. I was going to slam the door shut but I remembered Raj and gently closed it. The door of Regis' shop was closed too.

# 13

WHEN WE TOUCHED DOWN at Timehri airport, Nar grabbed my shoulder and touched Bram. "Home, boy," he said.

I looked at him and he grinned. He stretched himself to his full height and looked around. I thought he was going to bring on the rotation thing. I rubbed Bram's head and he smiled.

Patches of white cloud sailed high overhead. A few kites danced and sang in the high winds. They were the first kites I had seen for the Easter season.

"I must secure broom and clammacherry to make two box kites as soon as I get home," Nar declared. "And I am making two for your two boys too, Bram."

I took in the surroundings in one sweeping glance and breathed in the fresh air that swept over the vast, flat terrain. The twenty five mile ride to Georgetown was smooth—there was only one 'dead' gooseneck turn—and at times I felt that the driver was too casual.

At the bus park at Georgetown Ferry Stelling there were over twenty buses and twice as many vendors

"Get your pine here! Sweet! Sweet! And cheap."

"Yes," Nar said. "The only slice I had tasted in St. Lucia was anything but sweet."

"True," I said, as I sank my teeth into a slice, and craned my neck to find '**Journey to Hope**,' and Hustler.

A young man, with two pairs of track boots hanging from his neck came up to me. "Countryman, this is good stuff...banned stuff. Only two thousand dollars," he said, and deposited the white pair in my hands.

"Ron!"

I turned around quickly.

It was Hustler for sure. He was pushing his way towards me with a broad smile. He grabbed my hand. "Ron, me brother, you didn't tell me you were going foreign?" He saw the boots and the young man. "Don't bother with that," he said, as took the boots from my hands and pushed them back into the guy's hand. "Parika have better and cheaper." He looked around and said in almost a whisper, "How things, nah? You bring anything for your old friend?"

"Later..." I winked at him.

"Look, how many of alyuh? I going now, now." His alert eyes shifted and danced as he searched for more commuters. We followed him. I looked for his dark blue bus, but Hustler suddenly stopped and pointed to a white one. '**Merry Time**' was written in white in front.

"But..."

"The owner of Hope says I too rough. This belongs to Shopman Ramroop in you own village. A new baby...she fast, fast." He held one of my arms and guided me to the front. "Let we talk," he said.

As soon as we were out of the car park, he said, "The Coolie people vex, vex because Shopman take me to drive he bus...Coolie people mean, mean, and they save up for the bandits! As for Black people them ah dog...Them hate me because me does save and black people does spend wild, wild." He cursed.

When we arrived at the floating Demerara Harbour Bridge, he raved, "The flipping bridge does get mad, mad and bruck, bruck, bruck every time somebody fart." He sucked his teeth.

"Oh, it okay today." He smiled.

After we had crossed the bridge, he pointed to two police-men standing at a junction. "The damn police always pon your tail." He cursed and accelerated.

The wetness of the North East Trade winds slapped my face as the bus sped along the wide smooth highway to Vreed-en-hoop. Soon it mingled with the putrefying smell coming from Versailles sugar factory, located not far from the bridge.

"I don't know why they don't scrap the stinking estate," Hustler said.

But soon the smell dissipated. Hustler slowed down after he took the left ninety degree turn at the Vreed-en-hoop junc-tion and we were on the West Coast road with the Atlantic Ocean on the right. The North East Trade winds swept through the bus. Acres of yellow fields of rice glistened and rustled on the left. Combines and tractors appeared in some sections. We passed a few tractor drawn trailers loaded with bags of paddy. They were heading in the direction of the huge silos, situated on the left just a few miles away from Vreed-en-hoop.

Hustler said, "People get bumper rice crop this year. No rain like last crop." He inhaled loudly. "I like the smell of paddy." He glanced at me. "Indians go get richer. I hope the damn govment find  market for the rice..."

"Oh yes..." I yawned.

"But you look tired." He accelerated.

My eyelids were getting heavier. My head drooped and jerked forward a few times.

"...must stop driving bus for the Indian...I must be a bloody ass or what? Yes."

"Yes," I repeated.

"What?"

I sat upright."Oh, no. What did you say?"

He stared at me.

"Sorry," I said and closed my eyes again.

Then it was that smell again. The bus had covered about fifteen miles. We were passing Leonora sugar factory. I opened my eyes. Sugar cane waved in the fields nearby. When we slipped past Uitvlugt sugar factory in the next village I said, "They have to close down these two, also."

"You know," Hustler said and laughed.

Minutes later. "Hey, Ron...your old school."

I looked over my shoulder. "Our, Nar."

When we alighted at the bus stop, I instinctively glanced at silk cotton tree. Goose bumps rose on my skin.

"Ron...Ron..."

"Oh, Hustler. Yes?"

"You seemed lost. When do I see you again?"

"I will get a message to you."

"Home," Bram said quietly and took a deep breath. He hugged Nar. "Hope everything works out well."

As we were about to go our separate ways we heard, "Hey, teach!"

It was a woman approaching us with a little boy clinging to her side.

"Who? Me?" Bram asked, looking at the woman.

"Yes, you, guru," she said. "So glad to see you. I waiting for so long. Please, I would like you to do my Hawan on Sunday."

He agreed and before she left she glared into her son's eyes, imploring, "I want you to grow and be somebody like uncle Bram, you hear?"

"Boy," I said, "No rest for the Godly... And as for that new Toyota..."

"Ah, go home."

As soon as I rattled the gate, Curly screamed, "Daddy come!" He dashed to me and clasped his hands tightly around the waist.

Alesia and Jenny came running seconds after. They were smiling broadly. They both hugged me and I bent over and kissed them.

When I straightened up, I saw Geet. We looked into each other eyes as she approached. She gently embraced me. "Welcome home," she said. When she stepped back I saw her wipe a tear from her eye.

As soon as we got inside the house, the children busied themselves emptying the suitcase while Geet and I talked.

Geet asked, "Nar come?"

"Yes, why?"

"Meena gone."

"From what you hinted in your letter, this is not surprising," I said.

"She too wutliss," she replied and screwed up her face. "Is a *dogla* man too. What a disgrace…! Anyway, you must be hungry. I have hassar curry and dhal puri."

A few relatives and friends visited later that evening. One chided, "Man, Ron, why didn't you tell us you were going? We woulda plan a big farewell."

"Okay, next time."

And another said, "Me too glad you make it, boy. You should have gone a long, long time ago. This govment fish up."

"True."

"Now you there, fix us up nah," someone said.

"Sure."

My neighbor told me, "You look young, neighb."

"Yes. I didn't have to dodge traffic cops."

We laughed

My brother held me by the shoulders, "You get fair."

"Naturally. St. Lucia is closer to the United States."

Curly ran his finger through my hair as he straddled my legs. "Dad, some of your hairs drop out."

"The boys in the school I teach, bald their head."

"Not true, dad."

Early the next morning I stood on the road next to my home and looked directly into the rising sun. People hailed and greeted me with newfound enthusiasm and interest as they passed.

That set me wondering. Why did we look up to people who had migrated and returned? Well, I came up with the following:

*A man had to be good, really good, and loaded with assets before he could secure that elusive visa whether by fair or foul means-he deserved praise.*

*A man who had gone to foreign was moving out of a relatively backward society and would return a wiser man — he should be respected.*

*Any man who had returned from foreign must be loaded with greenbacks and since a few greenbacks could literally buy the whole village — he was a man to be friendly with.*

*Any man who was already in foreign was the ideal man to help one get to foreign — he was a man to stick close to.*

On the following Sunday the boys planned a softball cricket match—twenty overs and nine men per side. Many spectators turned up to the playing field as usual to witness what they thought was another Sunday betting match. Normally in matches like these the stakes were sometimes as high as five thousand dollars. I remembered how the rules were drummed in our ears before the start.

*"Batsman must run everything. He only run when ball hits bat,"* the umpire had pointed out once.

*"Whichever batsman hits the ball in old retired policeman Dubraj yard get six runs but he has to pay for the ball,"* a captain had once suggested.

*"If the ball bust in two, the match draws. Okay?"* another captain had suggested. *"And if the umpire cheats don't pay him and the match draw."*

"What's the bet today?" a spectator inquired.

"No bets. No rules. Festival match...Ron's match. Married men versus Bachelors." The spectators were disappointed.

I scanned the field. All my friends were there except one — Kalli Snake Eye Balgobin, my cane cutter friend, the same one who was Bram's cousin, who wanted to come to St. Lucia and who once told me, "Teacher does pass for grass." We had become friends since we started to play for the same cricket club in Zeelugt. Once, after we had a drinking spree, he had complained, "They tell me since me take up with graduate friend, me turn big shot. They say me English improve and me Maths too because you does teach Maths good, good and me glad, glad because one day me going foreign." Kalli never missed a cricket match, hence the name Balloil, and he wouldn't have missed one in which I was the beneficiary, and certainly not one followed by food and booze. And so when someone told me he had gone to Barbados, I wondered how society would treat him when he returned.

"Ready, Ron?" the umpire asked.

I blocked my first delivery. As the bowler was running up to send down the second, I heard, "You ask him if Girdo son marry a black girl."

I wasn't looking at the bowler when the ball left his hand, but I knew it hit the pitch in his half, behaved like a leg break, hit the pitch again, evolved into a half break, and uprooted the middle stump.

As soon as I entered the players' section, another friend pulled me aside. "Is true Girdo son take a black girl?"

I shrugged and freed my hand from his grasp. "Don't know. Don't live near to him."

"Oh. But you hear Nar wife left he and…"

The sudden swell of noise drowned his voice — the last of our batsmen was bowled.

We made twenty runs and the bachelors wiped them off in two overs.

We assembled for the fete in the bottom flat of Alim's house. He was a very close friend and his house was close to the ground.

They served fish broth, stewed chicken, boiled beef and curried goat. We spoke quietly, mainly about cricket while we ate.

On the table there were Banks beers, vodka and rum. At first I drank Banks, switched to vodka and then reverted to Banks. Most of the older guys who started off with Banks diverted to rum and stuck with it.

They played songs by the Indian playback singers, Mukesh and Rafi. We hummed along.

The man in charge of the tape recorder—they called him Drake—switched to the Mighty Sparrow and Bob Marley.

"Drake, you mother..."

He cursed louder.

A few screamed along with Sparrow and Marley.

Some began to speak loudly.

"Ron, tell us where you work," Alim said as he moved closer to me.

"Boy, the place where I work they call Soufriere..." I said.

"Hey, turn down the music," someone shouted.

Drake turned off the music.

"You ever hear about the Montserrat volcano?" I continued.

Some nodded and one asked, "What the place name again...Sou...who?"

I spelt the name slowly and explained its French origin. "You see, St. Lucia changed hands more than a dozen times between British and French, like a whore (I remembered what Regis had said)." I told them about the patois and the French.

"Oh, is like we then. Guyana is a prostitute. We change from Dutch to British."

"Yes. That's it. The difference is we don't speak Dutch..."

"Is like how we speak broken English and even the white man can't understand. Not so?"

"That's right," I said.

"Yes, is like how we have Dutch names and yet we speak English?" someone added.

"Yes, we understand...but come back to this volcano, Ron," Alim said.

"Well, they connect. I mean under the sea. Okay? But the mountain in Soufriere split in two... they say forty thousand years ago and...*gason*, the crater still boiling. If you see smoke and sulphur. We usually drive in the crater and bathe in the sulphur."

"Eh?" All eyes were riveted on me. "But Ron, you really, really brave. You not afraid of *gason* or whatever?"

I paused and grabbed a beer. "*Awa*...ah mean nah, and *gason* mean boy. But the sulphur could cure A.I.D.S. too."

"Eh?" Their disbelief echoed even louder.

"Okay. I joking; but people come from all over the world to bathe in the sulphur water."

"So is a tourist country?"

"Uhuh."

"Foreign dollars must be flowing there, boy."

I smiled.

"What the salary like? Like how much you get per month?" another asked.

I told them right away.

"Wow!"

"You know," one of them joked, "that man IMF, ah could kill him. Every time he land foot in Guyana, the money going up faster than me dick."

"But Ron, this IMF really pissing me off. You know why they here?" another said. "This fishing govment borrow money to build hydro. Yes...hydro, saying we going to have light even in we pit latrine. But you know what we have, eh? We have hydro between we legs!" He stomped his feet and I feared that he was going to crash the beer bottle on the table.

"Take it easy," I said, "I know..."

"You know all them people who leave them work in the city and gone to work for the hydro does come out here and burn twenty dollar notes when we drinking, eh...and we poor like church rat and can't even buy a beer." Some of the contents of the beer bottle spilled as the bottle shot out above his head.

174

"And ah hear a man thief a whole bulldozer...a whole bulldozer! He bury it in the sand!" another snorted, and shook his head. "Ron, you right to leave this flipping deh bad country and go. Me have to cut cane till me dead." He gulped his beer and concluded, a little more relaxed, "Anyway, Ron, we too glad for you. But you mustn't forget we."

"No, I wouldn't. I would see how I can assist," I said.

"Ron, me going with you to St. Lucia..."

"Me too..."

"And me also..."

"DAD, WAKE UP!" Curly was pulling my feet. "Mom say to take us to the beach to the picnic to fly our kites."

I glanced at my watch. It was after ten. I stretched and yawned.

"Please, dad." He rubbed my cheeks.

We left shortly after for the Easter Monday picnic on the seashore north of Zeelugt. I tagged along with a headache and an upset stomach. Along the route, one of the guys who were at the fete hailed, "Had a nice time, Ron?"

"Very."

When he got closer, he asked, "Is it true Girdo son living with a black gal?"

I dismissed him with a wave of the hand and as I was walking away, he flung, "Me hear Nar wife left he because he too have a black gal."

My head throbbed. I closed my eyes and tried to recall what I had said.

"Them boys too wutliss," he chuckled behind me.

On the beach, the strong North East trade winds tempered the warm sunshine. The picnickers were spread along the hundred yards embankment.

Men crowded the four or five bars. I ambled up to the El Dorado bar to take 'one' for my hangover, and was offered many more by my friends who were delighted to see me; I took a couple. The men laughed lawlessly and spoke aggressively. A few moved closer to the music set, and wined and gyrated even when slow-beat music was played. A young man staggered, slid down the sea wall and was venturing out into the muddy waters of the ocean. His friends encouraged him.

One of them approached me, as I rejoined Geet and the kids. "Mister, give a twenties, nah."

"Don't," Geet ordered. "He is a rum sucker."

Suddenly screams pierced the air. We looked around anxiously. A few people hurried in the direction of the screams.

"Don't bother," the gentleman standing next to us said. "It's only a fight. When coolie people drink rum, they want to be noticed."

Geet grabbed my hand and pulled me away to the flat, grass-matted embankment. Women and children sat carelessly and rocked to the blare of Indian music. The children held on to the strings of their kites. Man, box, bird, diamond shaped and star pointed kites claimed the air and darted to and fro crazily. Geet and the kids struggled to hold theirs still. Some children ran behind fallen kites. After a while Geet lost interest and gravitated to a small group of women. They spoke in hushed tones and giggled. Mainly they focused on the female who was dancing. A few imbibed alcohol, and others tugged at the sleeves of their husbands' shirts.

Curly abandoned the kite, held my hand and steered me to the 'Odd and Even' gambling board. He placed a dollar on Even and lost. He placed fifty cents on Odd and won. He shrieked. He invested all on Lucky Seven, lost and looked sad. A young man disputed with the man rolling the die. The man withdrew a cutlass from under the gambling board and the young man ran. I remembered the previous year when I operated one, and a man wrapped his fingers around my neck. I ended up with an immensely sore throat and a handsome surplus of cash.

On Curly's insistence, we diverted to the greasy pole event. There was a large and noisy gathering of people. Men staggered, some with bottles in their hands, and approached the starting line of the pole—it was tied slightly inclined upwards across the twenty-foot wide trench running parallel to the seashore. Four large bottles of El Dorado rum dangled at the finishing line.

The first competitor placed his left foot first, but before the right could touch the pole, he fell into the water on his back.

Everyone laughed. Someone said, "He is a damn amateur."

The second took four steps, staggered and stopped. As he pushed off, one foot went to the right and the other to the left. He fell straddling the pole.

"Oh God...he balls burst!" The spectators roared.

The next one had hardly inched a foot, when he began shrieking. He tilted backwards and landed heavily on his naked back.

Curly said, "Ouch!"

A lean one was making some progress until someone shouted, "Take care you fall and break you biscuit leg."

He looked around, overbalanced and dived into the water. His swimming trunks appeared on the surface of the water.

The crowd erupted. Curly rubbed his belly and laughed.

Firefoot James stepped up. The crowd applauded. He was a Kali Mai disciple who was a famed firewalker. He took out a small bottle from his pocket and gulped down whatever was in it.

Someone shouted, "Bush rum won't help you."

He took two quick steps and stopped. He held out his hands like a tight rope walker, took another four and stopped. He was three quarters of the way. But then he lost his balance. He tottered to the left, to the right, to the left and to the bottom of the trench.

"Too bad...just a little more eh?" said the girl standing next to us.

It was then Claw foot Rajah Mohan marched up to the

starting point. The crowd hummed with expectancy. Everyone one knew Claw Foot—his toes were so spread out that it was actually a semi circle of about nine inches in diameter and at a cricket match one Sunday, he had walked around the cricket field on the two-inch wide board on top of the fence after he had consumed a forty ounce bottle of white rum.

The boatman reapplied grease to the pole while Claw-foot took out something from a bag and applied it to his foot bottom.

"Tar!" someone shouted.

Claw-foot took out a big bottle from his bag.

"Christ! Bush rum!" a man said.

Claw-foot drank and burped. He dropped the bottle and actually dashed halfway up the pole. The crowd was stunned into silence. Claw-foot looked around and waved. He feigned a fall.

Curly went, "Oooh."

Suddenly Claw-foot was off again. One...two...three...four steps and a lunge. Clawfoot was home!

The applause rang out.

Geet and the girls found us. "Let's get roti and curry," they implored. They pulled me along the numerous food stalls with an array of Indian and Chinese dishes. Eventually, they stopped and pointed. I bought, and they ate and complained about the pepper. They pointed to the ice-cream cart. I bought and we left for home.

I tried to picture Regis on Zeelugt's foreshore today. I could see him smiling. There were over a thousand people there. I could see rivulets too on his forehead. There were only two Blacks present and one of them was a policeman.

Despite my aches and pains, I awoke early the next day and waited for Hustler as planned. He arrived looking exuberant as always. When he stepped out of '**Merry Time**' to greet me, I drew back. "Wow!" I said.

He was wearing a dark, multicolored dashiki shirt. "You

look like an African Prince," I said.

The front of the shirt reminded me of Bram's embroidered patterned shirt-jack. The black pair of serge pants fitted his trim body perfectly. He was grinning from ear to ear.

"Jump in," he said. "Let's go home to Vergenoegen." During the five-minute drive he was his normal self; he criticized, cursed and laughed.

When he pulled up at a restaurant and bar, he pointed, "Ron, you remember there? Of course you do. You born and grow here."

"True."

As we passed the largest buildings in the village I asked, "Do they still have dances there?"

"If! Every Saturday night God make, Perseverance Hall have dance until the wee hours of the morning. Boy, black people love a dance."

The blare of Indian music floated from the restaurant and bar. When we entered we found it was crowded. A Black and an Indian who sat at the same table, hailed Hustler.

"My friends." Hustler waved to them, and then tilted his head towards me. "You remember Ronald...? He just came back from America," he shouted above the music.

The friends came over. They looked at Hustler. "Man," the Black one said, "You not only ugly, you have to be the blackest Blackman God ever put on this earth." They laughed.

"I proud, boy. Black is beautiful!" Hustler curtsied.

"Beer or rum," I asked Hustler as we stood at the counter.

"Don't matter," he said. He began swaying to the music. "This Indian song is very popular here."

The waitress brought the XM Gold that I had ordered. Hustler gulped half a glass without chaser.

"What would you like to eat?" I spoke through my funneled hand.

"Let's try plantain, cassava, duff, callaloo and saltfish," he replied. He was dancing with more frenzy to the rock music that was then blaring from the punch box.

I beckoned Hustler when the waitress brought the food.

"Before you eat, I have something for you," I said, and pulled out a necklace and bangle from my pocket. "Volcanic rock," I said.

He lunged forward and hugged me. "My wife and daughter will really love this." He held and caressed the gifts for a while before he deposited them in his pocket.

Hustler drank, danced and reminded almost everyone in the bar, "This is my schoolmate...my good, good, good friend. We were in the same Form at Burn's."

Some recognised me. "Come back here to live, Ron? You left Zeelugt?"

"Nah, he living in New York," Hustler said.

He was silent for a while as he drove me home. "Ron," he said. "Why people can't live like they do in Vergenoegen, eh? Look how Black people and Indian get on so good, good."

"I would love that."

On the following day, I had an errand that took me past Georgetown to the Agricultural School at Mon Repos on the East Coast of Demerara. The floating bridge was up to its old tricks, according to Hustler. I ferried across the river.

Suddenly Big Ben chimed. I looked up; it was ten o'clock. Erected some sixty feet above ground level on Stabroek market, Big Ben made its presence felt miles away. Once when it had stopped, they discovered that the hour hand had fallen off and instantly killed a donkey below.

The market square buzzed. I stood by the large iron gate at the entrance and looked around for Alim. A man came up to me with his right arm outstretched. Wrist watches lined it from elbow to wrist. "Countryman," he said, "These come straight from Japan."

I shook my head and pointed to mine. He walked away and then dashed to a crawling vehicles shouting, "Take it at half price...Buy one, get one free." The vehicle stopped.

Just then, Alim joined me at the entrance.

"Ron, there was a shoot out up the East Coast last night,"

he disclosed immediately. "Three people died and...Eh! Eh!"

A figure had dashed across us. With his shirt flapping behind him, and his arms and legs pumping, he was galloping towards Regent Street.

"CHOKE 'N' ROB! Stop him! Stop him!" The distinct screams of a hysterical woman just a few yards away from us resounded in the market.

My hand reached into my pocket. The prolonged cry rose sharply above the clamour around. Several people dashed towards the woman. Alim and I were roughly shouldered out of the way. Between sobs, the woman vented her anger and tragedy. "Damn thief...he...he... took... took... all... My gold chain...!My purse...! God ...all fifty thousand dollars...!"

One gentleman asked, "Which direction did he go?"

She pointed uncertainly, "There...I was going to buy a TV... Lord!"

Everyone craned his neck and looked in the direction where the finger pointed.

"Where are our efficient police?" someone asked.

"They guarding the president's palace!" a gruff voice shouted.

While we hung around, I told Alim how I was relieved of my wallet in Georgetown about a year ago.

Alim smiled. "Boy," he said, "don't be ashamed. You ever hear of the Prime Minister who was wearing a Rolex wristwatch and was passing over Guyana in an aircraft? Well, the mistake he made was to hang his hand through the window. When he alighted in Barbados he was wearing an old Timex watch! Boy, we specialise in this."

Although he made me smile, I clutched my wallet tighter, and pulled my shirt collar closer. Satisfied that my small gold chain was concealed, I grabbed Alim's hand and steered him out of the crowd.

"Mugging happens every day," he said calmly. "You want to see more action like this? Gunplay? Stick around one of the money exchange places... any Cambio."

"I have no US to change at the Cambio!" I said.

I implored Alim to drive to the seawall. Passing, we saw crowds of people at the U.S. and Canadian Embassy head-quarters and the Customs Department on Main Street. It was very windy at the sea wall and I began to feel better as the car sped along the east coast road to Mon Repos, to the Guyana School of Agriculture where I had to see someone.

On our return journey, just outside the capital, we ran into small pockets of men at the intersection of a cross road. We stopped when we noticed on one corner of the street, just opposite a Chinese restaurant, a small table next to an elec-tricity pole. On it was a microphone and an amplifier. A drinks crate was on the ground next to the small table.

Minutes later, an Indian man jumped up on the crate.

"Good afternoon, my brothers and sisters," he said, paused and smiled. "I want to make sure you hear me clear-ly...We have to remove this corrupt government..."

The mike began to screech and squeak. He looked in the direction of the restaurant. Another fellow, also Indian, came out from the restaurant and fiddled with the amplifier. In a few minutes, he got it working.

"Yes. I was saying..." He plunged into his speech. "...and the leader of the opposition is a confounded racist."

A young man flung back, "Like you mother man!"

The small gathering came alive.

I asked Alim, "Who is the politician?"

"I don't know him. There are about five or six new par-ties," Alim disclosed.

The politician droned on, "The main opposition party is a band of soup lickers, and I say you must brick them whenev-er they come to speak to you."

WHAM! A brick landed on cue on the table next to him. He looked around anxiously. Two more landed in quick suc-cession. He cursed. The crowd roared.

"That's why black people mashing alyuh backside. Coolie

people ah crab!"

A fourth missile found its target. He grabbed the mike and scampered for shelter in the Chinese restaurant.

We drove away chuckling. In the coming months just before Guyanese went to the polls there would be many more meetings like this. The problem, I thought sadly, was that if they followed a similar pattern of previous elections, racial overtones, insinuations and slurs would once again generate tension.

Two days later, news reached the countryside, "They burning down Georgetown! They looting Indian stores!" It turned out that one vehicle was set on fire and riotous protestors had metamorphosed into looters who had a field day until the Special Service Unit was called in.

There was a strike on the sugar estate. The newspaper headline read:

### Opposition Party Incites Union to Strike.

The strike was short lived.

"So relieved, Ron," Alim said afterwards. "We definitely don't want a recurrence of the three month strike."

"I remember it well, Alim. I was asked to volunteer to cut canes."

"Asked to volunteer...hah, I like that." Alim laughed.

"Lots of civil servants too."

"Yes. Employing scabs was a dumb thing. They did more harm than good."

"Whoever said there was no art in cutting cane?"

For the next two days, people walked about uneasily and whispered. They stayed away from the capital whether they worked there or not. They lurked in the dark and watched.

On the third day I asked Alim, "Is it safe to go fishing?"

"We go tomorrow."

Most of my friends who had played in the cricket match gathered at Alim's home minutes before six a.m., well armed with nets, roti, fried eggs and salt fish, and a few beers each in their back packs. Riding bicycles, we left for the backlands, which was tens of square miles of endless fields of green sugar cane and yellow rice.

The boys opted to go in the rice section.

"Yes," Alim agreed, "The trenches there would be bubbling with fishes from the rice fields."

When we got there, I stood and surveyed the surroundings bathed in bright sunshine.

Huge red combines and puffing tractors raced across the acres of yellow fields. Birds — doves, red breast robins, kiskadees, blackbirds, blue sakis and some other tiny ones — fluttered up from their path in flocks. The reapers, mostly East Indians, bagged and deposited the paddy onto tractor trailers bound for the silos.

In a few months time, I thought, the whole scene would be transformed into one of solitude and serenity when green seedlings in knee deep water would wave and rustle in the gentle North East Trade winds.

"Alligator!" one of the boys screamed.

We dashed towards him. The alligator trapped in his net heaved, flounced and swirled desperately.

"Don't pull the net. Allow him some slack," someone advised.

The alligator escaped but the net was torn to shreds.

Apart from that, luck ran our way. We caught nearly twenty pounds of fish including hassars, houris, patwas, lukananis and sunfish.

At around three o'clock when we re-entered Zeelugt, we saw groups of men gathered at the head of the street where they normally assembled in the evening to play cards and to lime.

Nar was there. Immediately he came up to me. "Bad news," he said, pouting his mouth.

"Sorry. I heard Meena..."

"My cousin, Jai, is dead."

"How? When?" I asked.

"His tractor turned over and pinned him. He was taking a load of paddy to the silo."

"Sorry. Where...?"

"They already take the body to the hospital for a post mortem, and they bringing it home immediately after. Could you stay around to assist?"

Many people had gathered around when the corpse was unloaded from the trailer of the tractor. I helped to place it on a slightly inclined galvanized sheet. We covered the corpse with blocks of ice and set a tub at the foot of the sheet to collect the water.

"Have you ever seen anyone rot while he is alive?" someone asked.

"No. Why?" asked Nar.

"Just slip some of that 'dead man' water into his drink."

"Something to think about," Nar commented.

Most of the villagers turned up for the wake. The men gathered in the open bottom flat of the house. I joined those who were playing cards. My partner and I didn't survive too long in the game. He was annoyed. "Ron, since you gone to St. Lucia you forget to play cards."

"True," I said.

"Nah," the fellow sitting near to me said, "Ron only checking out the girls."

The guys around laughed, and I smiled.

The fellow then leaned over and asked quietly, "Ron, I hear Girdo son living with a black girl? True?"

"Don't know."

I immediately excused myself and joined the set of men playing dominoes. They made a lot of noise. I didn't play but ate salted biscuits and drank coffee while I watched.

Near to midnight, the crowd had thinned out and the place was relatively quiet. I approached the group of men and small boys in a corner.

"...You know this bacoo is a really, really small man, but

he bad fo days," the man, the villagers called Uncle was saying. When he saw me, he stopped. "Oh. Hi, Ron. Come join us
*beta*."

"Thank you Uncle. I never tired hearing you tell old time
stories."

"Yes," he continued. "The bacoo bad fo days especially if
you don't feed him with bananas and put him back in his bottle where he live."

"What he do?" one boy asked.

"You sure you want to hear?"

"Yes, Uncle," the boys said together.

Someone began crying upstairs. We listened. The sobbing
subsided.

"Okay," Uncle said. "Somehow the bacoo get out of the
bottle and he didn't get bananas."

"Papa!" exclaimed the boy sitting next to me.

"So when the man who own the house come home that
night, the bacoo…"

"Ron!"

"Oh, Nar…Yes?"

"Before you go I want to see you."

"Okay…Yes Uncle, continue."

"The bacoo pelt brick all over the man…the man try to put
on the light…the light not coming on…and…" Uncle
stopped. He was breathing heavily.

"Shit!" The boys were wide awake. Their eyes were glued
on Uncle.

The elderly man sitting next to me whispered, "*Beta* Ron,
you know Nar wife left he and take a *dogla* man because he
take black gal in Barbados. Gidharry self tell me that."

"Bar…Listen, pappy, that not true." Abruptly, I turned to
Uncle. "Tell the boys what happen, Uncle."

"*Beta*, hah…The Bacoo start pelting cup…spoon…
fork…plate and everything at the man."

"*Rass*," one boy said.

"And not only that…" Uncle got up. "Oh God! Oh God!" he

exclaimed as he jogged on the spot. He stopped. "Yes. That was how the man was bawling and trying to get out of the house." Uncle pulled out a rag from his pocket and wiped his face. "But, papa!" he continued. "The bacoo close the door and start to slap up the man." Uncle bit his lips and slapped the air in front of him. Then he dropped on his knees and clasped his hands. "Oh God, me go give you a whole bunch of Cayenne banana, plus milk, good, good cow milk, and me not drinking rum again." He got up and smiled. "You know the Bacoo stop beating the man."

The boys breathed a sigh of relief. Uncle turned to them and said, "If you don't behave and don't go to school, the Bacoo coming for you."

"Uncle, you was the man?" one of the boys asked.

We laughed.

I went upstairs to look for Nar.

Loud singing and praying accompanied harmonica music. Bram sat in the middle of the group of mostly females. Raj's sisters were among them.

A female relative of the deceased arrived and there was an outburst of wailing and screaming.

Bram and the group stopped.

When calm returned, they resumed.

Minutes after, a close friend of the deceased entered. There were renewed outbursts.

The group stopped.

The friend was consoled.

The group resumed and continued for about fifteen minutes.

Another sympathizer arrived. She cried the loudest. She pounded her chest. She held on to Jai's wife, "Wha go happen with me poor Rajwantie...me poor Rajo and she pickney them...wha go happen..."

Bram and his group had to wait longer.

It was then I found Nar. He said, "I suppose you know all about Meena by now?"

I nodded.

"Well, I am not too sure if I am going back to St. Lucia. I will let you know."

It seemed that the entire village had turned up for the funeral that took place the following evening. Bram performed the burial rites.

"Our bhai Jai will be born again as a human being. And this time he could be sitting on a throne," he said. He chanted. It was touching at times. Spurts of hysterical sobbing and shrieking from women and children accentuated the pervading gloominess. Rajwantie fainted twice and her children clung to her.

The funeral procession left at three o'clock for the burial ground in the blazing afternoon sun. Only a handful of women joined it. Those who remained behind, screamed, chanted and consoled one another.

The coffin, borne by six male relatives, was laid down at intervals along the three hundred yards route to the burial ground for Bram to perform the rites. The final rites were read just before sunset. Most people around threw 'farewell' handful of dirt into the grave. I remained behind at the graveside with Bram and other relatives of the deceased.

Bram pulled me aside. "You hear about Meena?"

"Yes. Nar needs you again, Bram."

Just then Meena's brother came up to us. "Ron...Bram, is it true that a black girl get a baby for Raj?"

Bram and I looked at each other.

"I suspect Nar too has a sweet woman in St. Lucia," he continued and left.

"Ron, did Raj's father tell you anything?" Bram asked quietly, looking away.

"No. I haven't seen him yet. I was so busy. I will see him on Saturday."

"I don't know," he said, "how this thing has come about...But people talking about Raj and a black girl."

"Beats me."

Early Friday morning, Geet called from outside, "Raj father here."

"Christ, I had planned to see him tomorrow." I scrambled the two parcels and was out in a flash to meet him.

He smiled and shook my hand. "Mawning," he said meekly. "Me coming to see you since last week to give you this parcel to take back for me boy. Bram say he full up already and me must ask you."

"I will take it. He sent these, but I was busy. Sorry." I took his. He cuddled his two.

I invited him in. The place was wet with overnight rain. He braced his fenderless bicycle on the fence, removed a bag from the handle and walked ahead of me. A brown line of dirt stretched from the back of his head and along the middle of his white shirt to his behind.

He sat on a bench. "Me hear something," he said hoarsely.

I gripped the back of the chair on which I was sitting.

"Me hear...me hear a man rob he." The wrinkles on his face twitched.

"Nah," I said, and relaxed my grip. "When we left, we understand that the man who this man gave the money to, he has gone to Barbados."

"Oh." He glanced around and began rubbing his thin wiry hands. "How he doing? Alright?"

"Me want to ask you something."

I sat upright.

"Me hear he take up with a black gal," he said in one quick breath. "Tell me the truth, you know."

"Look, over there they have mostly Black people and the girl you heard about is someone he does go to work with. They work in the same place and she has a car."

"Yes, me hear about the brown kar."

"Eh?"

"What me hear is he serious about she! Bram say..." he said, pounding the bench with his fist.

I raised my hand. "Nah, man. She is just a friend. I tell you

189

they working in the same place."

"Ah hope so. If Raj marry a black gal, he go put me to shame." He paused for a while and exhaled loudly. "What the church people go say? He mother already ah cry. I hope he don't do like Nar and have black sweet woman."

"That is not true about Nar," I said slowly. "And look, Raj is young. He must get friends, new friends. They don't have many Indians there. Besides, the people there are very, very friendly and nice." I held up my hand to him. "Okay?"

He looked around, and leaned forward closer to me, "Let me tell you. You know Shopman Ramroop?"

I nodded.

"You know he get a nice, nice lil daughta?"

I knew Shopman had a daughter, but remembered her vaguely. I nodded again.

He sat upright. "Well, he come and ask me for Raj to married she." A glow appeared on his face. He watched me steadily in the face, his mouth agape. "What you think?"

"Oh, yes?" I said with a broad smile.

"Imagine a rich man like Ramroop, a churchman too besides," he said, looking up to the heavens and opening his hand at the same time. "Well, what you think?"

"Well...I...I..."

"Me son lucky, lucky. He go get enough money to study to become docta. Me know he can't come now 'cause this govment go lock him up. But we can do the wedding in St. Lucia."

He looked at me seriously again. I waited.

"Oh, me get this letter too. Give him." He got up and slowly walked out to the pavement, then turned abruptly and said, "Tell Raj what me tell you about Ramroop daughta. It in the letta, but still tell him how he lucky."

When I retired to bed that night, sleep didn't come easily. I thought of Raj and my return to St. Lucia.

BLAM! BLAM! I sprang up. Rapid gunshots echoed in the still night. Geetangali clung to me. Suddenly the door to our bedroom was thrust open and the children were on top of us.

"Everything okay," I said as I spread my arms around them.

Then all was quiet...dead quiet. I glanced at my night-dial watch. Five minutes to two! Slowly I disentangled myself and tiptoed to the window. I parted the curtains and peered. The night was pitch dark: Zeelugt was having its dose of scheduled blackouts.

Lights began appearing in most homes, and torchlights combed the area.

People shouted to neighbors and to others across the streets. Garbled voices multiplied. The night was charged with tension. Some men appeared on the streets. Despite Geetangali's pleas to remain indoors, I joined them. The men were armed with garden tools—cutlasses, forks, shovels, spades—and wooden batons, pieces of iron, machetes and even home made shotguns. They gathered in little pockets. We whispered.

"Bandits or police?" someone asked.

"Bandit or police, this thing really aggravating," another answered.

"Somebody has to put a stop to this eye pass."

"Yes, we must form back the vigilante group."

"Ron, you must help us organize."

We waited. We spoke louder. By the time it was realized that the threat was gone, the plans to reorganize the vigilante were almost completed. The men began to disperse quietly. A few lingered around until daybreak before heading to their Shanti Town headquarters. I knew, for sure, they would relive the past event, pass judgments and come up with airtight solutions.

Alim came to my home just before nine. "Ron," he whispered, "Let us go to Shanti Town. You can't go back to St. Lucia without gambling and trying some bushrum."

I slipped out of the yard when Geet went into the bedroom.

We found several groups of four men sitting on rice bags with dollar notes and cards in the center.

"Babylon!"

Men, bags, cards, money and bottles of bushy disappeared among the brushes.

Baldeo — the same one who lost his squatted land — rode up. "Inspector Brandon and two more police coming up the street."

"*Rass!*" Quickly we put up a drink crate as the cricket stump, and got hold of the wooden bat and a ball.

Brandon and his men came up and looked around. They pouted and sniffed the air. They left after an eternal five minutes.

The cards didn't run my way. I had a cup of bushy, though. I felt it scorching a trail all the way down to my intestines!

I left hurriedly for home. Geet was waiting for me at the gate, arms akimbo. "Where the hell you been?"

I raised a surrendering hand. "Am..."

She slapped the hand aside. "No ams...You been to gamble and drink bush rum. You can't stop a dog from sucking egg, eh?"

"I want to go the toilet."

She allowed me to slip through. "But you ain't hear anything what happened on the other side of Shanti Town?"

I stopped, shrugged and moved off again to the toilet.

"Nar chase Meena and her *dogla* man with a cutlass."

"Eh heh?"

She followed me. "But she really bare face, eh. She say she come for support money for she and the children."

I stood by the door of the toilet and looked at her.

"And to add insult to injury, she say diabetic man don't have sex drive."

"So where is Nar now?"

"The police lock him up."

"I think I am going to suffer from diarrhea."

# 14

JUST BEFORE MY TRIP back to St. Lucia on Sunday morning, Geet found me in the living room, slouching on the settee and resting my head in the palms of my hands.

"Still feeling sick? Take some more tablets," she said. "And don't worry...the vigilante will look after us. And listen, next September, we going with you. Let the children finish this school year here. Okay?"

"Alright."

Several of my friends accompanied me to the airport. We arrived at least one hour before departure time. In the parking lot we, well they — I was forced to drink one beer — spilled beer all over the place, screamed about a lot of things, and turned up the music full blast and danced. People stared at us. The friends reminded me, "Write soon...drink some Heineken for we...get a black thing like Girdo son and a spare wheel like Nar, and don't forget to send for we."

I ran into Bram in the departure lounge, and as I was about to inquire for Nar, I saw him coming through the sliding door. He was struggling with a bulky hand luggage. He waved when he saw us.

Before I stepped into the aircraft, Bram came up alongside me, and asked quietly, "Did Raj father see you?"

193

I nodded. After a few seconds, I asked, "How is Nar doing?"

"The police place Nar on a bond to stay away from Meena."

"But is it not she who sought him out?"

"Yes, but you know how things go. All Nar wanted was to get on the plane today."

It was still daylight when we touched down at Vigie airport but by the time we reached Mon Repos, the sun had disappeared behind cumulus clouds.

"Ah wonder if Regis around," Bram said loudly, as we walked towards the shop. The windows were closed but there was no Coca-Cola sign. On the other side of the shop, two strips of wood were nailed across the door. We looked at one another, shrugged but said nothing. Then as we turned around to move off something else struck us. All that was there to remind us of Madison Square Garden was a bald rectangular spot.

"It looks like, it looks like...Nah. It can't be." Bram was thinking aloud.

"I know what you are thinking," Nar said, looking at Bram. "You are thinking that Regis moved out."

We were transfixed for a moment, looking from Garden to shop and back. Bram limped off, leading the way to the house.

In the gathering twilight, we passed a small, yellow, black and white car parked in the pathway directly in front of the house. The door was closed.

"Like Raj too gone," Bram said.

Bram's folded right fist was poised to descend on the door when it squeaked open. Raj, dressed in white shorts and vests, appeared.

"*Bonswè*. I didn't hear you all come," he said yawning, and waving his hand.

"Good evening. How are things with you, man?" I asked.

"Okay...for a while." He extended his hand to Bram. Bram

hesitated before he shook the hand, and I quickly added, "Take the old man suitcase, nah. You don't see he is struggling?"

He didn't take the suitcase, but reached out and patted Nar on the back. "How things?"

"Okay."

"How are things back home?" Raj inquired as soon as we entered the bedroom. He stood by the window.

"Good, man, good. I enjoyed it," I answered, as I was unpacking. "I have a parcel for you."

He took the parcel, looked at it, and resumed looking through the window. "Do you like it?"

"What?" A strange question to ask about a parcel, I thought.

"The car, *gason*...the car."

"Eh!" I straightened up. "You mean that small car out there is yours?"

He nodded.

"It looks nice. Toyota?"

"Uhuh."

"How much?"

"Ten grand."

"Good price."

"Felicity father has to work in Soufriere and he has to use the car."

"Never mind, Raj. How is she?"

"Okay, man, okay. We make up." He was smiling. "I usually drop her home on afternoons. She comes here sometimes."

"That's nice. Oh, I have a letter for you." I delved into my hand luggage for the letter.

He ripped it open immediately. He read. "Christ!" he said and sat upright. He read on and sucked his teeth. "Man, I don't know what's wrong with these people. Here, read this letter."

I hesitated, but he pushed it into my hand.

*Son Son*
*Me don't here from you. You not send me nothing.*

I stopped reading, "Raj, is my fault. I delivered the parcel late."

"It is alright, Ron. But it is not that. Read."

*Me ask Bram about you. he say ask ron and nar. Me ask nar and he say ask ron but me hope you alrite. we is alrite. You ma worried bout you. Don't make anybody take them eye and pass you. A black boy chop up a lil coolie boy on the highway and rob he. Meena left Nar. He too wicked. You know the black sweet woman he with? He not good anymore. me has good, good news for you. shopman ramroop ask me for you to married he daughta savi. me too glad for you me son. you go get money to studie to become docta. you must go to hawan with bram an pray to lord Krishna everyday. Write soon. you papa*

"He told me about it, Raj...about Shopman Ramroop."

"I don't want anybody to fix me up." He pounded his hand on the sill of the window and sucked his teeth.

"Look, I told him Felicity is just one of your friends from the work place."

"You shouldn't have told him anything," he said angrily.

"Look man, he even knows about the brown car."

"Christ!" He looked up at the ceiling. "Is him!" he hissed, pointing to the other room.

Scenes of the day we had left for Guyana flashed before my eyes.

"I would have moved out if I didn't buy this car," he said. He looked at the letter again. "You know what. I am really serious about Felicity. I don't care if she is black or white or brown. I...I love her."

"I know that."

He looked through the window and scratched his head. Then he turned to me, "I am writing them...I am writing

196

them tonight. I am going to tell them about her."

"Hold on." I said, raising my hand. "Why don't you wait until you go home? You could explain and make them understand. Don't you think a letter so soon would be too blunt?"

"That would be ideal. But you know I can't risk going home. Not yet." He sat on the bed.

"You were lucky, Raj. Now all recipients of Government scholarship have to surrender their passports until they repay."

"I heard that."

"Anyway, try to work things out...And, by the way," I said. "What has happened to Regis' shop and the Garden?"

"Oh, I hear he has gone to Martinique. I understand Rasta Paul is from there, and he fixed him up."

"But they didn't seem to be getting along well of late."

"And you know what, Ron? Regis wanted to become friendly with Felicity again. He met her after the cockfight and asked her how she could love a Coolie she knows nothing about."

"She told you that?"

"Yes. She said that while she was having dinner with her father, she told him that and what happened at the cockfight."

"Oh, yes?"

"And he dropped his knife and fork, left and returned about fifteen minutes later...and resumed eating without uttering a word."

"I think Regis was trying to get back at you for what you did to him on the last night."

"Whatever? But she said he left for Martinique the next morning, and I told her about the US dollars business."

"For whatever reason he has left, it looks like Bram has lost everything," I said unwittingly. "Good for the bastard!"

"And you?"

"I got the rest of mine in cash."

"You mean when we left he came?"

"Yes. And as soon as he gave me, I invested it in the car."
He smiled.

I tapped him on his back. "Look, let me take a quick shower. I want to drive in your car."

He stopped me in mid stride. "Hey, what's the situation with Nar?"

I told him what I knew. "I think he is getting over it."

"Now we really have to find a *djabal* for him."

Before I stepped into the shower, I told Bram and Nar that Regis had left the island.

Bram bit his lips. "I know that. I know the crook would get away!"

"Raj got his money...And the car is Raj's."

"Eh?" Bram managed.

"Hah," Nar said.

Raj and I didn't go for the drive. We examined the car. I circled around and ran my fingers lightly over it. Opening the door, I poked my head inside, withdrew it, looked at Raj and said, "It really nice. And tape too besides...Reggae and dub music, boy."

"Oh, by the way, Ron, your tape recorder...the transformer got burnt. Sorry."

"That's okay. We have yours."

There was a broad strip of black that contrasted heavily with the yellow. Both front and back bumpers too were black. The rims of the wheels were sprayed in white. Inwardly, I nicknamed it Kiskadee.

Raj stood apart, with folded arms. A permanent smile was fixed on his face.

Nar joined me, did almost the same things I did to the car—except poking his head inside—and said, "Toyota car, durable, shapely looking, and colorful too. Almost reminds me of the bird we have home...the Kiskadee."

"True. True," I said and smiled.

# 15

THE CRIES OF BIRDS awoke me one morning and as I entered the living room. The birds especially the blackbirds and the ground doves were always there in the mornings and afternoons. They competed with fowls under the house for the rice and other food left over that we normally dispatched through the kitchen window for their pleasure. A smiling female clad in bright green tracksuit greeted me. She occupied the center of the almanac. May was already here.

"Raj, how is Felicity?" I asked that evening.

"Okay. Why you ask?"

"You said that she usually comes to spend some time with you."

"Oh. I told her that the boys were back."

"That's no reason for you not to bring her."

After nine the following Sunday morning, I was in the bedroom sorting out my laundry when I heard familiar voices outside. I knew Raj was there splashing water on his car. The other voice was a female's. I peeped and saw Felicity.

"Ron, come a minute," Raj called.

I opened the door and said, "Hi...oh, it's you. This is a surprise."

"Hello, good morning." She was clad in dark top and blue

jeans.

"Nice of you to come," I said.

Raj steered me aside and whispered, "Listen, I didn't expect her to come. But take her inside and see how you can make her comfortable. I want to finish washing this thing."

At first, she protested but then said, "Okay."

In the living room, I pointed to the only soft chair. She sat, folded her hands across her knees and concentrated on the floor.

"Would you like to have some tea or coffee?" I offered.

"Thanks, but I am okay." She looked at her feet.

I sat on one of the hard chairs. "The weather looks okay today," I said.

She looked up. "Yes, it is fine."

I heard Raj splashing water on his car. Bram and Nar's voices rose and fell in their bedroom. It seemed they were having a disagreement over something connected with money. Felicity looked in the direction of the bedroom.

"I think Raj has a nice car," I said.

"Oh...Yes, I like the color," she replied and smiled.

"In Guyana, we have a bird..."

Just then, the curtain to the dark room was pushed aside and Bram emerged.

"Ah, Bram, you remember Felicity?"

He quickly buttoned his shirt and they exchanged courtesies. He sat at the table. She played with her wristwatch. I thumbed through a book on the table. I peered outside. Raj was wiping the car.

The curtain in the doorway of the dark room moved again, this time with a lot of flourish. Felicity looked up and squinted. Nar emerged. "Every flipping day..." He saw her. "Oh, hel...hello... Good...good morning."

"Nar, meet Felicity. I don't think you have met," I said.

"No...but I have heard...heard about her." He went up to her shyly and they shook hands. He sat and began the rotation thing. She studied him.

"I hope good things," she said, smiling.

"Well, Mr. Reg...Regis told us...us most pleasant things about you."

"Oh! I thought Raj did," she replied, raising her eyebrows.

Bram opened a book, Nar grabbed the newspaper and Felicity looked through the window.

I looked at her. She began to turn. I looked away quickly in Nar's direction. His head was buried in the newspaper.

Bram closed his book and looked at her. "By the way," he said, "when last did you see Mister Regis?"

She replied, "I told Raj that Mr. Cauldron went to Martinique about two weeks ago."

"I was hoping to meet him."

"I could take a message to his wife. We live in the same street in Gros Islet."

"Thanks, but I would like to meet him myself."

"Felicity, I heard so much about 'Gros Islet Night'. Is it much fun?" I asked feeling a little more relaxed.

"Ron, Didn't Raj tell you? You will enjoy it. Let him bring you."

Raj had told me about it every time he had gone.

Bram opened his book again and flipped the pages. Nar was still concentrating on his newspaper. Felicity was waving to Raj and I was looking at her.

Then Nar folded his paper noisily and looked at her, "Miss, you...you work at the hos...hospital in Vieux Fort...don't you?"

"Yes. Raj said he told you all."

"No Miss, Regis did," Bram said.

"Oh."

"Miss, what I...I mean is that I am a dia...diabetic and I could do with some ex...expert advice."

"Glad to be of any help. But you have Raj right here."

"Yes, that is true," Nar agreed quietly and turned away.

"But what would you like to know?" She sat upright, and looked at him.

"Like...like to know about...about a good diet plan."

"Okay. I will send a booklet with Raj."

"Thanks."

Felicity looked through the window. Raj was drying the car with a plastic chamois. She turned around to face us. "Well, how do you all like it here?" she asked.

"Things are nice here," Bram was the first to say.

"Things..." Nar began.

Just then Raj came in. "That was quick, eh, Ron? Anyway, Felicity and I are going out on some important business."

He turned to Felicity. "You know Bram and Nar?"

"Yes. Ron introduced us."

Raj quickly slipped on a shirt over his vest and they left immediately.

As soon as the engine of the car roared, Nar said, "Pretty, shapely and..."

"Yes...nice car," I said, and laughed.

"Not the car, you fool," Nar said, sensing my sarcasm.

"Okay, Nar, she is okay, alright? Why didn't you tell her?" Bram said.

"Well..."

"Seemed lost for words," I said and got up.

AT SCHOOL on the following Friday, Raj called. It was one of the rare phone calls I received at my workplace from Raj. I quickly accepted his invitation to Gros Islet night. "Felicity says you must come."

Immediately I packed and left for home. I dressed, sat on the steps and waited. They arrived at exactly 4:21.

Felicity lived in a small brightly painted house. The inside was comfortably furnished. I was sipping a juice when a big, broad shouldered man strode into the living room. "My father," Felicity said. We spoke for a while—he was a friendly man. Mr. Linus Johnny was a police sergeant who worked at the Gros Islet police station. Later two of Felicity's cousins dropped in, and after we were introduced, one of them told me, "I know Feli since I born." He looked at her and smiled. "Yes, she was always a bright girl...and she loves her church."

"Ah, come on, Daren," she blushed.

"And Raj, you lucky boy," Daren said. He punched Raj lightly.

They spoke of things with which I was unfamiliar and laughed—Raj was at home.

Later Felicity's step-mother arrived with her two little girls. Felicity introduced them. We spoke briefly. They were very polite and affable. .

Daren decided to join us for Gros Islet night. "I always enjoy a street lime," he said.

When we got there it was before eight. The street, thickly lit with decorative bulbs and florescent tubes, was already swarming with people. At the first corner of the street, music blared from four speakers. Chicken and fish sizzled on the grill of a glowing coal pot. There were some white people around. They drank beer that a woman sold from a small cooler. We drank a beer each.

Further up, we ran into various food stalls alongside one another under tents covered with tarpaulins and galvanized sheet. Plaited coconut branches separated some. Thin smoke hovered around those where there were sizzling sounds of something being fried. Many people, especially whites circu-lated the stalls.

Raj steered me to one of the stalls. Lobsters—the biggest I had ever seen—and seababs piled on one another adorned the counter. The pungent, yet enticing smell around made the mouth water.

"Ron, you must try the lobster," Raj said.

"You can say that again."

We looked around to find seats. Tables lined the middle of the street in a haphazard way. There was not a vacant seat. Many stood and ate. Suddenly a group of young people just next to us got up noisily. We quickly dropped into the vacant seats.

"This is great," I said as I swallowed my last piece of lobster. "Tastes better than our big sweet water shrimps back home."

"Uhuh," Raj said as he nibbled at his.

Just then a group of four white people came near to us. In one hand each was balancing his plate crowned with either lobsters or chicken and in the other holding his drink. By their attire and comportment I could tell they were tourist. The Friday night Gros Islet street jam was a well known tourist attraction.They stood and looked around. The six people, who sat next to us and were only drinking glanced at them smiled and got up.

When the foursome were settled one of them looked in our direction, pointed to his lobster and said, "Very…delicious," above the noise.

"Really…really," Felicity said, nodded and smiled. She was still munching hers.

All of them looked at us and waved. We did the same.

"From where…how do you get it?" one of them asked between bites, raising his voice.

Felicity looked at Daren who shouted, "The fishermen trap them…right here off shore." He pointed to the sea. "In cages."

The whites nodded. One asked through his funneled hand, "All year round?"

"No. Seasonal…May to August," Daren said.

When they were finished, they came over to us. We shook hands. One said, "This here is awesome!" His hand described an arc, covering the surroundings. They left.

Immediately a group of young men took their place. One of them called out to Daren, "Daren, gason, you trying a beer?"

Daren said to me, "Come meet these guys."

The guys bought beers for Daren and me. We spoke…well, we shouted into one another's ears

Music drowned us from eight massive juke boxes piled on

one another in two rows. The DJ, huddled in a corner with an earphone apparatus clamped on his ear and surrounded by numerous blinking electronic equipment, was swaying to the music.

All around, revelers, especially locals were hopping to the hot tempo of West Indian soca, rap and reggay music. The many whites among them danced with equal gusto. They looked at one another, smiled, gyrated and flailed their arms. When the tempo changed, they all shifted gears.

Felicity held Raj around his waist and they began to sway to the music. When a rare sentimental song came on, they embraced and danced suavely as they looked into each other's eyes.

"A wonderful couple," Daren said. "But Ron, let's get some more beers."

We sipped our beer. Now and again, I glanced in Raj's and Felicity's direction. They were still dancing closely.

"Oh, hi Daren." A young lady approached Daren, and despite his protests, she pulled him into the crowd. When he returned he was all smiles. Perspiration dripped from his face. "Ron, you have to shake your waist," he said. "This is fun."

I moved the waist for a few seconds. Felicity and Raj joined us. She held his hand and nestled up to him.

"My God, so hot," she said and fanned herself with her hand.

Raj unbuttoned his shirt all the way down to his waist. He blew air on his stomach. "Time to cool off," he said. He bought beers for all of us.

After more beers, I began to sway to the music.

Felicity looked at me and smiled. "That's the spirit," she said. She pulled Raj and they disappeared into the crowd again.

The same young lady came again and claimed Daren. She held his arm and steered him away. Left alone I looked around to see if I could recognize anyone. I didn't see a familiar face. The merrymakers appeared and disappeared from view in the blink of an eye. The place was jam-packed. People were streaming past me, back and forth. The din was tremendous. Everything seemed to be vibrating. The dancers moved around effervescently, touching, jamming and bouncing into one another. They were erotic. Their faces shone and the exposed parts of their bodies glistened in the bright light.

When Daren rejoined me this time, his shirt was plastered to his back with perspiration.

"Boy," he said, "This is wild." He pulled the back of his shirt away from his back.

"I am hungry," I told Daren rubbing my stomach. "You?"

"Sure am too. Let's find something light though. Fish cake and fig salad will do."

We snaked our way up the street to find the fish cake and salad. Consumers yelled at sellers over the counters for attention. As soon as a piece of barbecued chicken or fish left the grill it was snatched up before it rested on the counter.

Along the way, music blared from many music sets. As the music clashed and bounced, so did the revelers around. Some who did not take to the street sat anywhere they could fit their backsides. Others squatted on the pavement. They drank, cursed, ate and laughed uninhibited. They spoke a lot of patois.

Some couples walked along soberly hand in hand and looked into food booths and bar. Others cuddled in dark corners.

A young man with trinkets hanging from his neck and wrapped around his arms appeared suddenly and approached a group of white people. They looked at him and shook their heads. He moved on.

We were lucky to find fish cakes.

"Let's find Raj and Felicity!" Daren shouted in my ears as we lingered around for some time.

"Let's take fish cake for them," I said.

We wormed our way back to find the couple. It seemed as

if everyone had taken to the street. Some danced wildly and screamed along with the enticing music.

We ran into Raj and Felicity in a secluded corner. They were in each other's arms.

Abruptly we turned to move away.

"It is okay. It's time to go home," Felicity called out to us. She looked at her watch. "It's after one."

Daren gave them the fish cake. They ate in silence.

Suddenly two angry voices very close to us rose above the noise. Those immediately around moved slightly away. We saw two young men pointing fingers in each other faces. Each had a beer bottle in the other hand. They screamed at each other. Most of it was in patois. They each took a step forward. They glared at each other. One of them raised the beer bottle. Those around backpedaled further away. Two young men—their friends, I assumed—stepped in and dragged them away.

"Don't worry Ron, these things happen sometimes."

Those around resumed their drinking and dancing.

When we left the crowd had not thinned out much. On our way to Felicity's home, she asked, "Had a good time, Ron?"

"Great," I said.

On Monday afternoon, I came and found Raj and Felicity sitting under the breadfruit tree. "Hey, Ron," she greeted as she stood. "Raj says he is waiting for you to play cricket."

"Only if you join us," I returned, and she laughed.

We played cricket. They left for Gros Islet just before Bram and Nar arrived.

On Wednesday afternoon, I heard laughter coming from inside the house as I approached.

When I entered Raj said, "Ron, Felicity is cooking the dhal." He rubbed his stomach. "She is actually cooking the dhal, Ron." He broke in laughter.

She feigned to throw the spoon at him. They left around five thirty.

Bram and Nar arrived after six.

"Ron, lots of chicken in the dhal tonight," Nar said, as he dipped his roti in the dhal and licked his fingers.

I shrugged.

"This really tastes good," Bram added. He looked at me and smiled.

When I arrived home after seven on Friday evening—we had a staff get together—I found Raj, Felicity, Bram and Nar sitting around the table. Each had a malta.

"Hey, Ron, join us," Raj invited, and placed a malta in my hand.

"What are we celebrating?" I asked.

"Well...well, nothing...nothing really," Raj said.

We chatted about mundane things and there was much laughter.

Suddenly Felicity asked, "Raj, why didn't you bring me to meet these guys before?"

"What? Well...am..."

Both Bram and Nar stared at the floor.

"Hey Raj, it is getting on to nine," I said quickly, looking at my watch.

Raj glanced at his watch. "Oh yes. True, Ron." He put a hand on Felicity's shoulder. "Let's go."

When Raj returned that night, I asked him straightaway, "What did you tell her?"

"I told her everything. And Ron, why didn't you tell me what Bram and Nar told her the other day when I was washing my car? I would have tried to work around it."

"I didn't think it was important. And anyway, now that the truth is out I am sure you feel better."

"Yes. She is a very understanding person."

I patted him on the back.

"And Raj, now that everything has been cleared up, do not say anything to the boys."

He raised his hand. "Okay, peacemaker Ron."

When Felicity came the next afternoon, she was in her

usual pleasant mood. Bram and Nar looked at each other and smiled.

One afternoon in the second week since she had started visiting, she was standing in the doorway. Raj and I were outside in the yard fiddling with the car.

"You two got to be twins," she said, causing Raj and I to look up immediately.

We looked at her, but she was staring past us. We turned to see Bram and Nar approaching. They were blushing.

"Hi, there," Bram greeted her. "It's so nice to see you."

All of us were inside the house when Nar told her, "Thanks for the booklet. It is helpful. I need some medication. Back home, top quality drugs were hard to find."

"Raj can..."

He raised his hand quickly. "Forget about Raj...he never remembers."

Raj shrugged.

"Okay, Mr.Nar. I will help you out. But Twins Drug Store in Robb Street, Georgetown, had good stock when I was there."

"Eh?" Nar sat upright.

Bram stopped reading, "I knew it...I knew it."

"Didn't Raj tell you?" She looked at Raj.

Raj shrugged.

She told them.

"Anyway, I am not going back to Guyana for a long, long time," Nar said. He stared at his feet.

"I understand, Mr. Nar. Raj told me," she said softly.

When I arrived home the next day just after five I found Nar tidying the living room. Their curtain was missing. I smelled dhal puri.

Felicity and Raj arrived shortly after. Felicity was invited to dinner.

"Dhal puri is my favorite," Felicity said, as she tore the roti and dipped it in the chicken curry.

"Eh?" Both Bram and Nar looked at her.

"I was boarding with an Indian couple in a village just outside of the university compound."

"What else we don't know, Miss Johnny?" Nar asked, and laughed.

One day she left very late after she initiated a conversation with Bram. "Mr. Bram, I hear you are a priest in your religion. Tell me, what do you think of Christianity?"

"Eh? Oh, yes, Miss Johnny, I..."

"You can call me Felicity."

"Ok, Felicity. I am...I think Christianity...all religions, for that matter, have good principles and teachings. It is up to the people to stick to them."

"I agree with you totally," she said.

"Hinduism is not just a religion. It is a way of life, a philosophy and a guiding principle," he told her.

"Christianity is, too."

He told her about Pagwah.

"Oh yes, I remember this big fire..." she said.

"Holika, they called it."

"Yes, and all the water and the red thing and the powder...and...and the sweet things...Boy it was real fun." Her eyes were fixed on Bram. "But what I like most is the festival of lights..."

"Diwali."

"Yes, I know. Raj explained about it. I actually helped to make the little vessels..."

"Diyas," Bram said, looking steadily at her and smiling.

"So symbolic," she continued. "The triumph of good over evil...the return of a prince...the demise of the Devil..."

"Rawan and..."

"Celebration of the harvesting season," Bram added.

"Yes, Mr. Bram. I like the Hindu religion," she said.

"Bram..."

"Ok, Bram."

"Felicity, you must have been to a Hindu wedding?" Bram asked.

"Oh, yes, Bram. A few times...they are very colorful and long."

"Think you could get married in Hindu rites?"

"Why not?" she said, and laughed.

"Just joking."

One evening she borrowed the Guyana Mirror newspaper from Nar.

"Mr. Nar, tell me something about this IMF. I am somewhat confused. I asked Raj but he said to ask you."

"Oh, yes?" Nar pushed aside the novel he was reading. "Okay, Miss Johnny. In Guyana the money has been devalued..."

"But what is responsible, Nar? Sorry, Mr. Nar..."

"It is okay. You can call me Nar."

"Felicity." She pointed to herself.

"The government borrowed a whole heap of money from the IMF to invest in development, build hydro and so on. Well, corruption and squander mania followed...projects flopped...no regeneration of funds...and now they have to pay back. That's why." He pounded the table.

"But whenever the money is devalued, won't commodities become more expensive?"

"Naturally and..."

"And if there is no salary increase, the people will not be able to buy. Not so?"

"Naturally... And not only that, the IMF recommends retrenchment in the public and civil service. And there are cutbacks in social services like education... "

"Terrible," she said.

"And the Government had to cut down on foreign imports to save foreign exchange."

"I can understand. When I was there, I saw it all. Yes, the people had to line up to get flour and other basic food items," she said.

"So you see why we here?"

"I see."

211

FELICITY AND RAJ came and left almost every day. Sometimes Raj didn't return until the following day.

One evening, Bram and Nar left immediately after they had eaten. "Visiting a good friend by the gas station," Nar said.

"We going at the friend by the gas station," Bram said the next evening.

Two days after, Nar said, "Will be by the friend," and they left.

The next evening, Felicity and Raj came and left. Bram and Nar came, ate and left. I sat at the table to prepare some schoolwork.

BAM! BAM!

I sprang up and headed for the door. Before I could reach it, it flew open and Laljeet entered.

"*Gason*, where the other guys?" he queried with a slight frown.

"Gone out."

"*Gason*." He threw an arm around my shoulders. "*Gason*, Ron, let's go and celebrate."

I smelled beers.

"Why, Lal? This is Wednesday night."

"*Gason*, I know, but one beer, *Gason*. *Wi*." He tugged at my arm.

Since I had returned from Guyana, I had not visited Lal. He worked in Castries and arrived home very late in the evenings. He hardly drank alcohol—he had told me that the doctor had advised him not to because he had high blood pressure—and if he did drink, it wouldn't be during mid week.

Any way, ten minutes later, we were standing at the counter of the little refreshment parlor some hundred yards away from Lal's home. He gulped his beer. I sipped mine.

"*Gason*, I get it," he whispered and peered around.

"Good. What is it?" I said.

212

"I got it yesterday, *gason!*"

"Oh, yes." I waited.

He rocked his body. "I sent in the application last week."

"Congratulations. When do you begin?" I extended my hand to him.

He ignored the hand. "I am leaving as soon as possible."

"But..."

"U.S. I get five year multiple, *gason!*" He held my eyes compellingly with a fixed stare. His eyes shone like the stars outside, and his mouth was half opened. I reached over and patted him on the back.

He rocked faster. "Not only me. The entire family got too." His right hand came up in a clench. He had his third beer in the other. My eyes roved over the sign in the shop. It read: *Credit is like sex. Some get it, some don't.* I smiled. I thought the same could be said about obtaining a visa.

"I moving with me whole family. See what happened to Nar," he threw in.

"Great. How many times did you try in Guyana?"

"Three."

I patted him harder.

He brought his face closer to mine, "I have a problem."

"Oh."

"I have a contract, man...a two year contract."

Somehow Raj's contract flashed through my mind. "So why don't you let the contract end?" I suggested.

"Ron, the contract finishes next year. And the family does-n't want to wait. They don't like here."

We concentrated on the beer for a while, making circles on the counter with the bottles.

"Look, don't they have a clause about terminating con-tracts?" I asked.

"Yes, you have to give them one month notice and you don't get pay for the last month."

"Well..."

"Man, I won't get pay for May."

213

We drew more circles on the counter.

"Anyway, *Gason*, I have some things I could give you tomorrow."

This, I assumed, meant that he had already decided to go soon.

"I am booking a direct flight. I want to be in New York by the first day in June."

I was now sure that he had already made up his mind.

"*Gason*, I am having a Hawan on Sunday coming. I know you don't like those things, but you must come. This one is special. I don't think Raj would come. He become Christian…I sure he will marry the black girl from the hospital."

Raj arrived just before nine that night. He barged into the room and flung the attaché case on the bed. He opened it and plucked out a letter. "Read," he said, and slumped on the bed.

*At home*
*8 may*
*Dear Son son we ok. me read you letter you friend give me after he gone. You ma worried bad bad bad. She say you must be careful of them black people. Don't do like nar. Shopman Ramroop say he waiting to fix a day for the weddin. Everybody saying how savi so pretty she go make you a nice hindu wife. And shopman saying to everybody he go make you become docta. me hear you buy yellow car glad glad. write soon you ma worried and sick*
*Pray to Lord Krishna*
*You papa*

"Raj, I don't know…"

"Is okay." He took the letter and tore it.

Later, when Raj was settled, I told him about Laljeet's visit.

"Oh yes. Glad you told me."

All of us were invited to Lal's Hawan on the last Sunday in May. It was bright and sunny. The gathering was a large one, compared to what it was on the one and only time I had attended; it could have been around twenty-five. Five locals were present.

Bram was the officiating priest. At this special Hawan, he went through with what I thought for him, after so much practice, must be routine — he read in Hindi and translated in broken English; he chanted and sang; he admonished the sinners and the nonbelievers and let them know exactly in what form they will be reincarnated; he blew the conch and rang the bell; he squeezed his eyes shut, opened them and scanned the gathering; he made the place smell of camphor and caused much smoke.

"Our dear bhai is moving on. Lord Krishna blessed him. May he prosper and move on further."

Lal closed his eyes and swayed along with Bram.

The locals with hands folded across their legs, sat upright on their chairs and shifted their gaze from Bram to Lal and back most of the time. For the most part, I sat on the patio. I noticed the weather was changing. Dark clouds drifted slowly overhead.

About halfway through the ceremony, I saw Raj gazing intently past me down the pathway leading up to Lal's house. I turned around and saw Felicity, with hands on hips, struggling up.

Raj touched me on the shoulders and was gone. When he reached her, they spoke for a while before trudging down to the highway.

On the Monday afternoon Raj and I went over to Lal. "We have decided to rent the house," Raj told Lal.

On Tuesday, it rained intermittently. Bram and Nar came home later than usual. Felicity did not come.

It poured for most of the day on Wednesday. Bram and Nar were soaked.

Nar said, "It couldn't get worse."

Felicity did not come in again.

On Thursday night as soon as Raj arrived amidst the drizzle, he announced, "Ron and I moving over to Lal's place.

This place is becoming too much congested."

The book that Bram was reading slipped out of his hand.

"Laljeet left us some things over there..." I began to explain.

"It is okay, Ron," Bram interrupted.

Nar scratched his head. He embarked on the rotation routine. "It does get worse. I think..."

Bram said, "Is okay, Nar. We will have more space."

"The girls could sleep over," Nar mumbled.

I stared at Nar.

"What?"

"Nothing." Actually Raj had told me he wanted Felicity to sleep over. "The weather," he had said.

"Brown curtains going," I thought I heard Bram say. He wearily got up and went up to the almanac. The 'X' stood out like a landmark. It rained for most of the night.

# 16

"THE HURRICANE SEASON is here, sir," the students screamed, as howling wind and pelting rain drowned my voice in the classroom. The following day was terribly hot and humid. The weather was most unpredictable. And whenever it rained water swirled around our house.

"Raj," I said, "you don't think we should return to live with Bram and Nar?"

"Don't be stupid!"

At school, Adrian told me jokingly, "Ron, prepare for it. A torrid hurricane season is predicted. Get torchlight, buy up food, nail your window and listen to the radio," and afterwards said he was serious.

We bought a radio/cassette player. Earlier I had suggested to Raj that we buy a fourteen inch television but he had said, "Man, I got a lot of expenses. The car and...Well, let's see how things go next month."

One afternoon Raj came home early. The weather was fine. He invited, "Come, let's play cricket." We trotted down to the playing field.

We went down to the playing field everyday when the weather was fine.

One afternoon I sat on the steps in my cricket attire and

waited. He parked the car, and walked slowly up. He entered his room and didn't come out.

"Let's swing a few beers," he greeted me on the Friday afternoon as soon as I arrived. "I will buy."

After our first beer, he said, "Felicity is such a good person."

I nodded.

He played with his beer bottle for a while.

I said, "We should tell Bram and..."

"Felicity is so intelligent."

"Sure she is."

He emptied his second beer and stared at the ceiling.

As we got up to leave, he asked, "What were you saying about Bram..."

"Forget it."

On the Sunday I was still in bed when Raj left. He returned after five, all disheveled and greasy fingered. "I could take a sledge and mash it up!" Of late, Kiskadee was giving him a hard start, or simply refusing to start.

"I am a mechanic, you know."

He glared at me.

"Come on, Raj. Relax...I will buy this evening," I said.

"Don't feel like it."

One night I checked the patio at least five times for him. At the very least, he would always hint to me when he would spend the night out. I was relieved when Kiskadee woke me at around three a.m. As I opened the door, he said, "Sorry to wake you." His face shone. He yawned. "Felicity and I went to a birthday party last night. We had such a wonderful time." He did a little dance, a skip and a hop.

At around eleven thirty one night, I heard a noise on the patio. I found him lying in the hammock in the dark.

"What's up?" I asked.

"Just thinking," he replied, and turned away from me.

Twice thereafter, I found him sleeping in the hammock.

Midnight, two days later, I switched on the light in the

patio and shook him awake. "Tell me what's bothering you?" I demanded.

He got up slowly. "Ron, I don't mean to be rude. Thanks for your concern, but you can't help."

"You used to confide in me...Try me again. At least I could listen."

He bit his lips and massaged his forehead.

After a while he said, "Alright," and reclined in the hammock.

"Let me set some tea to brew," I suggested.

He nodded.

When I returned, he began, "I don't want to disappoint my parents but I love Felicity and I am going to marry her."

"Okay, let them know."

"But they are bent one way, hardened, fixed in one path, and would never ever agree for me to marry in another religion, much less another race."

"But Raj, you also have to see it their way. Their customs...their traditions...their beliefs would never change."

"Yes, I understand that. But what happens to my life? Why should I succumb to customs...tradition...whatever...at the expense of my welfare? Yes, I know the people will blame them."

And immediately I recalled Bram had succinctly remarked, "*It could drive them to their grave.*"

I moved closer to him and rested my hand on his shoulder. "I understand your problem, Raj. But you have got to work out things."

He sighed and nodded. I retreated to my room.

For a few days we hardly saw sunshine. One day the heavens broke loose. Water pelted down from hills, swirled around our house and took with it concrete, rocks, gravel and debris at a tremendous speed. My colleagues laughed at my fears. One said, "You haven't seen anything yet."

"Like what?" I asked anxiously.

"Like the roof..."

"Don't bother with him," Adrian butted in. "We are prepared for those things."

Raj and I spent most of the following evenings indoors. The place was damp, wet and gloomy. I couldn't remember ever feeling so frightened and insecure during the rainy season back home. I had this nagging fear that the house would be blown away or just simply collapse any time.

One night I suggested again, "You best let us go and stay with the boys down below."

"Huh. Go back there? *Awa.* And in any case, I understand that around this time the weather always like this. This weather sucks."

As we were speaking, there was another torrential downpour. It lasted about fifteen minutes. Raj went down to drive up Kiskadee, which he had parked earlier by the gas station. I heard Kiskadee groaning and when I looked down, I saw it struggling to climb up the hill. I went down to Raj and said, "Look, man, why don't you park the car at the gas station? I think the water could sweep it away from up here anytime."

"You are really afraid, Ron, but you are right."

"And another thing...why don't you patch the exhaust? Kis...Your car is disturbing the whole neighborhood."

"What do you mean?" he chuckled. "Is it making all that noise?"

"It sounds horrible man. Seems too like the spark plugs need cleaning."

He laughed heartily and I joined him.

THE WEATHER IMPROVED and Felicity came regularly in the evening. At first I joined in their chatter. But then I began wandering off to the gas station as soon as she arrived, and there I always encountered the same set of boys. When I was around, they looked at me and whispered.

After a week, I asked, "Are you guys regular and punctual to school like this?"

No one answered.

Instead one asked, "Mister, where you from and what do you do?"

I told them. They conversed as if I was not there.

One afternoon about a week later, they offered me a chewing gum.

The next day as soon as I arrived one of them said, "Have a coke, mister."

I accepted.

A few days after, they held out chewing gum, coke and cake to me.

"Thanks," I said. "But I do not eat much sweet." I sat and listened.

"*Gason*, do you know the Rasta in Form five chatting the new girl..."

"I tell you Greg shouldn't be on the football team..."

"But the teacher like him..."

"*Gason*, I see Mr. Charles drunk, drunk on Friday night..."

"And I don't like how he teaching..."

One evening as I got up to leave, one asked, "Sir, a very, very, pretty young lady is checking out the other Indian, Mr. Raj. Nobody is checking you out?"

"Nah."

On a windy evening several days later, as I was about to leave for the gas station, I heard, for the first time, the raised voices of Raj and Felicity. They didn't shout, but their voices bore anger and frustration. And although I quickened my pace, the voices trailed behind me in the quiet night. I clearly overheard her saying, "You show no responsibility," and he rebutted, "But I am trying."

When I reached the gas station and looked over my shoulder, she was already on the other side of the road, flagging down a bus.

That night it rained as if all the taps of heaven had broken off. I couldn't sleep.

About midnight, Raj rapped on my door, came in and said, "*Gason*, I can't sleep. The blasted roof is leaking in the middle of the bed, man!"

We shifted the bed and placed a basin to catch the drops. He returned about half an hour later. "Man, the flipping thing driving me crazy, only pat, pat, pat!"

"Okay. Sleep here." He bedded beside me. I watched him toss, turn and roll. When he eventually slept, he began to groan. I must have fallen asleep after two a.m.

Next morning I was dozing on the bus on my way to work, when someone shouted, "Landslide!"

I peered through the window anxiously. There were about six buses parked ahead of us. Further up half of the road was covered with mud and silt.

"Part of the hill slipped," the lady sitting next to me said calmly.

I gazed at the hill. Supposing, just supposing, I thought, another part was to slip on the bus…BURIED ALIVE! Or if one of those boulders jutting out would become loose…CRUSHED ALIVE! A lump rushed up my throat. The school children on the bus were chatting excitedly.

A bulldozer arrived within minutes. It cleared a path wide enough for the bus to squeeze past.

"Look, another one!" some school kids screamed, as we approached River Doree. "Bet we see another one round the bend."

As soon as we entered the bend, their shrieks confirmed it. They counted five in all. They screamed even longer when they saw the tumultuous water pelting over the bridge of the River Doree. After a long half hour, the bus was able to crawl over the bridge.

The students at Soufriere Comprehensive were much noisier.

"Sir, you know the storm wash away three houses one time and…"

"He is lying, sir. Only one house collapsed."

"It is true. And Sir, mud has covered an entire house in Malgre Toute."

They were overjoyed when they were told that classes for the day were cancelled. I returned home around eleven a.m. and slept for most of the afternoon.

It was very bright and sunny when I awoke. I was standing on the patio yawning and stretching when I saw Bram laboring up. Apart from breathing heavily, he looked disturbed, as if someone had messed around with his altar.

"So glad to see you," I said. We hadn't seen or spoken to each other since Raj and I had moved out. I had always felt a tinge of remorse after we had left so abruptly without much explanation. "Come in," I said, and pushed the chair for him to sit.

He didn't sit. I inquired about Nar.

"These days Nar is coming home later than me. I even smell alcohol on his breath. Anyway, read this." He handed me a piece of paper. He looked away, scratched his head and sighed.

Trouble flashed through my mind. A cable! Just a few words:

*I coming B.W. 609. Friday 15 June 4.00 p.m. Meet me.*
*Balgobin.*

"Eh! You mean, Kalli?"

"Yes. Him."

"But the last I heard of him, he was in Barbados."

"Yes. That is where he is coming from."

"Well, I'd be glad to see him. You know, we played cricket together."

"But I am not glad to see him. He is my cousin, yes, but this man is real trouble."

"Did he ever indicate to you before that he would be coming?" I was puzzled how Kalli had known where to send the cable.

"Look, Ron, this man knows I am here. Before he went to Barbados, he went to see me wife for the address, saying he was going to give me a look up." He sat on the chair and exhaled loudly. "Back home," he continued, "he don't even say hello to me after he thief my bicycle...In fact, when I confronted him, you know what he told me?" He paused and took a deep breath. "He told me, 'Teacher does pass for grass. Cane cutter work for more money than U.G. man any day. Me could tramp on you...Me thief you bicycle?' Ron, this man is sheer trouble."

I laughed.

"What?"

I quickly explained, "It is the same teacher and grass thing he told me."

"Anyway, I told my wife to tell him over here they don't have sugar cane."

"Maybe it is only a look up."

A grunt of helplessness escaped his mouth; I could understand.

As Bram was about to leave, Raj drove up. He and Bram greeted each other coldly. I told Raj about Kalli's coming to sort of explain Bram's presence.

"Yes, heard about him. A very good cricketer, I saw him play."

"Same fella," I said.

"Could take you all to the airport," Raj volunteered.

Bram smiled.

On Friday the 15th, Raj drove Bram and me to the Vigie airport to pick up Balgobin.

Kalli Balgobin emerged from Immigration and Customs just as I pictured he would—with mouth opened. The open space on the top gum was still there. The thick crop of jet black hair on his head was plastered back as usual and the black beard was pointed. His tall, wiry frame glided towards us, with two equal sized brown bags, one in each hand. When he got closer, I noticed the small, squinting eyes doing the same things they always did—shift, dance and roll. Many, including myself, believed that it was because of those alert eyes that he was able to pick up those short pitched deliveries and dispatch them effortlessly to the boundary.

"What happen, cousin? Eh! Eh! What happen, Ron? Lord Krishna bless me eyesight," he exclaimed coarsely and loudly in Guyanese creole accent. A few people nearby looked around instantly. Bram looked away. Kalli dropped his bags to the ground, extended one hand to me, and the other to Bram. I squirmed as he gripped mine. Those bony hands still possessed deceptive strength, I thought.

On his shoulder bags, written in scrawls was 'M.C. Balgobin'—Mohandas Charran Balgobin. Once he had asked me to fill out a passport application form for him-I believe he never got beyond Division Two in the primary school. But since he had started playing first division cricket, he had preferred to be called 'Kalli', after the dashing little West Indian batsman, Alvin Kallicharan. His full name though, with appropriately acquired pseudonyms attached, was as intriguing as the man himself. It would read something like this: Mohandas Snake Eye Kalli Charran Ball Oil Balgobin. A few called him Gutter-mouth when they wanted to invoke his wrath and especially when he was on the cricket field and was either batting or bowling. I wasn't too sure how that particular nickname originated.

"Like you lose another tooth, Kalli?" I teased him.

"Another flipping bouncer!" The cigarette that he usually kept in the space would now roll, I mused.

"You remember Raj," Bram said.

"Oh. Girdo son! Me hear he going to marry a black gal." He laughed uproariously, drawing the attention of the people nearby again. Bram bowed his head and Raj glared.

"But why have you come?" Bram asked straightaway.

"Come to work. Me hear dollars flowing here." It was a loud, prompt and emphatic reply. He grabbed one of his bags, "Let's go home," he said, and tugged at the sleeves of Bram's shirt.

People stared again. "Balgobin, keep your voice down,"

Bram scolded. "And man, you can't get work here. It is only qualified people who get work here."

Kalli dropped the bag. "Cousin, what *rass* you tellng me. Me name Balgobin and me get work anywhere...anytime! You let me stay by you or what?"

More people stared.

"What you looking at?" he smirked.

The people looked away.

"Take it easy, Kalli," I said.

Bram stuck a finger in Kalli's chest. "You know I mad march you through the exit door, just like they rewind a cassette, and send you back to Barbados."

Raj bit his lips. I couldn't suppress the laughter.

Kalli turned suddenly to Raj, "Friend, me hear you get a yellow kar."

"Eh?" Raj said aloud, and turning away, he muttered, "I can't believe this."

"Ah, that must be it," Kalli shouted and pointed at the same time. He immediately grabbed one of the bags, pushed the other in my hand, and was guiding Bram to the car.

He jumped into the back seat, wound down the glass, and pushed his head out before we could all get aboard. He moved his head like the pendulum of a clock to take in the view and declared, "Look them hill and them mountains. Nice, nice place. Me could live here."

"Yes, nice place," I said absent mindedly, still pondering about this little historical development-Snake Eye Balgobin of all people would be living with Bramnarine Tiwari!

It wasn't long before he got bored with the scenery and turned to Bram. "Cousin, look how you get fat. Back home you does pass for grass. Now look how much money you making." He punched Bram lightly in the stomach and let go his tantalizing laughter.

"So what you name again...? Oh, Raj. So when you marrieding the black gal?"

Raj looked straight ahead.

"He aint't getting married. How are things in Barbados?" I asked.

"Barbados hard, hard like concrete. You know, since me gone there, the whole of Zeelugt come up." He sucked his teeth and continued, "Coolie people can't see you do anything. They too damn greedy. They does climb on you back and pull you down. Me said me going to go home and buy a mini bus, but now me can't even buy the steering wheel."

"You can't buy anything because you drink too much rum," Bram slipped in.

He looked at Bram. "People too ungrateful. They stab you in you back and juk you in you eye." He cursed.

"None of that!" Bram said.

"Okay, never mind, Kalli. Do you still play cricket?" I asked.

His eyes immediately lit up as he leaned forward and punched the seat. "Me blast a century last match me play home. You?"

"Only softball sometimes."

"You still have the bat?" he queried as he grabbed my shoulder and we both laughed. Looking at Kalli, I recalled the incident involving the bat most vividly.

We, the Packer Boys, were preparing for a very crucial match with the much-vaunted Wanderer, which boasted several first class rated players. Kalli, regarded as our best player, was more than excited, but he knew that something was missing for him to be up there with the others. "Ron, me want me own bat, bad, bad," he had told me several times before the match. "Lend me some cash til pay day, nah," he begged.

I gave him a small part. For a couple of weeks, he put his head straight and walked past all of the rum shops. His friends were flabbergasted. "Eh, eh, like Balgobin going mad," they declared. It was alleged that he instructed his wife, "Don't buy mutton and chicken anymore, greens better." Still he was short of the cash.

On the Friday afternoon before the match Kalli, mouth

wide open, staggered into my yard with a big, black bag over his shoulder. "Open it," he said.

I extracted a brand new Alvin Kallicharan autographed bat.

On Saturday morning, Kalli sent for me. I saw a small crowd including two policemen, Kalli's neighbor and a goat.

"But Ron," he told me the day after the incident, "this damn ram goat me neighbor have, he tie it on the fence in front of me yard, and it only bawling, bawling..."

"So you..."

"Yes. But when me see the two policeman coming up the street, me didn't take it for nothing, because police always coming up in Zeelugt on Saturday morning, since every Friday night they have fight." He paused to wipe the sweat off his forehead. "Hah. Me see the ram goat and a man was pulling it, and he turn out to be the very man me sell the goat to."

"So why you didn't get away?" I asked.

"Me tell me wife to tell them me not home. The wife tell them and the neighbor say 'She *rass* lie...Look, he bicycle there.' Okay, to cut long story short, me come out and the black policeman tell me he going to lock me up and that was when me send for you."

After I arrived, Kalli pulled me aside and said, "Man, the fool me sell the goat to, is a damn goat. Me think he woulda kill the damn thing the same day. See what you can do, man."

Kalli sold the bat to me, bought back the goat from the man, and gave it to his neighbor who told him, "Tie it back on the fence."

I allowed him to use the bat the next day. He scored an entertaining half century.

Here in St. Lucia, Kalli was talking excitedly in the back seat of Raj's car and Bram's mouth was set tight.

About mid way home, Kalli must have noticed, or hoped what he saw was a pub. "Me throat dry, cousin," he said.

Bram quietly seethed, "Nobody...nobody is stopping to

drink rum or drinking rum in my house."

"Eh, eh, don't get vex, cousin. Me only a making a joke," Kalli laughed. "Besides, a little rum good for the worms," he continued as he rubbed Bram's paunch, and was reaching with his other hand in his top pocket at the same time.

Bram pushed his hand away from his stomach. "Nobody is drinking or smoking in my presence!"

"Okay, cousin," Kalli said and looked through the window. "Better than Barbados," he uttered and glanced at Bram. "Me really like here!" he exclaimed and shook Bram by the shoulders.

"Behave yourself!" Bram snapped.

On arrival at Bram's place, Kalli dropped his bag in the pathway, stared with mouth agape and pointed a finger, "You mean that little bruck down place you live in."

"You want me to rent a palace? I could arrange that you stay with the Prime Minister."

But Kalli, espying Nar in the doorway hailed, "What happening there, cousin? You look fat. Like the black woman you have looking after you good, good." When he got closer, he held Nar by the shoulder and shook him, "I know alyuh too glad to see me, countryman."

"How long did the immigration authorities give you, Balgo?" Nar asked, as if he had just awakened.

"Who?"

"Immigration."

"Oh, the officer. One week. But when me get work, they go give me a whole, whole year."

When we entered the house, Kalli dropped the bag he was carrying on the floor. "Eh, eh...this like me old grandfather place in Zeelugt. No TV?"

"I going to Courts tomorrow to get one, my lord," Bram said.

Kalli sniffed the air. "Yes, me smell food...me hungry bad, bad. You get anything?"

"Some dhal and rice, I think," Nar offered.

Kalli licked his lips. "Yes, is dhal. Man, you know how long now me don't eat dhal and rice. Put it in a basin with plenty pepper."

When Nar returned with a green basin half filled, Kalli slumped to the floor against the wall, sat yoga style and dived into the basin with his long fingers. He gave the rice and dhal a thorough massaging, and for the next few minutes, we watched in awe as he attacked his morsel. In between the assaults, he mumbled, licked his lips, and plucked a few grains of rice that had escaped onto his shirt and deposited them in his mouth. He attempted to talk, but Bram held up a hand promptly, "Just finish. Okay."

When he finished, he belched like an old truck starting up. "Thank Lord Krishna," he said as he rubbed his belly vigorously. He then grabbed hold of the mug of water that Bram had placed next to him, tilted his head back, and leaned the top of the mug into his mouth. The water disappeared as quickly as his Adam's apple pumped.

"Super! All me want now is a good shot of El Dorado rum and a bed."

Bram stuck out a finger. "No rum…and you have to sleep out here on this floor."

"Floor? You know in Barbados…"

"Where did you stay in Barbados, Kalli?" Nar interrupted.

"Cousin, a nice big, big place. And in Barbados, if you see them big, big hotels on the beach and them white women with all them titty and backside outdoor. *Rass*, man me nearly go blind. Oh *rass* boy, if you see…"

"Shut up, Balgo!" Bram said.

Raj and I left about fifteen minutes later.

"I don't like that man," Raj said as soon as we stepped out of the house.

"He could be very irritating if you don't know him, but he could be fun too."

"Like the whole world know my business."

"I don't think Kalli meant any offence. I think the guy is

only repeating what he heard."

"Okay, maybe I am a little harsh on him. But I must do something about this. I am writing my parents tonight."

An hour later, he held out a letter to me and sat on the bed.

"I don't think you should," I suggested.

"But I must. I have to do this now. Read."

The main part read:

*I have something to tell you. Please don't feel bad. I can't marry Ramroop's daughter. I know you meant well for me. But I meet a girl. Her name is Felicity Johnny. She is a black girl. We work at the same place and I want to marry her. I really really like her and we plan to marry soon. I would want all of you to come to the wedding. (And it is not true that Nar had a sweet woman). I love you all…*

"Raj, are you really serious about getting married soon?"

"She is pregnant." He sighed. "It is already showing."

I scratched my head. Raj cracked his knuckles.

"Raj, why don't you take out the 'black' and the 'marry soon' parts?"

"No!" he almost shouted. "I am finished with this cat and mouse game." The finality in his voice startled me, but in those few seconds he seemed to have grown into a man. He got up and pulled himself to his full height. "Look, let's celebrate."

At the refreshment parlor we sipped the first beer in silence. After the second beer, Raj turned to face me. "You know, Ron, I am so worried what my parents would say, especially my mother. I am sure they wouldn't agree and they might not even want to see me again." He sighed.

"It would have been ideal if you could have gone home and tell them. But I know the contract..."

"Yes, the contract."

Two beers later he said, "Feli is the best thing that ever happened to me." He began to tap to the beat of the light music that the proprietor was playing. I joined him.

"I will make it up to them." He stopped tapping and clenched his fist.

"Who?"

"My parents and relatives. Who you think?" he asked.

"Oh."

After what could have been our sixth beer, he got up and danced. He staggered, collapsed on the chair and chuckled.

"Must get married before the end of August...a big, big hic...wedding, with lots of ...hic bridesmaids like...hic...we see in the...hic...movies. Yes, a big..." His hand toppled a beer bottle as he attempted to demonstrate how big, 'big' would be.

"Ah, shit! Anyway I applying for permanent...hic...residence, ah buying a property, ah furthering my...hic...studies, and I taking Felicity...hic...to Guy...hic...and, and I don't hic...care...what any...hic flipping...hic...body...hic...hic say...hic...hic, hic."

"To hell with Bram...to hell with Nar ...to hell with Regis!" I said and collapsed in fitful laughter.

We staggered home and turned up our tape recorder to its fullest. We played all eight cassettes we had. We hummed and sang along with them, as we staggered, danced and hopped about. We rode "No woman, No cry" with Bob Marley until our voices cracked.

"Yes...remove...remove...the        whole        damn nasty...brown...brown curtain!" I believed I shouted before I passed out.

# 17

I HARDLY SAW RAJ the following week. Most days he left before I was awake and came in after I was asleep. The weather too was on and off.

For that week also I did not see Kalli. The night before his permit expired to stay on the island, I decided to go over to see him and was glad, after some prompting, that Raj had decided to accompany me.

We met Bram and Nar in the living room and inquired about Kalli.

"He is staying here and we don't see him," Bram said. "Snake Eye gobbles down a whole heap of food every morning." He shook his head and sucked his teeth.

"Plus, he snoring like a pig," Nar added.

"Anyway, tomorrow the Snake is going home," Bram continued in the same vein. "His job hunting finishes tonight self, self. And in any case, he wasn't looking for a job."

"I will like see him before he leaves," I said.

"Well, you have to wait a long time. He leaves before six. He comes back after midnight every night...drunk, drunk!" Bram disclosed, slapping his thighs.

Then we heard crunching footsteps outside.

"Ah, cousin," the voice boomed, "ah come home early

tonight." The door opened and the effervescent Kalli entered. He saw me, came up directly and threw an arm around my shoulder, "Me so glad to see you. Me so busy looking for work that me ain't get the chance to visit you... and the rain just coming and going."

I reached up and punched him lightly on the chest. "Seeing tomorrow is your last day, I come to see you."

A whiff of alcohol escaped from his breath.

"Last day! Last day! What you talking about, cousin?" He skipped over to Bram, attempted to hug him, didn't succeed, and exclaimed, "Cousin, me get work!"

"Work?" Bram uttered.

"A job?" Nar 's eyes were riveted on Kalli.

"Cousin, me know alyuh too glad for me. Me get a job as a mechanic."

"Mechanic?" I said.

Raj covered his mouth with his hand.

"Selfsame mechanic," Kalli replied and smiled. He stared at us with his mouth opened wide enough to accommodate a lawn tennis ball.

"How?" Nar asked.

Kalli, looked us over once, and slipped on the floor yoga style.

"Me end up in a garage and fix a caburator or whatever *rass* it name and the big mechanic tell me, 'Garsa, you could work with me,' and me tell him, 'Cousin, me don't name Garsa, me is Balgobin, but okay.' That is how me get the job."

"As simple as that?" I said.

"Yes. Thank Lord Krishna, he bless me." He pushed his hand in his pocket and withdrew a pack of cigarettes.

"Balgo!" Bram wagged a finger.

The packet hovered in front of him in his hand before he slowly slid it back into his pocket. "Cousin Bram, tomorrow, you own, own cousin Snake Eye, yes, Gutter-mouth, working."

I had to laugh.

"Cousin Bram, you has to cook more lunch."

I stepped outside to continue laughing.

"Unbelievable," Nar muttered, slouched over the table and began to rotate the head.

"Me hungry," Kalli said suddenly. He sprang up and glided into the kitchen. He returned with a green plastic basin—it seemed like the same one he had used the first day—but this time it was filled to the brim with rice and crowned with pepper, tomato ketch up and red beans. He reassumed his yoga style posture, placed the basin in the fork of his legs, and launched a ferocious attack on its contents.

He used his left hand to squeeze all the items into one ball, nearly half the size of a football. Then with fingers opened like a shovel, he dug into the ball, excavated a sizeable portion, and levered it into his mouth. He repeated the process non stop until the entire ball had disappeared; very little escaped. What was caught at the back of the hand and on the beard was brushed back into the container. He then ran his left index finger around the entire bowl, and inserted the finger deep into his mouth. He made a sucking sound and withdrew the finger. It was as clean as a whistle.

This time, Kalli didn't even attempt to utter a single word during the assault. It was executed with unflappable concentration and relish. It was so reminiscent of one of his long innings at the crease. Bram, Nar, Raj and I were merely amazed spectators. Chuckling spontaneously, we looked at one another and shook our heads.

Finally, he poured the mug of water down his throat, belched and drawled, "Thank Lord Krishna." He looked steadily at Bram. "Cousin, let me take one?" he begged, patting the pocket with the cigarette.

Bram burst into mild laughter, "Alright."

Quickly, Kalli removed the cigarette from the pack, inserted it in the space in the upper gum, and lighted up. He pulled his legs from under him, stretched them out. He exhaled once, filling the room with smoke.

Nar walked over to Kalli, rested his hand on his head and ruffled his hair.

"What you want to tell him, Nar?" I said laughing.

"Kalli, this is long gone, but tell us…tell us what you did with your cousin's bicycle?"

Kalli looked at Bram, and smiled.

I waved Nar aside. "Forget about that," I said, and turned to Kalli. "Kalli, tell them about the time you chased your neighbor with the cricket stump."

"Ron, you was playing in the match, not so?"

"How can I forget?" I laughed.

"Well, tell them nah."

"Okay."

This was how I remembered it: I was standing at mid on when he opened the bowling. His first three deliveries, all gentle paced, were easily dispatched to the boundary. Some spectators booed, and one shouted, "Snake eye, we beating you like snake today."

In a flash he was on top of the spectator. "Say that one more flipping time and see if me don't wring you flipping scrawny neck!" he yelled, as he collared the spectator in his vice-like grip.

That section of the crowd heckled him. He spat at them and cursed. His fourth delivery was pulled over the mid wicket boundary. He kicked the ground and swore. I went up to him and asked if he was alright. I knew he was suffering from a hangover.

"Alright! Me knocking out the bastard middle stump!" He didn't only do that; he sprawled all three stumps and had the wicket keeper rubbing his head where a bail had hit him. But just as his left hand was coming up in a victory punch, we heard, "No ball!"

Kalli stopped in mid air, whirled around and glared at the umpire who, incidentally, was the same neighbor whose goat he had stolen. What happened next was not too unexpected.

"Bastard!" he roared. "Me break you frigging jaw bone!"

He then grabbed a stump, and with arms, legs and stump pumping, took after the umpire who was already well on his way to his home. A wave of spectators was sucked into the narrow street. Suddenly the wave stopped, stood still and then began to recede with the same speed. From my vantage point at the top of the fence, I saw Kalli, stump still in hand, being closely pursued by the neighbor who held a cutlass high above his head. The wave began to disintegrate after it cleared the narrow street. Kalli broke free and galloped in my direction. I lost sight of the umpire who apparently was consumed by the wave. That was the end of that match.

Here in this little house, Bram, Raj and Nar were rolling with laughter as I told them. Bram slapped Kalli a few times on his back. Raj did the same to him whereupon Kalli asked Raj if he wanted him to repair his car. Nar attempted to imitate Kalli chasing the neighbor. Kalli asked Nar about Meena and the black woman. Nar laughed and asked Kalli if he found a black woman.

I smiled. Kalli, like Regis, the unsuspecting common factor had done it. I owed him a big drink, I thought.

When we were about to leave, Kalli followed us down the steps. It was drizzling. He tapped Raj on the shoulders and quietly asked, "Cousin, when you marrieding the black gal?"

"Soon," Raj replied.

"Me see one who me could live with."

"Do that and I telling your wife!" Bram, with hands folded over his chest, was standing in the doorway!

237

# 18

TOWARDS THE END OF JUNE, the weather had improved. It still rained consistently but with less intensity. I was becoming acclimatized to it and even enjoyed the coolness it was giving the nights. I ventured out most evenings.

"You don't have to leave when Felicity comes," Raj told me one evening as I was leaving.

The first night Felicity stayed over, I realized how obvious it was that she was pregnant.

That night too, some of their friends visited and left close to midnight. There was much hilarity and banter. Raj invited me to join them. Sometimes, they slipped into patois and then, "Oh sorry, Ron, let me explain."

When they left I said, "Raj, boy, you really understand the patois now."

He tapped Felicity on her shoulder. "She teaches me."

She smiled. "*Awa.*"

"I know some but there was so much of it that I couldn't follow too closely what they were saying," I said.

"They want to be down to earth," Raj explained.

"How much down to the earth can you get?" I asked.

"*Salòp.*" He sounded like a St. Lucian.

"Raj!" Felicity said and slapped him on the arm.

The next time the friends came I hung around briefly before excusing myself. I went over to Bram and Nar. I was hoping to meet Kalli. Only once since he got the job did I meet him, and that was brief. Kalli wasn't there.

Nar said, "Kalli working overtime everyday, huh."

"Overtime, me foot. I believe he seeing a woman." Bram shook his head.

"By the way, Ron," Nar said, "what has happened with Raj? Does he have to get an inferno to remove the brown curtain or what?"

"They will be getting married soon," I said, "but what about you?"

"What about me?"

"Have you become Mahatma Ghandi? You don't want a woman again?"

"I have to support my two boys and I am applying for a U.S. visa."

"Just joking, Nar."

It so happened that the next day, Raj awoke me around six a.m. and said, "Ron, I am sorry. I have to get married soon...sooner than I wanted."

"But I thought you had said the end of August?"

"It has to be sooner. Two weeks time maybe. Felicity and her relatives are insisting."

"You letting your parents know, I hope?"

"I am phoning tonight to a friend in Georgetown to pass on the message."

"But..."

"It has to be done." He gritted his teeth and stared straight ahead.

Throughout the day, I thought of Raj and tried to anticipate what would happen. Kalli too flashed through my mind and I wondered if he was serious about the black girl.

I was pleasantly surprised to see Kalli that evening. Raj was there when he stepped on the patio.

"Ron, me come to tell you something. But it can wait for

next time."

"You can tell me." I ruffled his hair.

He glanced at Raj and smiled. Raj raised his hand and stepped into the living room.

Kalli studied the traffic down below. "Two things. Me want to borrow some money and..."

"Hold on. Are you not working?"

"Yes, but am...am..."

"Kalli, you have to ease up your drinking and..."

He raised a hand. "Is not that."

"What then?" I raised my voice.

"Me helping out a...a woman." He looked at his feet.

"What? You helping a woman and you don't have enough even to buy your own liquor?" I turned away and took a step towards the living room.

"Cousin, wait." The voice was hoarse.

"What?"

"Don't tell Bram," he pleaded.

"I can't promise. But I think Bram knows."

He exhaled and his head drooped. After a while, he straightened up, came across and held my hand firmly, "Cousin, lend me the cash nah...please."

"You in trouble with the woman? You will stop seeing the woman?" I shook his hand loose.

"Cindy. No...yes."

"Which?"

"Which what?"

"Will you stop seeing the woman?"

"Cousin, you confuse me. Yes...I will stop seeing the woman."

"Where Cindy or whoever live?"

"Vieux Fort."

"Are you going to Vieux Fort this afternoon?"

"Nah," he said quickly.

I loaned him the cash.

"What is the other thing you wanted to tell or ask me?"

"Me was going to tell you about Cindy and tell you not to tell Bram," he said.

Raj came out on the patio.

"Cousin, me could fix you car anytime. But is when you getting married?"

"In two weeks' time…two weeks. I will invite you."

"Me want to get married here meself," Kalli replied, chuckled and immediately rushed off, leaving me speechless.

Two evenings later when the weather was pleasant, I went over to Bram's and Nar's place. I wanted to see Kalli. He wasn't there. Nar and I spoke for a while. The conversation veered inevitably to Raj.

"Ron, is Felicity pregnant?" Nar asked. "You know, I saw her in Castries the other day and I am sure she is carrying a child."

"So why do you ask?"

"Is he sure it is his seed? Regis told us he and Felicity were friends."

"I thought you and Felicity had become friends. Why didn't you ask her?"

He didn't say anything.

"You haven't changed much. Have you?" I said, and left abruptly.

Raj and Felicity were on the patio when I reached home.

"We were waiting for you, Ron," Felicity said, and smiled.

Raj said calmly, "We are getting married this month…on Saturday, the thirteenth."

"Thirteenth!"

"Yes."

"But that is the day I have confirmed my flight home."

"I suspected that. But it can't be helped."

"Anyway, congratulations! I will see what I can do."

"Thank you," Felicity said softly.

"Ron, I would need you," Raj said.

"I would be there."

They left immediately.

241

The next evening, they were there on the patio again when I entered.

"Okay, Ron, this is the plan."

"Only two or three bridesmaids," Felicity indicated, "and a little reception at my home, and a two night honeymoon right here...maybe at Sandals."

"What about your relatives, Raj? Did you inform them?" I asked.

"Yes. I phoned the friend in Georgetown to tell my father. I haven't got a reply yet. I wish I could have gone," his voice trailed off. He shook his head, "But I can't take that risk. Not now."

"No way," Felicity laughed. "Guyana will claim him."

"Lock him up, you mean," I said.

We laughed.

Outside had become increasingly brighter although a few patches of dark clouds were hovering overhead. It was nearing sunset, and yet it was undoubtedly the clearest afternoon we had had in a long time. The wind had sprung up and was whistling through the vegetation.

Raj and Felicity strode hand in hand to Kiskadee, which sparkled in the crimson rays of sunlight. Kiskadee purred contentedly as it skidded off. I was sure the exhaust was fixed.

# 19

THE MORNING OF THURSDAY the fourth of July was bright and breezy.

"U.S. independence anniversary," Raj reminded me.

"I know."

"How many times did the US Embassy turn you down in Georgetown?" he asked.

I shrugged. "About three or four times. You?"

"Two."

"Trying again?"

"Not in the near future."

"Same here."

The chorused cries of flocks of birds disturbed the quietness. I looked outside and strangely at that hour there was a bustle of activity.

The bus shed was crowded when I got there. The people were loud.

"They said it is expected to hit Friday night!" a voice rose distinctly above the clamor.

I managed to get aboard the bus.

"They say this is a bad one," said the lady sitting next to me.

I looked around. Everybody was talking to somebody

else. The radio in the bus was also blaring.

I leaned over and quietly asked the lady, "What is a bad one?"

"Eh, Eh. You mean you haven't heard?"

"Matilda coming!" a few voices said together.

I pondered. I had an idea but didn't want to embarrass myself asking who or what was Matilda?

"This storm could be the worst," someone lamented in an afterthought.

How was it Raj or I didn't know or hear about something as serious as this?

Just then "…Matilda will hit on Friday night," sounded on the airwaves. The driver turned on the radio full blast. "Prune trees… clean yards… nail down windows… loose animals… buy food…"

At school, the chatter and excitement were even greater. A few students vied to enlighten me. They laughed at my innocence and ignorance, and made my fears grow.

"But nobody told me yesterday," I said.

"But it was far off, sir. They didn't know the course it would take. Guyana doesn't have storms, sir?"

"We have rain for days, but not high, high winds to blow off roofs."

My colleagues sensed my despair, and laughed too, but said that it was nothing to worry about. "It's okay. We are prepared for this." Their calmness eased my growing apprehension.

Slowly I began to realize that people here had an attitude prior to tropical storms and hurricanes. Tedious advertisements—buy food, store water, buy candles, fix your torchlight, clean the debris, secure your shutters and the like—ignited the populace into action. Urgency, not panic, was the order of the day. Anyway, why not joke about it as they seriously prepare? To become hysterical wouldn't help. I thought.

I phoned Raj.

"I heard," he said. "When we get home, we would see what to do."

Nevertheless, despite the admirable composure of those around us, Raj and I were battered into preparedness after we were hounded by skittish friends, frenzied weather reports, pockets of gusty wind and dark hovering clouds. We kept the radio on while we cleaned the yard, nailed shutters and loose structures, and moved things around.

When we returned from shopping, I dashed down to see the boys. Kalli wasn't there.

Bram asked straightaway, "Let's see. Do you have water, candles, matches...?"

"Yes, yes, yes..." I nodded as he reeled off the list in the same manner as a concerned mother would to her child whom she is sending off to primary school for the first time.

"Okay, don't panic. And tell Raj to park the car down below."

That was nice, I thought. "Yes. I will tell him."

Later when I returned up the hill, I told Raj. He smiled.

We fortified ourselves at least twenty four hours before the hurricane was expected to hit.

We waited.

At ten p.m. I was still on the patio looking at the heavens.

"Ron, they predicted tomorrow night, not tonight," Raj calmly reminded me.

I settled down in bed.

Suddenly water was pelting down from everywhere. Raj, Bram, Nar, Felicity, Regis, Meena, Kalli and I ended up in a tangled mass, clutching, grabbing...I began screaming.

"Wake up, Ron." Raj was standing over me and shaking my arm.

I sprang up and sat upright. "What...?"

"Take it easy, Ron," Raj said.

I nodded and he left.

My skin was wet with perspiration. I drank a glass of water and settled down again. Some time afterwards I fell asleep.

When I opened my eyes, I saw daylight. I sprang up and glanced at my watch. Eight o'clock! I dashed to the door and headed to the bathroom.

"Don't panic," Raj shouted from the living room. "They say everybody must stay home today."

I breathed a sigh of relief. I went into the living room and slipped into a chair.

"Take it easy, Ron. Today we would see if there is anything else to be done."

We shopped again. We filled all our containers to the brim with water. We gave the yard another go over. Not a nail or twig could be seen.

Time dragged.

At five p.m. we put the final nail into our fortress. The sun had disappeared totally by then.

Suddenly, the winds sprang up, lightly at first, and then it came in strong gusts accompanied by howls. The trees struggled, bobbed and weaved. Galvanized sheets and windows rattled. "This is it!" I shouted to Raj.

We retreated inside. We waited.

The howling died down to a gentle swishing. I ventured outside. It was as still as a hostage. In the far distance, lightning brightened the sky, and thunder rumbled.

I remembered what one of the students had said. "It could come so quickly...BUFF! Just like that, and blow away the whole house!"

Our house did quiver with the first gust. My dreaded expectations and fear grew with the passing of every minute. I watched the walls and roof closely. "Raj, you don't think we should go and stay with Bram and...?"

"Why?" he frowned, as he glanced sideways to look through the door at me.

"Oh, never mind."

He joined me outside on the patio.

It began to rain lightly but grew heavier by the minute.

The approaching darkness encircled the surroundings rapidly. Soon, hazy lights appeared all around. The wind roared and died with frightening regularity. Each time the intensity increased. The rain began to pelt down with venom.

The report on the radio was drowned. We sought refuge indoors. I clutched the radio to my ear. "Don't go outdoors... don't drive..."

"Only a moron would do that!"

"What?" Raj bawled.

"The man said that the storm is here!"

"All of us know that!"

I lifted the curtains and peered outside. Everything was blurred. Cautiously, I tried to open the front door leading to the patio. It resisted. The enemy was here for sure, I thought. I braced to defend. Sprays of water attacked me from my waist down. I withdrew hurriedly.

"The whole patio is wet!" I shouted.

"I know. But my room is flooded."

Water spouted through the hole we had patched on the roof some time ago. The hole was as big as a cricket ball. We quickly set about emptying the room. In five minutes, everything lay scattered in the living room.

Raj grimaced and cursed. After a while, he slumped into a pile of clothing and buried his head in it.

I paced the floor—whatever space was left—and waited wide eyed.

At around midnight, the wind dropped considerably. A steady pitter-patter of water rolled down the roof like a lazy locomotive.

I waited.

I sucked my teeth and kicked a few things in my way. Why doesn't the enemy get on with it and remove the flipping roof? I looked at Raj. He was curled up and motionless.

I thought of the wedding. I thought of Geet and the kids, and how they would be excited to hear about this. But what if our house should collapse?

Raj began to snore lightly. I chided myself for being a coward. Maybe I should sleep and let fate take its course. I settled down beside Raj. I closed my eyes. Sleep didn't come. My thoughts left.

Back in Zeelugt, we had our worst flood about four years ago. It was spring tide and the twelve feet high sea defense wall 'just went under,' one eyewitness had reported. Our coastline had succumbed under the severe battering of the spring tide. Chunks of concrete wall had disappeared and holes and tunnels appeared. The surrounding area was flooded within hours. Everyone worked feverishly to remove items from the bottom floor of his home to the upper flat, and sought higher ground for his animals and poultry.

The village boys reveled in these conditions. Small boats and other floating contraptions — some grotesque, like an old refrigerator — appeared quickly on the smooth surfaced water under which lay streets, yards, the bottom flats of houses, and pit latrines. The boys, oblivious of the seriousness and dangers of the situation, engaged in little boat racing competitions, and plucked escaping household items out of the water.

When the water receded — and that was about four hours after the tide ebbed — the entire surrounding was one big mess of debris, mud and slush. There was the fear of an epidemic. However, Zeelugt didn't suffer much from that. It moaned the loss of a seven year old girl who was discovered under a bridge.

A heavily loaded streak of lightning jolted me back to the present. Raj jumped up. A second set of thunder and lightning, more powerfully charged, made us sit upright and scan the room nervously. My heart pounded. Raj peered at the ceiling. The light bulbs flickered. Somewhere, somebody or something must have suffered, I thought. The wind roared and howled much more furiously than anytime before. Our little house trembled. The lights dimmed, flickered and then went out. This was it. I shuddered.

248

"Raj!"

"I here. The torch?"

"I have it." I flicked it on.

"Run it along the ceiling," Raj cried.

I ran the beam of light along the ceiling and the entire house in one circular movement. "It alright!"

Another flash of lightning confirmed that everything was all right. Raj lay huddled among his scattered clothing. "Pull down the curtains!" he screamed.

"The curtains already down!"

"Switch off the torch and lie down!"

Whether it was fear, resignation or calmness Raj showed, I couldn't tell.

"Okay." I slouched among some clothing, pulled a few pieces around me and stared into the darkness.

"I pray nothing happens to Felicity," he murmured.

Soon, I realized that the darkness was less frequently cut by the streaks of lightning. The rumbling of thunder too, began to die away in the distance. I welcomed the steady flow of rain again. I felt my eyelids getting heavier, my head was drooping...the car was going down. "Hold it back, hold it back!" I screamed and tried to grab it.

A hand was shaking my shoulder. "Wake up, Ron...Wake up."

"The car, man, your car!"

"It's alright. You dreaming."

Outside was bright. "Is everything alright, Raj?"

"Come. Let's go outside."

We stood on the patio. The concrete in front of our patio was gone. Mounds of stones, sand and debris had replaced it. I stepped cautiously outside and peered at our house. The little thing was intact.

I gazed down at the highway and saw clusters of people moving about. Their excited voices floated up. Something was happening down there, I thought. I clambered up the railing of the patio to get a better view. I saw many people around a tree lying across the highway. It seemed that a vehicle, a red one, was entwined in the branches. I looked across to the gas station. The yellow car was still there, along with about a dozen others.

"Ron, come here," came Raj's shrill voice from the back of the house.

I treaded on loose stones and debris to reach him. A mango tree was resting snugly between the wall of the house and the incline on the hill.

"But how? This thing could have crushed us and to think we didn't even know." A slight tremor ran through my body.

"It must have come from up there," Raj said calmly. I followed Raj's finger to a spot about a hundred feet up.

We circled the house. We probed and inspected.

"What the...?" we shrieked, jumped back and looked up anxiously.

A slight gust of wind had revealed that two zinc sheets had come loose.

We stood back and gazed admiringly at our house.

"Strong little house," I said.

"Yes, like David standing up against Goliath!"

Most of the gravel and silt on the eastern side were washed away and a little stream appeared in its place. All of our five garden beds lay under a pile of mud and silt.

Curiosity pulled us downhill to join the noisy crowd around the tree. It was clearly evident from where the breadfruit tree had come. The landslide around that area extended about fifty feet. The vehicle was a red mini bus. The owner was visibly distressed.

"I parked it in my gap," he said, "and when I awoke and looked, it was gone!" He quickly rounded up some able bodied boys and men and they began hacking away at the branches of the mango tree with cutlasses and axes.

We ran into Bram and Nar.

"We were coming up. How are things?" Bram asked. I told him about the cricket ball-sized hole, the mango tree and our garden.

"How about your place?" I asked.

"Okay, except that the water passed through the bottom of the house and all the fowls and roosters disappear."

The crowd swelled quickly. The chatter rose. People flitted about, inspecting affected houses, corners and areas like spectators looking in at display booths at a fair.

"Christ, I never see something like this before," one elderly man said as he looked at a house that was battered into shapelessness.

A young man who was hurrying in our direction shouted, "*Gason,* the road by the ravine cut in half like when you cut cheese with a dull knife."

Some laughed. Others shook their head.

"Mama, look how that bus twist up," someone commented

"Simply unbelievable!" Nar said.

Then we noticed people were detouring with some haste in the direction of the ravine. Boys and girls sprinted. We followed briskly.

Spectators had lined both sides of the ravine. Water tumbled downstream with breath taking speed, curling, churning and boiling. It lashed viciously against the banks, creating a tremendous din, and carrying off gravel. Numerous floating coconuts, resembling the heads of brunettes, popped in and out of the strong current like erratic butterfly swimmers, tumbling over, or overleaping one another. Now and again, trees, branches and logs of all sizes bobbed up and down, and somersaulted over rocks and banks.

It was chilling to think of the fate of any house, animal or person trapped on the embankment.

"Guyanese," our neighbor who was standing alongside us, said calmly, "every time there is a storm, the banks of the streams overflow. But, mama! This is the worst I have ever seen."

"Nobody...just nobody can predict with any certainty

what horrors and destruction the awesome power of the water would inflict," Nar told him.

He stared at Nar for a few seconds.

"Time to start cleaning and rebuilding," someone uttered.

"The stark reality is that we have to live with this," the neighbor said, hung his head and left.

"God's work," Bram said aloud.

"No. The devil at work," a spectator looked over his shoulder and addressed Bram as he moved off.

Slowly the people began to disperse. Groups of men reappeared with spades, fork and cutlasses and other tools. They began to remove debris, level mounds and hack away at fallen trees.

While we patched the roof and cleared the debris with the help of a few willing neighbors, we learnt through our radio how the rest of the island had fared. Reports, the announcer said, had indicated that the banana farmers took a battering through landslides and floods. He said that it was too early to estimate the damages, but he was certain that it would have a tremendous effect upon the economy. The news was far worse than we had feared.

"Further," he said, "Communication is at a stand still...telephone lines are down...But thank the Lord our broadcasting equipment are all intact." He understood that some main bridges had collapsed, others needed clearing, and numerous landslides had blocked most of the roads.

"I hope many people took the pre-storm warning and bought candles and batteries because reports coming from the electricity corporation indicate that there are many fallen poles," the announcer continued.

He reported that two people were slightly injured, and one person had died, but the cause of death was not yet ascertained. Then he promised to give an updated report every hour on the hour. "We must all pray to the Almighty. It could have been worse," he concluded.

"Got to call Felicity," Raj said suddenly.

"But the lines…"

He was already hurrying down to the phone booth next to the gas station. He returned shortly and said, "Lines are down, and the people at the gas station say no vehicle can reach Castries much less Gros Islet."

"She must be alright. The report said just a few casualties," I told him.

"I am not worried about that. She must be okay. I want to know if it would affect the wedding plans."

"In a couple of days, I think things should be normal in certain areas," I tried to reassure him.

"I hope so." He didn't sound too optimistic.

# 20

FOR THE REST OF SATURDAY and the whole of Sunday, the updated reports didn't do much to change our mood or boost our optimism. On Sunday morning when I looked outside, I saw an unusually large number of people on the highway. It appeared as if everyone was dressed for church.

"Thanksgiving services," Raj said. "It will be like this all over the island."

"It is becoming clearer," one reporter said, "that the storm almost totally devastated the banana industry, the tourist sector and the economy…" And after he had gone into details, he turned to the human side of it and reported, "Up to this time the only fatality is the elderly woman…"

We set about putting our landscape back in order and resurrecting our small vegetable garden. After a while Raj trudged down to the telephone booth. When he returned he said, "Telephone lines still down."

"Don't think servicemen will start working until tomorrow," I said.

He went down to the telephone booth at least three more times and each time he returned, he plunged the fork deeper in the ground. He hardly spoke.

Both of us left for work around 8 a.m. on the Monday

morning after we had listened to the six a.m. news. Again, it was not promising: "Workers will be trying to restore some utility services today. Drivers are asked to take precaution as the roads will still be wet, slippery and damaged..."

It seemed that there were landslides every fifty yards where roads hugged the hillside. Traffic was held up as workmen cleared the road. Eroded sections of the main road itself compounded the problem. Debris appeared in unusual places. Most of the flat sections of Vieux Fort were swamped. The runway at Hewanorra had become a lake overnight. At the River Doree I had my longest delay. A tangled mass of the limbs of trees had gathered on the bridge. While men hacked away feverishly at it, commuters in the bus vied to relate what they heard and saw during the peak hours of the storm.

On both sides of the highway, the damage was extensive, especially in the banana fields, which lay flat and swamped. The banana plants on the hillsides were a twisted mess, except for a few sticking up defiantly here and there. Most of the buildings along the route had lost their roofs. Many were ruined.

When I arrived just after eleven, only staff members, handymen, a few members of the community, and several students were on the school premises. Classes had been called off indefinitely until the environment was declared safe and useable. Most of the classrooms were still about three feet under water, mud and silt. Our worst calamity was the library. It was completely destroyed. We formed work forces and tried to see what could be salvaged.

"Cousin!"

"Kalli!"

It was just before noon, and there stood the grim-faced Kalli blocking the doorway to the staff room—one of the few rooms that had not been severely damaged. I jumped up and rushed to meet him before he could call out again. I grabbed his arm and hustled him into a secluded corner.

"What are you doing here? Who told you I am working here?" I asked angrily.

"Don't vex with me, cousin." He held my arm tenderly. "Ah find out. Ah come to ask you something. Me didn't go to the boys since before the storm — the big, big rain."

"I know. They are worried about you," I said as I pointed my finger in his face.

"They not worried. They mad with me."

"I glad you know. But why? How you know?"

"You think Bram go tell me wife?" He was looking at his feet.

"Tell her what?"

"That me living with Cindy."

I held him by the shoulder and steered him further away from the staff room. "Kalli, you mean to tell me that you really are living home with Cindy after you promised?"

He stared at his dirty boots again and scratched his head and beard. "Man, cousin Ron, she ask me to nail up something before the... what you call it? Storm...wi, the storm. Man, it get late and me stay over."

"You lying, Kalli. If this is the first time you stay over, how they would be mad with you?"

"Okay, me stay over before."

"What her parents say?"

"Cousin, she don't live with her parents. She live alone with she two sons."

I wanted to ask him more about Cindy and her two sons, but changed my mind. "So why didn't you go home on Saturday morning?"

"Cousin, *awa*. The road break up bad, bad, *salòp!*"

"What did you say?"

"Cousin, that is what everybody saying."

"Okay, the road has broken up. But what happens today? Are you going?"

"That is what me come to find out. What me must do." His eyes held mine.

I let him squirm for a while and then said firmly, "I am going home in about half and hour. Wait for me. You are going with me."

As soon as I rejoined him, he said, "Oh *rass*, me never see something like this in me born life! *Awa*! If you see..."

I shut him up with a stare. He inquired about Bram but I did not reply. He spoke aloud to himself all the way on our journey home. "It was the devil heself that night. Me never see anything like this in me born life. *Rass*, it look like the world was ending...Me nearly piss meself!"

I turned away and smothered my laughter most of the time.

He lingered behind as we walked down the pathway to his home. Just when I was beginning to wonder if Bram was home, the door flew open and he appeared in the doorway.

"What happening, cousin? Me so glad to see you safe," Kalli suddenly cried over my shoulder. He rushed past me and when he got to Bram, he attempted to hug him.

Bram pushed him away. "Snake, I thought the storm carried you away."

"Nah. Me stay by me mechanic friend."

"You have a good mechanic friend. I must see him one of these days," Bram said.

"Shit!" Kalli responded.

ON MONDAY EVENING, while I was relaxing on the patio, I looked up at the sky and thought how different it was just two nights ago. Just then I saw Raj striding up, despite the uneven ground. Beyond him, at the bottom, Kiskadee was parked.

"Hi, Ron, lovely afternoon, eh?"

"Yes, lovely."

"I had to take Felicity home."

"Oh."

"The road is clear."

I wasn't too sure what he was talking about. He put his

attaché case on the rails and caressed it. "The wedding is still on for the thirteenth of July." He paused briefly and rubbed the palms together. "You want to see it?" He opened the case before I could have answered and held out a small velvet box, "Open it, Ron. Open it." The sparkle of the diamonds matched the twinkle in his eyes.

On Tuesday afternoon, he came at around four o'clock. I was outside still trying to restore the garden, and to work up a sweat. I saw Kiskadee turn into, and up the pathway in haste. It made a heavy grating noise as its rubbery legs skidded on loose gravel. It stalled and then rolled down gently for a few yards before it stopped. Raj alighted and started jogging up.

"Take it easy, man," I said.

"It is okay," he panted. "I have something to tell you. You have to take me to church on Saturday. You know what I mean, the person to give me away."

"But isn't your father coming?"

"Yes, but he doesn't know about these things. He can't fit into these things."

"But I don't know much either."

"Ah shoo..." He fanned his hand.

"And I don't have a suit." I added.

He scratched his head.

On Wednesday afternoon, after my stint in the garden, I was in the kitchen making some lime drink, when I heard crunching footsteps on the gravel. I peeped through the curtains and saw him almost running up with a bag held over his shoulder, and the attaché case swinging by his side.

He entered the kitchen, took a deep breath and said, "I got it," and pulled a black suit out of the bag. "Like it?" he queried, and before I could respond, "Yes, it is nice," he continued. "And my father is coming tomorrow afternoon," he added as he searched his attaché case.

I offered him a drink of limejuice. He gulped down two glasses, licked his lips and continued, "Alright, good. You have to try on the suit...And you have to pick up my father at the airport. He is coming tomorrow at four p.m. Felicity and I have something to look after at that time. You have to go for him. Hire a bus or anything. I would pay. Here, try the suit."

"Hold on. Is that my suit?"

"Sure, it is."

"But how do you know my size? How did you get it so quickly?"

"Listen, I have a friend your size and I borrow it. Ron, come on," he pleaded and then continued, "If it don't fit...but it must fit...make it fit." He grabbed the envelope he had extracted from his attaché case and smiled. "See you," he said quietly and was gone.

This was one of the few times I had ever laughed aloud all by myself.

Later that evening, I went over to find Kalli and asked him to accompany me to the airport. Earlier, I had wanted to ask Bram, but I changed my mind. When I arrived to pick him up on the following day, Kalli was immaculately dressed in a white shirt — really white — neatly pressed, and with long sleeves buttoned down to the wrist. It suddenly dawned on me that this was the first time I had ever seen him wear a white shirt outside of the cricket arena. It fitted snugly into a pair of black pants held firmly to his narrow waist by a brown belt with a conspicuous lion head buckle. The high top white boots were certainly new. His beard was neatly trimmed, and his black hair too, neatly plastered with some kind of sweet — smelling pomade.

I looked at him and nodded. He laughed. We arrived at the airport nearly thirty minutes before the scheduled time of arrival. Kalli's excitement and garrulousness grew with every beer he imbibed. He glorified his boss and then cursed him, "He nice but he too mean. Me pay stick like chewing gum. But when me come back from Guyana..."

"Oh yes? I didn't know you were going home. But why are

you going home?" I asked.

He sucked his teeth. "You know me think me run mouth cousin tell me wife that me have a black woman. He tell me the other day that me wife say if me don't go home soon, she go left me...And he say that she say me could go home and come back." He smiled. "Boy, imagine everybody home begging me Snake Eye for a drink, hah." The smile disappeared. "But is a flipping waste of money to go home and come back." He was quiet for a while. Eventually, he said, "You know, Cindy too nice."

"Wait! Are you still seeing Cindy?"

He quickly threw an arm around my shoulder. "Cousin, she does still come and see me, but me ain't living with she." He looked away and burped. "But she too nice. No matter she lil mèg."

When the announcement of the arrival of Girdo's plane blared over the intercom system, Kalli was swaying on the stool at the counter of the bar. He pulled himself upright and tugged at his sleeve to look at his watch. He peered and did all manner of things with his eyes before he mumbled, "Quarter past four...Me going to piss."

When he returned, all the oil from his face had disappeared and the hair had been freshly combed. The white shirt, which had acquired a few brown spots in front, was once again tucked into the pants but not as neatly as before.

We lingered around the vicinity of the exit door. Kalli became impatient. "Me hope they don't fatigue the old man," he growled and cursed.

The few people nearby looked sternly at him. Some were amused. He glared at them and they looked away.

Old Girdo emerged slowly through the exit.

"Look. Is he!" Kalli shouted and advanced.

I waved as I walked briskly towards the old man.

Old Girdo stopped and peered around.

"Mr. Girdharry!" I shouted and moved closer.

He dropped his bag and brought his hand over his eyes as

if he was blocking out sunlight. He turned his head to the right and then to the left again.

Upon reaching the old man, Kalli threw an arm over his shoulders and cried, "How you does, old boy?"

The old boy pulled back a little. He looked closely at Kalli and squinted. When he looked up and saw me, he smiled and extended a hand. I gripped it.

"Glad to see you, Mr Girdharry."

Dressed entirely in white as Raj had said he would be, with his thinning white hair sticking out of his head, he looked very distinguished, and reminded me of Bram and the Hindu priests back home.

"Where is Raj?" he asked.

I explained.

When we boarded the bus, Kalli sat next to the old man.

"You see this place," Kalli said, as he touched the old man and pointed to somewhere outside "is only hills and mountains." His index finger remained slanted upwards to a hill we were passing. "You could come down on the other side of the island."

"Oh." The old man's eyes opened wide and the rivulets on his forehead twitched.

"And you see them varleys down there. When rain fall, water does cover all them house tops. And last week, we is had a hurricane storm, and it mashes up the whole damn place."

The old man gaped. The destruction caused by the storm was still very much evident.

"There is where we live, Mr. Girdharry," I pointed out as the bus came to a halt.

"There?" He screwed up his face and shook his head slowly from side to side.

It was already five o'clock when we stepped on the patio. After I took the old man's handbag and put it in the living room, I said, "Would you like to eat, Mr. Girdharry?"

"Not yet."

We sat on the patio and awaited Raj.

Kalli asked, "Uitvlugt still grinding?"

The old man nodded.

"Mohan gone to Barbados?"

"Don't know."

"Flour on the market?"

"Nah."

"They lock up Jagroop?"

"Nah."

"So he still making bushrum?"

"Don't know."

"But how come you don't know?"

"Kalli, leave Mr. Girdharry alone," I said.

The old guy's eyes roved over the surroundings.

"Is in this house Raj live since he come to St. Lucia?" he asked.

"No. He was living with Bram and Nar," I told him.

"Oh." He exhaled. "And Nar still living with he sweet woman?"

"Mr. Girdharry, Nar never lived with another woman," I said.

"Okay, *beta*." He continued to survey the surroundings.

"Lots of bushes, eh?" he suddenly commented loudly.

"In between them bushes, they have houses and banana," Kalli said.

"Plenty hills and mountains too, eh?" the old man said. He looked at Kalli.

"Yes, old boy. And if you see them pitons…"

"Ron, *beta*, where is the big house Bram and Nar live in? You must show me."

"Big house! I living there too. Let me take you," Kalli volunteered, and sprang up. The old boy straightened up.

"Sit, Kalli!" I elbowed him, and turning to the old man I said, "I don't think they are there, Mr. Girdharry."

The old boy reclined in his chair and closed his eyes. "Ron," he said suddenly. "You know the *beti* Raj getting married to?"

"Yes, she working at..."

"Yes, I know she. She too nice. She..."

"Kalli, shut up!" I told the old man about Felicity.

We sat and waited. The sunshine that sliced through the shadows was growing dimmer. I looked at the highway. I glanced at my watch. Six! One...two...three vehicles whistled by.

Just after six o'clock, Kiskadee turned into the driveway. When Raj stepped onto the patio, Old Girdo stood. Both father and son were rooted to the spot as they stared into each other's eyes. Raj took an uncertain step forward, opened his arms and attempted to embrace his father. The old man extended his right hand as if he was a traffic cop stopping vehicles at a pedestrian crossing. He waved Raj away. He slumped in his chair. Raj recoiled, and stood waiting.

"But why, Raj? Why, son...why?"

"Why what, pa?"

"Don't make me get vex. You know why, Raj. How you can do this thing to you ma, and Ram and Govind and Seeta and Jasmin. How?"

"I can explain, pa..."

"Explain! Explain! How me can explain to all me family, me friends, the church people...Zeelugt. How? How? How?" He pounded his clenched right fist into his right thigh.

The hurricane was over for the rest of the island, I thought, but it seemed that for Raj it was just beginning.

Raj slowly raised his right hand, "Is my life, pa."

"Is a stray dog life!" the old man screamed, and sat upright. His right hand shot out again, and slapped the arm of his chair with his palm. Suddenly he sprang to his feet and for one moment I feared he was going to punch Raj. "*My life...my life*, when me sweat blood, and Ram and Govind too, to send you to high school and U.G. Yes U.G. And now you telling me *my life...my life*. You shame all of we. Me sorry me come. Why you think is me alone come? They shame...me shame." He shook his head and pouted.

"Pa…"

"You know how black people killing Coolie people back home and take advantage pon them. If was an Indian no matter she not Hindu, we woulda come around, but a black girl! My God, Lord Krishna! Why you punish me so, Raj? Is obeah, they obeah you? Raj, cockroach eat you brain? Eh? Raj, cockroach eat you brain?" He broke into a sob. His nostrils flared and his chest heaved. He began to cough and sank slowly onto his chair.

"Kalli," I said, "Go across to the gas station and get…"

"Me wish you dead or me dead! Me mad take a cutlass and chop you piece, piece. You not me son!" Old Girdo was on his feet.

Raj backed away to the rails of the patio and stared at his father, mouth agape. He slowly turned his back to us, dropped his shoulders and wiped his forehead. The tears trickled down the old man's cheeks. I couldn't see Raj's face.

I saw Kalli open his mouth and I quickly reached out and covered it. I grabbed Kalli's hand and was about to steer him out of the patio when the old man said quietly, "Ron, you…you…how you let this happen?"

"You see…"

"No. Me don't see…me don't see!" He gritted his teeth and clamped his mouth shut. He trembled. His face contorted.

Kalli looked up into the sky as if he was trying to locate a bird or an aircraft. Suddenly he took a few quick steps nearer to the old man, placed his hand on his shoulder and smiled. "The girls here…"

"Shut up!" Raj screamed.

The smile vanished from Kalli's face. I reached out and squeezed his shoulder.

A knife edged period of silence followed. I welcomed the ear piercing cries of birds that alighted on a nearby mango tree. Kalli aimed and threw an imaginary stone at them.

"Bastards," Kalli said, vexed.

264

"Me shoulda listen to Bram," the old man sobbed quietly. "If only me did listen to Bram and…"

"Bastards!" Kalli screamed, as he shooed the birds away.

Raj, eyes squinting, looked directly into his father's face and mumbled, "Bastard."

"Shopman Ramroop rich, rich and he daughta too nice," the old man continued as he pouted and shook his head wearily.

"So, pa, you really come to stop the wedding?" Raj asked.

"Is you life," the old man retorted with a wave of the hand.

The light from the street lamp below gradually replaced the gloom that engulfed the patio. Raj took a deep breath and stood erect. He walked to his father, and stood directly in front of him. Placing his hand on his father's shoulder, he looked into his eyes, and said quietly, "Pa," before stepping into the house.

The old man slumped into the chair. I leaned over the rail of the patio and stared into the darkness. Kalli sidled up to me and did the same. After a while, I glanced at the old man. He seemed to be breathing lighter.

"Dinner, Mr. Girdharry?" I asked.

"Nah, me not hungry…Me want to go to Bram."

"Bram is not here," I said. "He and Nar went home yesterday. Maybe while they were going, you were coming."

"Me know. They…" Kalli began.

"Kalli," I said, holding up the palm of my hand to him, "see some food for Mr. Girdharry."

"Yes, eat something, old boy. Ron say they is have dhal and rice and fry fish and hot, hot pepper. You musn't take in wind."

For a moment, a smile appeared on the old man's face but then he buried his head in his hands. Kalli left for the kitchen, returned with the plate of rice, dhal and fried fish, and gently placed it in the old man's hands.

"Nah," The old man said and pushed the plate away.

"Come on, old boy," Kalli coaxed. "Me tell you, this fish

really, really sweet."

"Please, Mr. Girdharry," I said.

"Alright," he said, "But not too much." He slowly slipped his fingers into the plate and executed a slow, mild version of a Kalli—style method.

"Old boy, what about..."

"Shut up, Balgo," I said.

The rest of the evening passed quietly. Raj did not come out of his room after he left us. Finally, I told the old man to sleep in my bed. He slumped into the bed without removing any of his clothing. Facing the wall with hands between his knees, he began to snore at first lightly, then the snoring picked up like a growling dog getting angrier by the second. I held Kalli and guided him to the nearby bar. I thought I owed him a drink.

# 21

I BEDDED on a sponge mattress on the floor in the living room. Mosquitoes buzzed and attacked early. I slapped a few on my exposed arm before I pulled the bed sheet over my whole body. The mosquitoes hummed even more around my head. I got up and lit a mosquito coil. I must have dozed off way past midnight.

"Damn!" Something slid across my back. Jumping up, I flicked on the light and peered around. I turned over the sponge and stomped on it. I shook it. I saw nothing.

I dashed to the kitchen, grabbed the cutlass and plunged it into all the cervices and dark corners of the living room. I uncovered nothing. I decided to leave on the light.

I glanced at my watch: 4:10. I sat on the sponge, braced my back against the wall and watched. Replays of the two mornings when I was bitten by the centipedes screened across my mind. The same sinking and nauseous feeling welled up in me. I wiped away the bead of perspiration that trickled down my cheek.

"Ron."

"Old…Mr. Girdharry, is everything alright?" I was on my feet.

"Not too well. But me don't sleep too much," he replied.

"But, Ron, me don't know what to do." He was wearing the same attire. The wrinkles suggested that he had slept in them throughout the night. His face appeared puffed up.

"Raj and you didn't talk last night?"

"Nah. They go vex with me. They send me to stop the wedding. You think he go call off the wedding?"

"Mr. Girdharry, please sit."

He looked at me for a few seconds and obliged.

"Listen, Mr. Girdharry, these days, young people don't care about color or religion. They want to be with people who they know, and can trust and can help them along."

He looked at me straight in the eye and nodded a few times. His mouth was set tight.

"Mr. Girdharry, Raj will become a doctor," I pressed on. "When two bright young people like Raj and Felicity like each other so much..."

He held up a hand. "But, Ron, you think they will want to see he and she?"

I was now sure that what I was saying was irrelevant. But, encouraged, I said quickly, "Not now maybe, but with time they will come around. You can help..."

Raj appeared in the doorway of his bedroom, rubbing his eyes. On seeing his father, he inquired softly, "Did you sleep well, pa?"

The old man nodded and stood. "Raj, me don't..."

Raj's right hand shot up like an angry schoolteacher as he stepped up to his father. Holding him firmly on the shoulder with both hands, he said, "Pa, there is no turning back. I am going to marry Felicity." And then he pleaded, "Pa, don't turn your back on me. I understand how you feel and how the others will feel. Don't go home. Come to the wedding. I won't go home for a long time if that is what you want."

"Raj, but..."

"No buts, pa."

The old man stared at the floor. Raj's hands still rested on his shoulders. Eventually, he looked up and said quietly, "Me will come to the wedding but me don't know what me want. And, oh, here..." He pulled a crumpled envelope from his pocket. "Me forget to give you the letter Seeta send you." Immediately Raj opened it. He bit his lips and shook his head as he read. "It doesn't matter anymore," he said, and dropped the letter in my hand. "Read," he said, as he backpedaled to the bedroom. There was no date or greetings.

*You have shamed us. You have neglected us. You are not my brother. The girls at church used to talk so highly of you. One of them was hoping you would make her happy. Savi is pretty and rich. You are going to marry a black girl! They obeah you? Just like they do Nar? I don't want to go to church anymore. You are killing ma. Jasmin is crying. She stop going to church. You are a stray dog. I hope we don't see you again.*
*Seeta, your sister lost forever.*

The old man left for the patio. I followed him and put a hand on his shoulder. Raj joined us. He was wiping his face with his towel. He looked up to the sky and inhaled. Daylight was taking over as overhead clouds drifted hurriedly out of sight. Raj looked at his father and then turned to me, "Ron, today, I am getting married and I should be happy. Nothing or nobody is going to spoil my day. Are you with me?"

I nodded.

He drew himself to his full height and combed his hair back with his fingers. He strode into his bedroom. I sat on the patio. Occasionally, I glanced at the old man. Most of the time, his head was in the palms of his hands with his elbows resting on the rail of the patio. I tried to picture what was going through his mind.

*Back home, in his Hindu home, there would be various little reli-gious functions to appease the gods before the wedding itself. He and his wife would be dressed in traditional Hindu garb, she flaunt-*

269

*ing a brightly colored sari, and he, clad in white dhoti and koorta. He would be tapping to the loud beating of tassa and drums while he sat with the pandit who did Dwaar Pooja to remove all obstacles in Raj's and his dulhin's married life. He would be pleased to see lots of women and children about. Everyone would be excited and well dressed especially the females who would be adorned with ornaments and brightly colored dresses and saris. After the pooja, he would go across to the men who cook bags of rice, hundreds of puri, pots of dhal, and different kinds of greens and vegetables in huge pots sitting firmly on the ground, part of which was excavated to accommodate large chunks of firewood. Yes…he would be glad that he had invited most of the villagers as Hindus normally did.*

"Ron," Old Girdo suddenly called out to me, "where the *beti* live?"

I told him.

"Oh."

Time jogged along.

A few of Raj's friends dropped in.

"Congratulations, my boy. You have taken away a St. Lucian beauty," one said.

Raj smiled.

"Now that you would be controlled, we won't see you," another said.

"*Awa.* Nothing will change," he responded.

"Spending the honeymoon in Guyana?"

"Ask my father. Look him there," Raj said, pointing to the old man.

"Oh, hi Mr. Girdharry. Pleased to meet you…You have a brilliant son and you will get a wonderful daughter-in-law."

The old man blinked. "Oh. Yes."

When the friends left, the old man asked, "Son, the *beti,* what she name?"

"Didn't I tell you? Her name is Felicity John…"

"Oh, yes," he said. "Nice name." He rested his head on the rail of the patio.

Raj left one more time for his bedroom but as soon as he reentered the patio."Son, the *beti*. You give she jewelry?"

"Dad...Pa, she has her own."

"But you suppose to give she. Is custom, eh?"

"This is different, pa."

"Raj, you not listening to me?" the old man snapped.

Raj withdrew into the bedroom, slamming the door behind him.

"You see...you see how this woman make him turn against he own father," he cried, beating his clenched fist against his thighs.

I entered the bedroom and found Raj sitting on the bed with his hands propping up his head.

"Raj," I said, "At least hear him out. You are making things hard for him and yourself by being so curt and irritable. Now he is blaming Felicity for your behavior."

"Okay, okay," he said quietly, raising his hand in submission.

I returned to the patio immediately.

The old man was pacing the patio. "Me not going to any wedding. Me going home. Ron, see me things and me ticket. Take me to the airport."

"Listen, Raj under pressure. You promise to go to the wedding...Please."

Raj came out on the patio.

"Raj," I said, "did you give Kis...ah mean, your car, a good cleanup?" Actually I had seen him giving Kiskadee a hurried cleaning the day before.

"No. But what is that you said? Something about Kis...?"

"Raj, I think your car looks like...like a Kiskadee."

"Ha," he laughed. "You know what. You are right. Let's go and give my Kiskadee a good pluming."

As we stepped off the patio Raj looked over his shoulder and said pleasantly, "Pa, do you want to help us?"

The old man looked up quickly. "Eh? What? Well...am...okay...okay," he stammered.

271

Just after one, Raj started to get dressed. He twisted, turned and looked over his shoulders as he preened in front of the fulllength mirror (minus a semicircular piece broken off from the top) stuck on the wall. Once Raj said, "That blasted tailor, Prospere, mess up this jacket. Look, it..."

"Raj, nothing is wrong with the jacket. Look, you haven't buttoned it properly."

"Mama!" he laughed. He turned to his father, "Pa?"

"Nice." Old Girdo mumbled, passed his fingers through his white fluffy hair and said, "But the jacket shoulda be white."

"Do you have white shirt and pants?" Raj asked with a hint of impatience and when the old man nodded, Raj said, "That will do."

The old man went into the bedroom and when he returned about five minutes later clutching a white hat and looking as solemn as a judge, he was neatly and simply dressed.

"You look smart, Mr. Girdharry," I said.

The old man smiled and tugged at his sleeves, which was buttoned at the wrist.

"Ron, you look nice too."

Actually the black suit that I had donned was not exactly my size. The sleeves covered the palm of my hands, the shoulder projected ludicrously, and the pants that had to be secured by a belt, bulged generously at the ankles.

The old man came up to me and gently pulled the sleeves up to my wrists. He patted me on the back before walking slowly to the patio. Soon, he returned and went up to Raj. "Son," he whispered, "when we come back, where the *beti* and the *lukni* going to sleep?"

Raj scratched his head and walked up to his father. He held him lightly by the shoulder with one hand, and said, "Dad...Pa, let me explain. After the wedding, we are not coming back here. I am marrying in a Christian church. And then we are leaving on our honey..." Raj stopped.

272

Old Girdo looked steadily at his son's face, blinked and then looked away. Raj threw the comb he had in his hand on the bed, held the old man firmly by both shoulders and said slowly, "Dad, this wedding is different from Hindu wedding. You must stay with Ron and he is going to explain everything. Alright, pa?"

Little rivulets appeared on the old man's forehead. "But son, you is Hindu."

"But, pa..."

The old man looked down at his feet and then moved off to the patio again.

Just before two p.m. Raj called from his bedroom, "Ron, come and adjust my tie."

I adjusted the dark bowtie and stepped back to look at him. He pulled his shoulders up, slanted his head back and waited with a faint smile on his face. The dark, threepiece tuxedo suit did justice to his trim, athletic figure. The white shirt under the suit presented sharp contrast and definition. To complete his simple outfit, he wore a pair of black pointed shoes—genuine leather, he had told me—that projected prominently from under the tapered end of his trousers.

And though his neatly trimmed moustache appeared strange on him—he had never allowed one to flourish so illustriously before—it gave him a mature look, and balanced perfectly with his closecropped wavy hair that was cut short recently. He looked regal.

"First class!" I said.

"Ready to go!" he sang, brushing away gently an imaginary thread from his trousers.

At exactly two p.m., young and old Girdharry, and I eased into Kiskadee, which had at last succeeded in reaching up to the steps of the patio since the storm. Old Girdo sat in the back seat. I sat infront. Kiskadee whistled smoothly along the highway in the bright afternoon made extremely pleasant by a gentle caressing breeze.

None of us spoke much. I looked at Raj and the old man.

I closed my eyes and my mind drifted back to Guyana...to weddings...to the one I had enjoyed the most...to a Hindu wedding...to the one where I learnt much. If Raj was marrying in Hindu rites, his wedding, I assumed, would have followed the same pattern.

*It was a Sunday morning. Iswar, my very close friend, dressed in dhoti and koorta, and wearing the symbolic crown on his head boarded his chauffeurdriven car at his father's home in Zeelugt. His friends and relatives were aboard a fleet of about a dozen vehicles parked ahead of his car, awaiting the signal to drive off. Bram and Nar were in my car.*

*Iswar's father emerged from his house wearing dhoti and koortah too and clutching his Gita. He stood still for a while, looked around and smiled. As soon as he entered the car, we left for the bride's or, as she is called in Hindi, the dulhin's residence on Main Street, Georgetown.*

*The dulhin's father and relatives warmly greeted Iswar, his father and the entourage.*

*The two fathers embraced and expressed their elations in public for bringing their two families together. These gestures indicated that the parents no longer had the duty to search for suitors for the couple and they looked forward to the strengthening of this new relationship.*

Back here in St. Lucia on the road to Gros Islet, in Raj's car, I opened my eyes and glanced at Old Girdo as if I half-expected him to be smiling, wearing his church attire and offering his benediction. I found him with his eyes closed.

"Pa?" Raj called out suddenly turning his head slightly.

"He is sleeping," I whispered.

"But, son, me still feel her ma and pa shoulda come and ask home for you." Old Girdo was awake. He leaned over and touched Raj.

"But, pa..."

"Is custom, son...But never mind." He reclined and closed

his eyes again.

"But son, what me have to do at the wedding?" The old man was sitting upright.

"Nothing, pa."

I could understand how Old Girdo was trying to grapple with the situation. It was not easy for him to see his most educated offspring...the pride of his life go astray like this...Yes, this *beta* who was a university graduate. He had been denied that auspicious moment when he would have been in total control. No doubt he would have had a taste of this when Ram and Govind got married. But this should have been the climax of his fulfillment. The moments of joy, the fanfare, the accolades, the chants and the revelry among his people would not be there.

"We are here, dad, Ron." It was minutes before four p.m.

About a score of people, mostly women and children, stood at the entrance of the church. They turned and looked at us when we alighted from the car. They smiled. Old Girdo looked around anxiously.

"This is the Roman Catholic Church, dad."

The old man placed a hand on his hat and tilted his head up. He then shifted his gaze to the entrance. Raj held his right elbow and gently propelled him to the entrance. At the door, he removed the hat from his head and hesitated. I held him by the left elbow and he walked between us. An immediate hush fell over the congregation, but whispers trailed us as we walked up the front of the aisle that ran down the center of the church. Eyes turned and stared as fingers pointed and tapped the air. The whisperings thickened into a buzz. There were nodding of heads and smiles all around.

*At Iswar's wedding, after the two father's embraced, we entered the yard at which the wedding would take place and stood outside the enclosure, the maroo — it was a small enclosure made of strips of bamboo — around which invitees had gathered.*

*At the entrance of the maroo, the dulhin's mother dressed in a*

*yellow sari and holding a brass pan — with flowers, mainly flamboy-*
*ant, and a little fire — awaited Iswar. She circled the pan over*
*Iswar's head. Another lady also dressed in sari came and did like-*
*wise. She was followed by a second...a third...and a fourth. This*
*was their way of welcoming Iswar into their family.*

*When Iswar entered the maroo the dulhin's father offered him a*
*seat. He then proceeded to wash Iswar's feet.*

*Iswar sat on the dulha's bench between six to nine inches high.*
*His father sat next to him.*

*The mother then escorted her daughter, Satie, the dulhin, wear-*
*ing a red sari and a veil, into the maroo. Satie sat on Iswar's right,*
*with the mother next to her. The mother's brother entered and sat*
*next to his sister.*

As we walked down the isle of the Church, Old Girdo cautiously turned every now and again and studied the congregation. He grabbed my hand once and it seemed he was
about to say or ask something. I squeezed his arm and whispered, "Sit in the front row."

He peered around, sat and clutched his hat. After a while,
he leaned over and rested his elbows on his knees. He
yawned. I wished Kalli was here to keep him company. "Got
to work and collect me pay, cousin, but me is coming. *Wi!*" he
had told me.

As the Best Man, I went and stood alongside Raj at the
front of the church and facing   the altar. In front of us, two
crucifixes of the same size were on either side of the pulpit
that stood in the middle on a raised platform. A larger cruci-
fix was on the wall directly behind the pulpit. There were two
doors on either side of the wall. I kept my eyes focused on
them.

Meanwhile the murmur behind us had become louder. I
glanced over my shoulder. Old Girdo was sitting on the edge
of his seat. His eyes roved over the congregation once again.

Then a sudden hush, this one more charged with awe, fell
over the gathering once again. I turned and saw the amply

robed priest approaching us with a smile. An elderly woman entered from somewhere in the back and went straight up to the organ that was partly hidden behind a table in a corner. She pressed the keys once, twice, stopped and waited. She craned her neck every now and again and looked in the direction of the entrance.

Abruptly she slumped over, and the organ bellowed.

Raj and I turned with the entire congregation to look at the entrance.

*"Here comes the bride,"* signaled the momentous entry of Felicity Johnny in her long, white, flowing and laced wedding gown, wearing a seductive smile and stepping lightly, confidently and majestically closer to her beloved, and into holy matrimony. Mutterings of approval and admiration floated spontaneously like sparse confetti.

Felicity's right hand was tucked perfunctorily into the vertex of the left arm of Linus Johnny, who donned a brown suit.

Behind her a short train, consisting of two pretty girl coaches — her step-sisters — completed the bridal posse. Their poise and composure were admirable.

In turning, I brushed slightly against Raj. A quiver raced through his body. Then I remembered her condition. Indeed, it was showing, but I had to look closely.

*At Iswar's wedding, after the dulhin's father had washed Iswar's feet, and everyone was seated, the pandit read and chanted for a while. Some females who stood around the maroo chanted along with the pandit. Some of the boys who came with Iswar left the area to join the others on the street where loud music was being played from the trunk of a car and they imbibed a variety of liquor.*

*The pandit instructed Satie to bite off the ends of the stems of five mango leaves, which he gave her one at a time and to keep them in her mouth. She then placed the leaves in her mother's right hand. As the pandit read and chanted some more, the mother's brother removed the mango leaves from his sister's hand separately, and circled each over Satie's head. Both mother and father then placed dough — it had a piece of gold in it and was symbolic of the dowry —*

*in Satie's hand. She handed over the dowry to Iswar who passed it on to his father. Both mother and uncle left the maroo immediately.*

*Iswar's and Satie's tied the nuptial knot, pledging to be life companions.*

*The invitees clapped.*

*The couple proceeded to offer rice to the fire This act symbolized fertility and prosperity in their marriage.*

*The pandit then instructed Iswar and Satie to circle the fire seven times. Satie lead for the first four times thus expressing her supreme devotion to her husband.*

*Together, the dulha and dulhin took seven steps forward to the North which was seen as a form of purification and was also indicative of their quest to seek fulfillment of their spiritual and material needs.*

*The Pandit recited the marriage vows, to which the couple responded affirmatively. When Iswar then applied a red sindhoor – a married Hindu woman was always expected to wear that – to Satie's forehead she moved over to sit on Iswar's right side.*

*Satie's father then requested Iswar to eat a kind of 'sweet meat' – a mixture of Dahi, ghee and honey – which I was told was symbolic of the bliss that should be experienced in a happy union.*

*Nar said, "Don't eat Ish, don't eat...he rich...let him give a cow...new car ...and... and a house..."*

*Someone replied, "We giving him a green cow...and a Mercedes...and state house..."*

*But seriously, unless Iswar ate the 'sweet meat', the union was not cemented.*

*Iswar ate not too long after.*

At the Church, as Felicity and her bridal procession walked down the isle, the congregation rose to its feet, all heads pointing down the aisle, all eyes glued on the bride..

Old Girdo's was a sort of a delayed reaction. From sideways, I could not really read the expression on his face. I was sure though, that he blinked a few times as his eyes were riveted to Felicity's face. *Was he taken aback that he could see her face before the wedding ceremony started.* His head dragged around slowly as Felicity stepped closer to the altar. A faint smile appeared on his face.

The congregation was hushed as the distinguished-looking and eloquent priest reeled off the marriage vows. Rajendra Rohan Girdharry and Felicity Patricia Johnny gazed steadily in each other's eyes and recited the vows like disinterested school kids lost in their own world.

Occasionally, as if by instinct, I glanced at Old Girdo. Every now and again, he turned his body and looked over the gathering. Was he expecting someone to approach him? After all he was the groom's father.

Towards the end, I thought I detected a slight droop in his shoulders.

*"I now pronounce you man and wife."*

The congregation broke into mild applause. Old Girdo sat upright.

*"You may now kiss your bride."*

Old Girdo stared wide-eyed.

*Back at Iswar's wedding It was an emotionally charged moment when the parents gave their daughter away wishing her absolute and life-long happiness, and exalting Iswar, their son-in-law, to love, cherish and care at all times their precious daughter in accordance with Dharmic principles.*

*The Pandit, parents, elders and friends showered a deluge of blessings on the couple, wishing them health, spiritual progress and a happy married life.*

*The way was then opened for the couple to be showered with gifts.*

*Indian music blared from a juke box.*

*Iswar's father rose from his seat. Satie got up and touched her father-in-law's feet. He looked around and smiled.*

In Castries, as Raj and Felicity turned to leave the church, I saw Raj whisper in her ear. She lifted her head, looked directly at Old Girdo and beamed. She unhooked her hand from Raj's and sashayed up to the old man. She placed her hand delicately across his shoulder and kissed him lightly on the cheek.

His face flushed and he looked around anxiously. I walked up quickly to him and threw an arm across his shoulder. "Are you alright, Mr. Girdharry?" I whispered.

He nodded.

After a while, he brought up his hand and gently touched the spot where she had kissed him.

We, that is, Old Girdo and I, followed the bride and groom as they made their way down the aisle. I scanned the congregation and was pleasantly surprised to see some of our countrymen way at the back.

Then out of the corner of my eyes, I saw another person noticeably dressed overall in white like Old Girdo. Bram! I must admit that my admiration for Bram grew tenfold. He looked up but wasn't looking at me. My eyes searched for Nar but he wasn't there. I saw Raj turn his head in Bram's direction. I couldn't see Raj's face, but Bram's widened with a smile, and his lips moved. Raj turned around immediately to look at me and raised his eyebrows in Bram's direction. The old man's eyes lit up on seeing Bram. When they got close, he embraced him as if he had found a lost son.

"Take it easy, uncle Girdo," Bram said quietly, as he tenderly pushed the old man away and looked into his eyes.

I inquired for Nar.

"Oh. Nar got a five-year multiple. He left for New York yesterday."

I was a little disheartened that Nar did not tell me, but I was happy for him.

A silvery welcome sign and showers of confetti greeted us as we entered the reception area at Mr. Johnny's residence. The place was small but it was exquisitely decorated. There were balloons, decorative crepe paper and fresh flowers everywhere. The three-tiered wedding cake with a miniature effigy of a bride and groom perched on top lay in the center of a small table lined with champagne glasses and other cutlery.

Raj and Felicity came up to me immediately. "You have to be the M.C."

"Nah. I am not good at that."

"Come on, you are Raj's best friend," Felicity pleaded.

"Suppose someone speaks only patois? How do I comment?"

"Just smile," Raj said.

They smiled and walked away immediately to take their place at the head of the table.

The guests—I didn't think that the number exceeded a hundred—gathered around.

When the floor was opened for speeches, a friend said, "I have known the bride and groom for some time. They are simply wonderful people..."

Raj and Felicity smiled.

"...and these two are models of excellence," a colleague ended.

The two stared at him wide eyed.

When Bram stood, there was a sweeping hush. "Congratulations, Raj and Felicity...You make a wonderful couple and with all sincerity, I wish you all the best. May Lord Krishna...God bless you."

"Thank you," Felicity said quietly.

An elderly lady got up. "*Boswe*, Felicity, *ou fe un bel tifi...*"

I looked at Felicity while the lady carried on in patois. She was nodding. When the old lady said, "...bon marriage," and sat, everyone clapped.

I smiled and said, "*Wi*, well said."

A lump rushed up Linus Johnny's throat. "...I know...I know Raj will make my daughter happy," he concluded and sat.

Raj nodded.

"Mr. Girdharry! Let's hear Mr. Girdharry!" someone

shouted.

Immediately, I said, "He is only speaking Hindi and he says, '*Tum say mahabat,*' which means *I love you.*"

Everyone put his hands together. Old Girdo shook his head approvingly and smiled.

Finally, I invited Raj to speak. When he rose one could literally hear a pin drop. He spoke briefly. It was emotional.

Once, he pointed to old Girdo, "...I am so happy he is here...He has done so much for me..."

I looked at the old man. His eyes were closed, but a smile lingered on his face.

"...*Wi*, I want to thank everyone for making my lovely wife and me, deliriously happy today."

The applause resounded.

In closing, I said, "...And man and woman are like the earth that brings forth flowers in summer and love...and from love slowly a gem forms of two human hearts, a man's heart and a woman's that is the crystal of peace the slow hard jewel of trust, the sapphire of fidelity..."

"Words! Words!" someone said.

"I was quoting from D.H Lawrence's 'Fidelity'."

"Oooh."

"A gem will emerge from this union," I said.

"Yea...yea...yea...*wi*...*wi*...*wi*..." the gathering shouted as they clapped.

After the ceremonial cutting of the cake and the usual by-play that accompanied it, Old Girdo, Bram and I, sat at the same table for the final stage.

Suddenly a hand dropped on my shoulder, and another simultaneously on Bram's. "Cousin!" Kalli's face shone and his eyes glowed. He was dressed in the same attire he had worn to the airport, but the hair was disheveled, and bristles sprouted on his neck just below his beard. He grabbed a chair and sat between Bram and me. He reeked of alcohol.

"But Snakeeye, you can't come drunk here," Bram sailed into him.

"But was only a small one, cousin." His thumb and index finger formed a circle to indicate how small the 'small' was. "But good God, cousin! This is a wedding. They don't drink at Christian wedding?"

"Not like you do in Zeelugt!" Bram glared at him.

"Kalli," I said touching him, "we will have champagne, wine and lots of meat."

"Alright. So old boy, how is you new daughta-in-law? You like she?"

Old Girdo smiled and nodded lightly.

"Black gals too nice," Kalli said, and laughed.

"Snake!" Bram scolded.

"But cousin, me ain't do or say anything wrong."

He looked around and waved to some people. He downed the half glass of champagne I had poured for him.

"Next wedding is me own...in Vieux Fort Catalic church," he said loudly.

Bram and I glared at him.

He rubbed his stomach and grinned, "Me feel so nice that me can make joke whole day."

When the food was served, Old Girdo looked at the plate and the knife and fork, and shook his head slowly. "Nah, me don't feel hungry."

Kalli surveyed the guests, then whispered to the old man, "Look, old boy, me know you want seven curry...with rice...and achar and puri...in puri leaf. But forget the damn knife, fork and shovel and grab the damn chicken with you hand like...how...how you does break the roti and dip it in the dhal." He grabbed the chicken leg, bared his teeth and was about to snap at it like a piranha.

"Snake, put it down!" Bram growled, almost hitting the chicken out of Kalli's hand. "I am not accustomed to knife and fork...But look how I am doing it...Don't shame us, Snake."

Suddenly Bram nudged me. "Regis," he said.

"Where? No...It can't be. He wouldn't," I said.

He pointed to the man who was with Felicity's father and then looked at me. "Why are you so surprised to see him here?"

"Yes. It's him...Never mind."

Regis was wearing a white suit. He was staring at the floor with hands folded across his chest and was listening to Mr. Johnny. Mr. Johnny bore down on him, and poked his fingers several times into his chest. Eventually he placed his hand on Regis' shoulder and Regis looked up into his face. A faint smile appeared on Mr. Johnny's face and Regis too smiled for the first time.

Bram and I were looking at them for some time hoping that Regis would look our way. And as Bram was about to get up, Regis turned and saw us. Bram and I beckoned silently and earnestly. Regis smiled, waved and came over slowly. His long, black tie floated in front of him. His shining pate was totally bald and his moustache was neatly trimmed.

"Oh, Mr. Bram, this is a surprise. Anyway, how are you? And you too Ron...Long time no see." He patted Bram on the shoulder. He leaned over and rubbed my head.

"Surprised to see you too, Mr. Regis," Bram said.

Regis looked around quickly. "Eh, eh? Where is Nar?"

"Gone to the States, *gason*," I said.

He laughed. "Hope he finds a white *djabal*."

He noticed the old man.

"Raj's father," I said.

They shook hands.

"Very pleased to meet you, sir," Regis said reverently as he assumed an upright posture.

He turned to Bram and whispered, "Bram, I am sorry..."

"You don't look *fou* anymore," Bram told Regis laughing.

"*Awa*, I am not *phaglee* anymore," he replied, and indeed suppressed his usual scandalous laughter.

Then Bram smiling got up slowly and passed his hand over Regis' pate. Pulling Regis' head closer to his, he whispered, "Mr. Regis, I hope you didn't forget the thing?"

"I was going to tell you…"

"Cousin, is this the man who thief you money?" Kalli butted in sharply, and without waiting for any confirmation, "Yes, is he!" He pushed the chair over as he attempted to get up. "Ah going to wring you flipping neck!" He made a grab for the neck, before either Bram or I could have intervened.

But Regis stepped aside like a rooster. "*Bondous!* Eh? Eh? What is this?" Regis back peddled. His face grew pallid instantly.

Others at nearby tables were attracted.

"Kalli, this is none of you business," Bram said, and pressed Kalli back into his seat.

After calm returned, Regis said quietly, "Mr. Bram, next week, I am coming back to open the shop again…and I am building back the Garden. I will pay you back." He left hurriedly.

Then we noticed Raj and Felicity who were circulating among the guests, heading towards our table. Felicity's eyes smiled. Raj was bridal happy.

Raj went up to Bram and they hugged. Felicity shook Bram's hands.

Felicity went over to Old Girdo. He stood up slowly and assumed an erect posture. They were about the same height. They looked into each other's eyes. She leaned over and planted a kiss on the other side of his cheek. He looked around, overcome by the gesture for a second time. Kalli giggled. Bram looked at Kalli sternly.

"Dad," Raj whispered.

"Dad," Felicity said.

"*Beti.*" He shook her hand. A smile appeared on his face. He looked down at his feet. *Was he was expecting her to touch his feet?*

She looked at Raj. They stared into each other's eyes. She looked at her father-in-law again and this time held his hand lightly.

"Dad, did you eat?"

"Yes, *beti*."

She released his hand and held Raj's. She looked at Raj again in the eye.

"Dad, did you have anything to drink?" Raj asked.

"Yes, son." He folded his hand.

"And dad, if you want anything, ask Ron. He will..."

"...And now the bride and groom will open the dancing floor." the DJ's voice boomed, followed instantly by the music.

Couples followed them on the dancing floor. After Raj and Felicity had danced, they brought over some of her relatives to meet the old man. Felicity's father embraced him and others shook his hand. For a moment the old man's eyes lit up.

"How is the family back in Guyana?" Mr.Johnny asked.

"Okay."

"Do you like St. Lucia?" queried another.

"Uhuh."

"How are things in Guyana?"

"Good."

"When are you going back?"

"Tomorrow."

When the relatives left, the old man leaned over and whispered something to Kalli.

"That's the spirit, old boy!" Kalli yelled, and promptly topped the old man's glass with alcohol.

The old man gulped down the drink. Kalli refilled the glass. The old man emptied it in two gulps and pushed it under Kalli's eyes. Kalli replenished.

Gradually Old Girdo's posture grew upright and he squared his shoulders. He began smiling at everyone and everything.

He asked Kalli, "You like this place?"

"Plenty."

He turned to Bram. "You does do pandit work here?"

"Yes, Mr. Girdharry. We have Hawan every Sunday."

"So Nar have a black woman?"

"No. Mr Girdharry."

He leaned closer to Bram. "How come you make Raj marry a black gal?" He tugged at Bram's shirt.

"I didn't..."

He turned away abruptly and touched glasses with Kalli. "*Wi*. St. Lucia too nice. *Wi*, cousin!" Kalli sang as he stood. Actually he had been rising at the start of every new song, gyrating for a few seconds and recoiling in his chair.

A few guests nearby looked at him, smiled and waved. And as he was about to respond, Bram seethed, "Shut up!" pressing him down onto his chair at the same time.

The tempo of the music picked up. The place became warm. My sixth beer was getting tepid in my hands. The old man began to tap the table. Once he turned to Bram, slapped him heavily on the back and invited, "Pandit, take a lil one nah," pointing to the rum bottle.

"*Wi*, cousin. It good for the worms." Kalli joined in and slapped Bram on exactly the same spot as the old man and certainly a bit harder.

Bram smiled. "It is okay, Mr. Girdharry. You know I don't drink." He turned to Kalli. The smile vanished and the tone changed. "And you, Kalli, you best watch yourself."

"Me going to waltz," Kalli said with a gleam in his eyes; but as he got up shakily on his feet, Bram pulled him down again.

"Sit you *rass* here and drink til you get drunk," Bram pounced on him.

Kalli smiled and obliged.

All of a sudden the old man went dead quiet. His head rested in his hands and drooped over the table. Kalli attempted to replenish his glass. He pushed Kalli's hand away. Soon he began to grind his teeth and complain about the noise.

I touched him and when he looked up, I said, "You okay?"

His eyes were barely open, but he nodded. Suddenly, he shot out a hand, grabbed Bram's shirt and said, "Where Raj? Tell him me want to see him."

"Raj has already gone with his wife on their honeymoon," explained Bram, placing a comforting hand across his shoulders.

"But why me *beta* don't tell me he going? Why?" His voice implored and cracked.

A lump rushed up my throat.

Suddenly the old man clutched the arms of his chair, forced himself up. He steadied himself and grabbed my arm. Staggering, he steered me out of the crowded reception area. Under the leaves of the banana plant just about ten yards away, he held me firmly by the shoulders in a vice-like grip that surprisingly hurt. He shook me violently and amidst the still audible blaring music in the fading luminosity of the evening, he stammered, "Wha...wha...wha...me...me...go tell them back home?" He sighed incoherently and embraced me tightly. Then he gently rested his head on my shoulder and sobbed quietly as quivers ran through his body. I felt a burning pain inside of me as if a centipede had just sunk its poisonous mandibles into my flesh.

# Other Jako Books

## Phases Poetry by Modeste Downes

"...impassioned poetry ... beautifully crafted images and metaphors that linger long in the memory ... Like that of Mr. Walcott, achieves the highest eloquence of passion.... produces an exquisite sense of beauty... A nationalistic and romantic poet with echoes of William Wordsworth, and Oliver Goldsmith"  —Jacques Compton, *The Voice*

## Death by Fire Novel by Anderson Reynolds

"The telling of the story is exceptional ... Extremely dificult to put it down ... A cunningly-woven tale ... A journey back into St. Lucian life ... (which) paints the dark side of the struggle for survival in a young country."

—Victor Marquis, *The Voice*

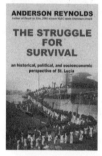

## The Struggle For Survival by Anderson Reynolds

"... Excellent work ... a 206 paged gem ... a powerful commentary ... A deep sincere analytical look into the state of things in the island today. The Struggle For Survival is truly a compendium of St. Lucian life from early times to the modern era ... I thoroughly enjoyed myself reading the book."  —*The Mirror*

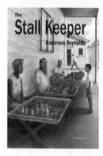

## The Stall Keeper Novel by Anderson Reynolds

"The Stall Keeper is a compelling story of provincial bigotry, religious experience and rivalry, faith, fanaticism, frustrated love, and the repression of intelligence and ambition, played against the beautiful wide open spaces and relics of post American (World War II)-occupied Vieux Fort."  —Allan Weeks, author of *Talk of the Devil*

## www.jakoproductions.com

CLIVE SANKARDAYAL was born and raised in Guyana. He holds a B.A. degree in English from the University of Guyana and he was a teacher and administrator at the Zeeburg Secondary School, West Coast Demerara. He and his wife now reside in St. Lucia where he heads the English department of the Soufriere Comprehensive Secondary School. In his role as an educator, Sankardayal also serves as an Examiner with the Caribbean Examination Council (CXC) for the English language. His poem, *Caribbean Man in Search of an Author*, won the 1993 Caribbean Union of Teachers' Poetry Competition, and *The Brown Curtains* was the 2005 Winner of the St. Lucia National Arts Award for Prose.